LOVE POTIONS

Warlocks MacGregor®

MICHELLE M. PILLOW

Michelle M. Pillow® - MichellePillow.com

Love Potions (*Warlocks MacGregor*®) © copyright 2014-2018 by
Michelle M. Pillow

Third Printing July 2018

Published by The Raven Books LLC

Second Printing July 2015

First Printing May 2014

Print ISBN-13: 978-1-62501-164-0

About Love Potions

PARANORMAL CONTEMPORARY ROMANCE

A little magickal mischief never hurt anyone...

Erik MacGregor is from a clan of ancient Scottish warlocks. He isn't looking for love. After centuries, it's not even a consideration...until he moves in next door to Lydia Barratt. It's clear that the shy beauty wants nothing to do with him, but he's drawn to her and determined to win her over.

The last thing Lydia Barratt needs is a demanding Scottish man meddling in her private life. Just because he's gorgeous and totally rocks a kilt doesn't mean she's going to fall for his seductive manner.

But Erik won't give up and just as Lydia lets her guard down, his sister decides to get involved. Her little love potion prank goes terribly wrong, making Lydia the target of his sudden embarrassingly obsessive behavior. They'll have to find a way to pull Erik out of the spell fast when it becomes clear that Lydia has more than a lovesick warlock to worry about.

Warning: Contains yummy, hot, mischievous MacGregors who may or may not be wielding love potion magick in an effort to prank their older brother, and who are almost certainly up to no good on their quest to find true love.

Warlocks MacGregor Series

SCOTTISH MAGICKAL WARLOCKS

Love Potions
Spellbound
Stirring Up Trouble
Cauldrons and Confessions
Spirits and Spells
Kisses and Curses
Magick and Mischief
A Dash of Destiny
Night Magick

More Coming Soon

Visit www.MichellePillow.com for details.

Author Updates

To stay informed about when a new book is
released sign up for updates:

michellepillow.com/author-updates

To all those who need a little magical mischief in their lives. Be careful what you wish for. Uncle Raibeart is looking for love.

Note from the Author

The term "warlock" is a variation on the Old English word "waerloga" primarily used by the Scots. It meant traitor, monster, deceiver, or other variations. The MacGregor Clan does not look at themselves as being what history has labeled their kind. To them, warlock means magick, family, and immortality. This book is not meant to be a portrayal of modern day witches or those who have such beliefs. The MacGregors are a magickal class all their own.

As with all my books, this is pure fantasy. In real life, please always practice safe sex and magic(k).

Chapter One

GREEN VALLIS, WISCONSIN, PRESENT DAY

A chill worked its way up Lydia Barratt's spine, and she stopped walking to look across the red brick street of downtown Green Vallis. The day was warm, and her lightweight linen shirt should've offered more than adequate protection from the elements. But suddenly, she was assaulted with a wintry bitterness that struck all the way to her bones, causing them to ache. Lydia didn't move as she saw the usual bustle of people go by, smiling and waving as they habitually did in the small town. The sound of engines burred along the streets, the car tires splashing in the puddles leftover from an early morning rain. It was just after noon and almost everyone was on their lunch breaks, eating in the diner or sitting out on benches that lined the street. There was no reason for her to feel ominous on such a beautiful, normal day.

Sheriff Johnson drove past in his squad car. She detected the impression of his arm lifting in a wave through the sedan's window, but couldn't make out his face. Automatically, she smiled and returned the gesture.

Lydia shivered again. This wasn't the first time the strange sensations overtook her, but they had been getting stronger in the last week. Before she died, her grandmother would've said it was a premonition of something to come, a forewarning to be ready. Lydia wasn't sure she believed in premonitions. But Annabelle Barratt had. In fact, her grandmother had believed in much more than that. She believed in the old magick, in those who could harness the powers of the earth and sky, those who lived forever hidden amongst normal folk.

People whispered that her grandmother had been a witch. What could Lydia say? That's exactly what Annabelle had been. She didn't fly around on a broomstick or have a hideous face covered in warts, but she was a naturalist, a green witch. Everything Lydia knew about herbs and making "potions" came from the woman. Her mother had died when she was born, and her father drank himself into his deathbed. Gramma

Annabelle had taken care of her and taught her everything she knew about the supernatural. Unfortunately, in grade school, the teachers didn't think her knowledge of vampire lore and ghost hunting was as practical as math and vocabulary. She was constantly behind the rest of the class. And, in response, Annabelle simply handed her a calculator and dictionary, while stating, "lesson over." That incident and many more like it pretty much defined her childhood.

Shaking the feeling off as no more than an oncoming illness, Lydia reached down to grab the handle of her small cart. The basket was close to the ground, overflowing with brown paper packages, and fixed to a long handle so she didn't have to bend over. The post office was within walking distance, just down the hill from the old Victorian house she'd inherited from Gramma Annabelle two years earlier. Almost every day she'd cart boxes down to be shipped, even in winter. If she didn't make the short walk, she'd never leave the house.

"Afternoon, Lydia."

Lydia glanced up and smiled at the man who spoke. Joe Ellyson was old enough to be her father, but she couldn't help thinking he was handsome in a weathered sort of way. The laugh lines on his face only added to his charm. "Afternoon, Joe."

"Got yourself quite a load today, don't you?" Brad Williams, Joe's new best friend said, glancing down at the cart overflowing with shipping boxes. The two had become inseparable, and Lydia wasn't sure she understood the connection. Brad was shorter, balding and had a slightly wandering eye. She noticed it especially liked to wander over her ass when he thought she wasn't looking. Bad manners weren't enough to get her to run the other way screaming, but the man definitely had a serial creeper vibe to him. He was the kind to get drunk and harass waitresses, or leer at bikini-clad women at the swimming pool. Had he been big and muscled, she would've been more concerned. As it was, he seemed a sad little letch. Brad had only recently moved to Green Vallis with his family—a spiritless wife and two obnoxious teenage sons who were suspected of vandalism. They'd never been caught.

"Yep," she answered politely. She'd grown up in Green Vallis. The town was small enough to be comfortable and big enough to afford some privacy—at least for most. Since she was grand-daughter to the "witch on the hill" everyone had known her business growing up. It's why she was so reclusive now. "Quite a load."

"Business going well, I take it," Joe said. He'd never married and spent a lot of time doing charitable works. Lydia always assumed he would someday take orders and join the priesthood. Maybe that was why he tolerated the obnoxious Brad. It was charity. Or penance.

"Real well." Lydia didn't want to be trapped in a conversation—not with the unsettling Brad staring at her chest. Turning the cart around so it was on the downside of the hill, she slowly backed away from them under the pretense of being pulled by its weight. It wasn't a complete act. The cart was getting heavier by the second.

"Glad to hear it." Joe nodded.

The men said their goodbyes continuing up as she went down. Lydia held onto the handle, turning sideways and leaning away from the cart for the steeper part of the incline. The weight tried to pull her faster, but she kept her feet braced. She nodded politely to those she passed, mumbling a soft greeting when necessary.

"I don't understand these men. Letting a wee lassie like yourself handle such a thing, especially when it's clear they know ya."

Lydia nearly lost her step as the Scottish accent came from behind her. She wasn't sure she'd understood the words completely. This time when she felt the shiver working over her body, it was liquid heat and not a cold chill. The low, honeyed tone of the voice was enough to make her stomach lurch—and not in a completely unwelcome way.

Well, considering she didn't have a boyfriend to help her out in that department, the sudden dampness between her thighs could be construed as slightly unwelcome.

Lydia didn't turn around, but kept walking toward the post office. If she didn't look, she wouldn't have to explore the curling in her stomach, the sudden ache in her neglected loins. She wouldn't have to see that the voice belonged to a short, fat, greasy man who was going to try to hit on her. Actually, she might just keep the voice in her head for later—when she had some alone time.

At the thought, she walked faster, not sure why her heart should be pounding in her chest, or why she was suddenly overtaken with the urge to let go of the cart and run home, packages be damned. The odds that the owner of a voice like that was talking to her and not someone else were slim. Men with voices like that didn't speak to her. Not in this town. Not in any town. She would just mind her business like always and keep going.

"Ya don't hear me, lassie?"

So much for that theory.

Lydia felt a large presence at her side and nearly tripped as it shadowed the sunlight. A warm hand grabbed her elbow to steady her. Her muscles tightened, even as her heart leapt in surprise, skipping a beat as she gasped for breath. Electricity shot up her arm from the man's touch, causing her to jerk. He didn't let go. It was like a blaze of fire that went straight to every nerve in her system. Even her scalp tingled.

"*Bòidheach*," he whispered, as if as surprised as she by the lightning contact.

Lydia couldn't move. Long, black hair spilled over the stranger's shoulders, the sides bound back from his chiseled features. Sinfully dark eyes met hers, as the man looked down at her from his greater height. At five-seven, she wasn't exactly short, but this man still towered over her. Or, perhaps it was the broad size of his shoulders that made him seem so gigantic.

The distant call of bagpipes on the wind filtered through her thoughts. The town disappeared as her imagination conjured visions of lush moors and warrior men in plaid kilts. So clear was the thought, she even spotted the tall peaks of a castle behind his shoulder. Within a blink, the image was gone and she was left once more staring into eyes that had the power to draw a woman in and lay bare her soul.

Three years!

Lydia tensed at the thought. Why was the fact

that she hadn't had sex in ages suddenly popping into her brain like the answer to some unasked trivia question? Her thighs tightened, almost clamping shut. She swallowed nervously, her body stiff, too stunned to move or speak.

Slowly, her eyes raked over him. The crewneck black cotton shirt he wore molded to his flesh, leaving no mystery as to the fine shape of his body. The long sleeve bulged at the shoulders, leading to a thick, muscled chest. Different emotions washed though her—fear and arousal, curiosity and apprehension.

He was by no means slender, for his stomach was nothing but a continuation of solid muscle. His heather gray, flat-front pants hugged to his perfect waist. Though loose by design, the material draped quite erotically over his thighs and calves, as a breezed stirred against them. Lydia's mouth went dry. The pants draped something else as well—the giant bulge nestled between his legs.

Her eyes widened, convinced by the size of it that his shaft was fully erect. She blinked several times. No, she was wrong. The bulge moved, growing as she watched it.

"Not that I mind ya staring, love, but I've got an appointment I must keep."

Staring?

Lydia pried her eyes away from the man's

crotch, completely mortified to be caught ogling him like he was a piece of meat she was about to kneel before and devour.

He gave her a playful smile and she knew he was teasing her.

She nodded, breathlessly saying, "Ah, yeah, yes, nice to you meet me. I mean nice of you to meet with me, me to meet you. Uh, I mean bye."

Lydia pulled her arm from his hold and made a move to grab her cart. That's when she noticed he held it up for her. With the incline, it would've rolled down the hill and her inventory would've been lost. She reached for the handle, careful not to touch the strong hand gripping it. Her body still sizzled from the zing his touch had given her.

The man's dark eyes glanced down to her chest. A slight smile curled his firm lips, adding mischief to his already amused expression. Lydia wanted to die. She knew without looking that her nipples had hardened and were pressing against the linen of her shirt. All her bras had been in the laundry and she'd not put one on for the quick walk down. Her breasts were by no means huge, and she'd thought no one would notice through the dark blue material. She'd been wrong.

"But, we've not met. I'm Erik," he paused, again glancing down to her breasts. She pretended not to realize they were poking like two hard beacons for the world to see. "Erik MacGregor."

Erik MacGregor. Even the man's name was sexy. Concentrating on making sure the blush stayed off her features, she said, "Ah, I'm…"

Damn it! What is my name? Think, Lydia. Ah! Lydia.

"Lydia Barratt," she finished. He extended his hand in a friendly gesture. Lydia didn't reach for it. She nodded instead, moving to pull her cart from him. If he touched her again, she knew she'd do something stupid—like faint dead away. Erik's touch was too potent. Men never affected her like this. "Good day, Mr. MacGregor."

"Erik, please." His hand tightened, not letting go of the cart.

Lydia nodded, but didn't say his name. She again tried to jerk the cart away, but he still didn't let go.

"Let me get that for ya," he said, not giving her a choice as he began walking.

"But, your appointment," Lydia said weakly, oddly touched by the gentlemanly gesture. In the last year of carting her packages down, not one person had offered to help her. Not that she needed help, but it was a sweet gesture.

"There's nothing sweet about me, love," he said.

Lydia blinked in surprise. Had she said that out loud? He winked when she looked at him, and she felt her cheeks heating. Glancing to the side, she was relieved to see the post office was close. "This is it. Thank you."

He turned, looking at the old brick building set apart from the others on the block. Mrs. Callister, one of the biggest town gossips, looked their way. The old woman had a pencil tucked behind her ear and a notepad in her purse for just such a rumor-happy occasion.

"I got it from here," Lydia said, taking advantage of his distraction to get away before Mrs. Callister's imagination could run amuck. His smile widened as she looked back from the front door of the building.

"Can ya tell me one thing?" he called after her. Dark eyes bored into hers. She really needed to find a place to sit down—preferably in a bath filled with ice cubes. Her heart pounded at a rapid tempo, and she didn't even want to think of what was going on between her legs. With her luck, her jeans would be soaked from their little encounter, and her total mortification would be complete. He motioned down to her cart. "What's Love Potions?"

Lydia needlessly glanced at the packages'

labels. Looking back at him, she said, "My business."

Before he could ask anything more, a young girl came out of the post office with her mother. "Hi, lotion lady!"

"Hi, there, ah, flaxen ringlet girl," Lydia answered in rushed cheerfulness. She couldn't think of the girl's name, though her mom came into her home-based shop at least once a month to buy lotions. It was quite possible she'd never gotten their names, only knew them by face. Though, to be truthful, Lydia could barely think of anything right now.

The girl didn't notice Lydia's distraction, giggling as she politely held the door open. Lydia gratefully pulled the cart inside, hearing the girl ask her mother, "What's flacken rings?"

As Lydia glanced outside through the glass door, she saw the Scotsman was gone. She took a deep breath. What on earth was that all about? "Gramma, if you really can hear me like you said you'd be able to, don't do this. I don't need the distraction right now. Hell, I don't need the embarrassment. I don't want a man in my life. Please make sure I never see him again."

Mrs. Callister grinned, catching Lydia's eye. The older woman's pencil flew over her notepad.

Grimacing, Lydia grabbed her cart and hurried to get in line.

MO CHREACH! That's definitely one thing in the town's favor.

Erik grinned, despite the seriousness of his day. As he climbed up the hill, visions of a slender goddess filled his head—and his body. Her eyes were the dark blue of the night sky and a great complement to her gorgeous lips. No less stirring was her smell, a sweet blend of lavender and mint, combined with the subtle scent of her sex. Sometimes having extremely good senses came in handy. At other times, it was a nuisance—like when he met a woman who was attracted to him, and he didn't have time to properly pursue their mutual feelings. When her pink little tongue had darted over her lips as those dark eyes watched his thickening erection, he'd almost burst through his pants.

Erik shifted his weight, sticking his hands in his pockets in what he hoped was a subtle gesture. Had he realized he'd run into such a beautiful woman, he'd have worn looser pants. Especially when the woman boldly stared at his manhood until Erik wanted nothing more than to cast a spell to freeze the town so he could play out the passions coursing in his blood.

Though, to be honest, he'd devoured her just as hungrily with his eyes—only he was lucky enough to recover first, able to hide his reaction under an easy grin. It had been years, decades perhaps, maybe longer still, since he'd felt such blatant need, such rampant uncontrollable desire. The kind of desire that made the beast in him want to take over his human form so that it could come out and play, the kind of liquid heat that made his magick surge to the surface. Even then, he'd usually seen the woman naked first.

All the MacGregors were lusty creatures. Being first and foremost a clan of ancient warlocks, it was in their nature. Sexual energy, like all of life's pleasures, gave brief surges of power to their magick. It fed them. And, if a man were so lucky to find his *fiorghrá*, he'd be powerful indeed. Each MacGregor had his own natural abilities and burdens. Erik's burden was the fact he'd been born a shifter. Somewhere in his ancestry there was either a dalliance with a puma shifter or a spell gone wrong. Either way, it just happened to be a dominant part of his genetics.

Most of the younger generation in the MacGregor clan had given up on finding their *fiorghrá*, and Erik was no different. It wasn't like the old days. Yes, at one time Erik had wanted to find love and marry. However, if he had sat around pining for it over the length of his long life, he'd have ended himself decades ago. Sometimes it was best to accept what could not be changed and move on. The clan elders—who also happened to be his parents, uncles and aunts— had tried to push the *fíorghrá* matter, but in the end there was nothing they could do. It wasn't like they could cast a spell when it came to the heart. To do so was forbidden and for good reason. Love couldn't be forced or else it wasn't love.

"Love Potions," he mused, walking faster as he neared the top of the hill. He owned a car, but had left it at the hotel. The day was too beautiful and his energy had been a little low as of late. The fresh air did him some good as did the simple pleasure of walking.

Erik grinned. Perhaps he'd pay her store a little visit and show the pretty little lotion lady just what really went into making a love potion. The real ones wouldn't make them fall in love, but it sure as hell would make them fuck like they were. A few of the right aphrodisiacs and he'd have her sprawled out on the floor for hours.

Erik sighed. The idea had merit, as far as fantasies went. He would never do it to her unwillingly.

The first step would be to get her out on a date. By the way she looked at him, that wouldn't be hard. And if she came on to him, offering him the delights of her sweet body, who was he to say no? Unfortunately, because of who he was, he'd have to make her forget afterward. It didn't matter that he felt a connection to her that went deeper than mere sex. With this being a new town, the elders wouldn't appreciate him stirring up trouble with the womenfolk until they'd settled in and could conceal any mishap with their combined powers.

Erik walked faster, the importance of his task weighing on him once more. Family responsibility called. For mortals, house shopping was merely a chore. For his family, it was more than a small burden. Their survival depended on making the right choice. There were too many considerations —size, security, natural elements in the surrounding area. It wasn't like the days when vast, private estates were easy to come by, and if their kind became exposed they would just pick up and move to a different country. Nowadays, land was developed and technology connected the planet. If his kind were discovered, they'd be broadcast all over the world. Sure, joined, they could drop a veil over the eyes of a town like Green Vallis, could erase the memories of a few, but there was no way to control a worldwide exposure with magick. The 1590 North Berwick witch trials in his homeland were proof of that, and back then they didn't have internet and viral videos to contend with.

No, they had to lay low, play it safe or risk the persecution of the old days, when witches and warlocks were hunted by mortals. To this day the words "Old Tolbooth" and "Inquisition" sent a chill throughout the clan. The residual effects of those times still lingered in human mythos. Warlocks were portrayed as evil monsters when in truth the MacGregors were simply a magickal clan—one immortal, supernatural species in a hidden world of many.

Actually, in a strange way, technology and science had saved his kind. With modern advancement came logic and understanding. Humans had explained away magick with reason and had given up folklore for the anesthetizing influence of too many movies. Fake magic tricks entertained them. Old magick, which had been a part of everyday mortal habit, had disappeared—like using ruins to create protection spells and hanging bells to ward off evil spirits. Superstitions were replaced by proposed fact.

However human exposure wasn't the only concern they faced. There were darker forces in the world that would love to see the MacGregors harness their power for evil. Though technically good by discipline, the ability to be bad was well within their reach. The balance of power inside each of them demanded restraint. Even Erik would admit there were times when the urge to let loose his energy, to no longer hide what he was, became strong. It was the love of his family that always brought him back from the edge, and he would do the same for any one of them.

Erik sighed, tired of searching locations. If only he had just magical concerns with this task, but he also had the matter of fitting the needs of his extended family. In too isolated an area they'd go mad with boredom, and bored warlocks were hard to keep out of mischief. Knowing he was going to be late for his appointment with the realtor, he let the wind take him, calling on it to speed his way. So far Green Vallis seemed like the answer to their prayers, and if all went well, as the signs had so far indicated, he'd be buying a house by the end of the day.

LYDIA WALKED into her home through the kitchen entrance. She let the screen door slam shut behind her, as she shoved the cart over to the side so it was out of the way. The kitchen was cozy with light floral curtains, the pink and yellow pattern really subtle against the cream colored walls. The old fashioned décor screamed of her grandmother's influence, and Lydia couldn't imagine changing it. Bottles of lotion cluttered the otherwise pristine countertops. Love Potions's line of self-pampering products had overtaken the house. As the business boomed, so did the hours she spent running it.

They rarely used the front door of the house, as the kitchen faced the driveway and walk down to the town. Lydia had kept it locked since the vandalism started. Off the kitchen was the living room, stairwell leading to three bedrooms and a bathroom and the small entryway by the front door. Her living room had been converted into a cozy display area. None of the locals seemed to mind stepping into the home to pick up purchases.

"Frank is up at the main house again," Charlotte said, glancing up from the table. "Rumor has it he's got a buyer."

Charlotte was her best friend and also happened to be her only employee. The woman was gorgeous, with the kind of all year tan, generous breast size and big almond eyes most women would kill for. If not for her sarcastic personality, she'd have suitors tearing down the door at all hours of the day. But after years proving she could rip a guy of his masculine pride with just a sentence and a look, the men had stopped coming around.

"Oh, yeah?" Lydia asked, still distracted by her little encounter on the way to the post office.

Lydia glanced around her kitchen, not really seeing it. The old Victorian house was originally part of a big estate, having been built for someone's mother-in-law. Later, it had become the servants' quarters before Lydia's grandfather purchased it for his bride. The "main house", as they called it, was the old mansion further up the hill that some old displaced English lord had owned. It had been uninhabited for years as no one in Green Vallis was rich enough to buy and maintain it.

Frank Fenton, the town's only realtor, had been salivating over the idea of selling it for years. Before that, his father had tried to sell it. Lydia's worst fear was that land developers would purchase the property and tear the historical mansion down, and even worse, turn it into a shopping complex. Annabelle had told her not to worry. Apparently her grandmother had cast some sort of protection spell over the house to keep it from falling into the hands of the wrong owners. If only Lydia believed in protection spells.

"That's all you got? Oh, yeah?" Charlotte demanded, wiggling with excitement.

"What?" Lydia paused on her way to the refrigerator. Charlotte's words sunk in. "You mean a serious buyer? A buyer, buyer? One with money? Not just someone curious to see inside?"

"Fletch at the hotel told me some Scottish guy is here to look at it. Frank told Maggie, who told Fletch that Frank is pretty sure he's got it sold this time. The man's references checked out, which means he's got money, and he's motivated to buy."

Lydia paled. A Scottish man? Erik MacGregor? He was going to be her new neighbor? Mr. I'm so sexy Lydia will be fainting every time she walks out of her house with just the thought of me being so close? *That* was who was looking at the mansion?

"Lydia, hon? Are you okay?" Charlotte instantly stood. "You're pale."

"I guess Gramma's spell wore off, huh?" Lydia took a deep breath and tried to laugh, but the sound was weak. Charlotte ushered Lydia to the chair. "Did Fletch say what the man wanted to do with the place?"

"Let me get you some tea," Charlotte said, instantly going to put water on the stove. "I just made some so it won't be long before the water's hot enough. And no, no one knows what the guy wants with the place. Fletch said he didn't talk much. Just grabbed some local brochures and asked for a room."

Lydia picked an opened box of tea off the kitchen table. It was one from her newest collections. "Drinking my entire inventory again, I see."

Charlotte made a face. "Leave me alone. It's your fault for having such great blends. Make tea that sucks, and I'll stop drinking it."

"So will the customers." Lydia chuckled. She leaned back and rubbed her temples, trying not to think about Erik or the way he'd made her a sensitive mass of nerves from head to toe. Maybe Gramma's imaginary spell would hold up and he'd go away. She took a deep, trembling breath.

"Maybe that's a good thing," Charlotte said. "Then we could keep up with orders."

"Being busy is good. No orders is bad." Lydia laughed, but the sound was halfhearted even to her own ears.

"Having dates is good. Working all the time is bad," Charlotte corrected.

"I wonder if they'll make it a museum." She bit her lip thoughtfully, trying to think of anything that would take her thoughts out of the gutter and put them back into her head. "That'd be great for walk-in traffic and for the town. Tourist places are always a great draw, and it would at least preserve the place."

Yeah, and the new owner wouldn't have to be anywhere near the business. He could leave town and I'd never have to see him again.

"So do outlet malls," her friend drawled.

"Ugh. I'd rather see it burned to the ground." Lydia wrinkled her nose in distaste.

"A bed and breakfast wouldn't be awful. It has enough rooms." Charlotte ran her hands through her hair, scratching her scalp while suppressing a yawn. "I'd do it if I could afford it."

"I met him." The words tumbled out. She could never keep anything from Charlotte. Lydia toyed with the opened tea box so she wouldn't have to meet her friend's eyes.

"Him, who?"

"The Scotsman." She tried to act unconcerned by it. "He helped me cart the packages to the post office, and then said he had to run to an appointment. Guess it must've been to see the house."

"Well?"

"Well, what?" Lydia asked.

Charlotte poured water into the cup before the kettle started to whistle. By the steam curling up from the rim, it was hot enough. Lydia grabbed a tea bag from her new line and opened it. The scent of mint and chamomile wafted over her. It was foolish considering she already had the tea packaged and would only have to do more later to replace it. For the moment, she didn't care. The herbal blend would help to calm her tingling body.

"The Scotsman," Charlotte prompted, rolling her eyes. "Well?"

"He's," Lydia shrugged, "all right, I guess."

Okay, so she *almost* always told Charlotte everything.

"Ugh, just all right?" Charlotte frowned, looking disappointed. "They're never like you hope, huh? Here I was having fantasies about a sexy foreign millionaire riding around on a horse in a kilt." She made a small noise of wonder. "Huh. If Scotsmen don't wear anything under their kilts and they ride a horse, do you think they chafe their manbits?"

Lydia took a deep breath, barely hearing her friend's attempt at a joke. The ache inside her would not go away, and not even the smell of tea helped. Adjusting her weight in the chair strangely turned her on. Poor Charlotte was in the same boat she was—no man, no dates, no lover and no prospect of them any time soon.

What was wrong with her today? Was three years with no man finally starting to take its toll?

Wasn't the libido supposed to shut off after a while?

She thought of Erik. He'd stared at her chest, and the thick interest jutting out against his pants had been unmistakable. Did she actually have a prospective one night stand? If he was to be her neighbor, then no. But if he was only looking and decided not to buy, then what harm was there in a small fling? She'd have to find a way around Fletch at the hotel. He'd tell everyone if he saw her going into a room.

"You feeling all right?" Charlotte asked. "First you looked pale, now you look flushed. Should I call Dr. West?"

"No, I'll be fine. I might be coming down with something, but it's not serious."

"You're never sick." Charlotte reached to touch her forehead.

"Just tired, then. How are we on orders?" Lydia needed to change the subject. "Did you check the computer today?"

"Yep, did it while you were gone. I even got most of the orders packed up in the living room ready to go. The majority of it was just lotion, so no big deal. By the way, we need to make a batch of lavender rose."

"I'll do it tonight." Lydia stood. "Why don't

you take off? It's so pretty outside. No use in both of us being cooped up."

"Actually," Charlotte said, her eyes gleaming with mischief. "I was thinking of a little recon work."

Lydia arched a brow. "You want to spy on Erik?"

"Erik, is it?" Charlotte smirked. Lydia instantly knew she'd messed up. "So, Mr. Scotsman has a name, does he?"

"Everyone has a name." Lydia tried not to look flustered and failed.

Charlotte hooked Lydia's arm and pulled her out the door. "Come on, walk with me. Let's just have a peek at this man you say is only 'all right'. If the town's lucky he'll be single and have lots of brothers. We're in dire need of some fresh dating material."

Chapter Two

Erik glanced around the dusty mansion's front reception hall, not looking directly at the realtor. So far he was very impressed with the property. The old Georgian style mansion sat high on a hill, overlooking the town below on one side and a long stretch of forest on the other. It was rare to find such a beautifully untouched location in America, though his family had lived in some wonderful places—Southern plantations, New York penthouses, even along an entire block in Philadelphia on the shores of the river—none really compared to those in the old country. There was a debate in the clan to move back to Scotland, but the truth was they were Americans now by legal paperwork and if the lot of them up and moved it would draw notice.

Foundation-wise the house was in excellent condition, even though it hadn't been lived in for some time. It didn't matter. A small spell and his uncles would have it as good as new.

"There's about eighty acres total, including the forest and a small stream in the woods. If you're an outdoorsman it's perfect for hunting and fishing. About six acres are the old gardens in back. Several paths wind through the area. The gardens themselves are a little overgrown, but I've been told by the local nursery that many of the trees and shrubs are salvageable. The owner has asked me to extend their services, should you have a need of them." Frank wanted the sale so bad he could hardly contain himself. Erik noted the man didn't even have to look at the listing as he recited the property's features.

"My brother, Iain, will see to all that," Erik told him, smiling at the thought. Iain would no doubt insist they put in another golf course, along with a shinty field. All of his family enjoyed playing the games. Well, everyone but his brother, Euann.

New York living had become difficult. Yes, they could blend into the masses better and disappear into a crowd, but after two decades of concrete and metal, they needed to refuel. Their magick could only borrow so much power-infusing life from Central Park and rooftop gardens before they killed every plant in Manhattan.

It was more than the beauty of the outdoors that called him to Wisconsin. They needed nature to fuel their magick. Power had to come from some place and though sexual energy could give a rush, it wasn't as steady and strong of a power source, not like borrowing from nature. Here the MacGregors could take from the forest as a whole rather than kill a single tree. They tried to live in peace with nature, which was why Iain was so conscious to plant trees.

Sometimes, though, magick didn't always go as planned, and there had been times they'd taken out a giant section of forest while fighting a powerful foe. Ah, but such were the good old days. Now the biggest threat to the clan seemed to be the members in it. Mischievousness ran in the bloodline.

"Very good, sir. As I was saying, the house has over twenty thousand square feet total and there are well over sixty-five separate rooms. There are also some outbuildings, including an old coach house from the late eighteen hundreds that could easily be turned into a garage or stables. There is only one road access in or out. The entire hillside you saw on the way up also comes with the property—all but a small lot. It will ensure the utmost privacy, just like you requested."

"What do ya mean, all but a small lot?" Erik broke in before the man could continue. He openly frowned, not happy to hear the latest glitch in his plans.

"The Victorian house you might have seen on the way up. It belongs to one of the locals. She's a nice woman and shouldn't give you any trouble."

Erik's frown deepened. So much for Green Vallis being perfect. He should've known not to get his hopes up. "So it isn't a rental? I thought ya said this property was completely secluded from the rest of town. My family is very private."

"A row of trees separates the two properties so you'll hardly even know she's there," Frank assured him.

"Will she sell her property?" Erik ran his hands through his hair. Maybe the town wouldn't be a complete loss. They could well afford it. Hell, given enough time, they'd probably end up owning half the town—like they did everywhere they went. "I suppose I could buy it as well."

"Uh…"

Erik felt that the man considered lying to him. He turned around, giving him a hard look of warning.

"Uh, no, no I don't think she will." Frank

admitted the truth after all. "But, she's a nice lady. Owns her own business. Very quiet. Never causes trouble."

Erik paused, tilting his head. "A business? What business?"

"Ah, you know, products for females. Lotions, bath soaps, candles, tea, that sort of thing." Frank swallowed anxiously. "She does a lot of internet business. Very respectable. Not a trouble maker at all. I assure you, you will have no problems with her. I doubt you'll even know she's there."

The man was nervous. However, excitement flooded Erik's veins overtaking his disappointment, as he asked, "Love Potions?"

Frank's mouth gaped open, as if he couldn't believe Erik knew that.

"I make a point of researching everything about the towns I'm thinking about moving to," Erik's voice was hard, but as he turned his back, he let a small smile come over his face. So, Lydia's house was just a few steps away, sharing the hill with this property. If he bought this house, it would be several weeks until the rest of the MacGregors joined him in full force. They'd wrap up their affairs and get the old house packed while he and a couple of his brothers got the new house ready.

He'd seen Lydia, how little and frail she

appeared. Getting the mortal to sell her house shouldn't be a problem—after he had plenty of time to seduce her first. What better way to ease the tension caused by the stress of moving? His arousal hadn't gone down since meeting her, but the pressure had lessened. Just thinking of her being so accessible made his body stir anew. Holding up his hand so the realtor wouldn't follow him, Erik said, "Ya wait right here. I'm going to look around."

"But—" Frank began, dabbing his forehead with a handkerchief. Erik shot him a look and the man instantly stopped protesting. "Yes, sir, I'll be right here if you need me."

"Very well." Erik decided to start at the top and work his way down. He climbed the long, wide tread, marble staircase. The craftsmanship of the woodwork was remarkable. It was the real deal—done in a time when people took pride in their trade. He threaded his fingers behind his back, not touching the dust on the old oak banister.

Erik was pleased to discover that some of the old furnishings were still in the home, covered by yellowed sheets. Many of them required small repairs, but were really a great find. With a little elbow grease and family magick, they'd be as good as new. The house was idyllic for what they needed with enough rooms upstairs for all of the MacGregors—Erik, his brothers and sister, their father, cousins, uncles and aunts. The whole clan could easily fit, each having their own private area. Those that chose to stay in the house would, anyway. The others could find places in town— close to the family, but away enough to be on their own. One thing was for sure. MacGregors always stuck together, from those early days in the barbaric Scottish countryside to today.

The first level was just as grand. As he walked by Frank, Erik again held up his hand, not saying a word. The man nodded and stepped back, letting him be. Erik was glad. Anything the man had to tell him he could see for himself.

The dining room was huge, perfect for large family meals together. There was space for the elders to practice their magick and still have a separate office to work out of. The vast MacGregor Empire only kept growing with each new property they acquired. It took all of them to keep the family business in order.

Beyond the offices, an entire back wing sprawled out with more bedrooms than he cared to count and plenty of space to build more bathrooms. After about an hour of poking around, he nodded to himself in satisfaction. This was it. This was their new home. He could well contain the situation with Lydia, and if worse came to worse, they'd cast a spell to get her to move. Women always seemed to respond unfavorably enough to a plague of spiders and roaches. The idea of muscling her out didn't set well with him, but the needs of the clan had to come first and they'd give her a more than fair price for her trouble.

"I'll take it," Erik said, coming back into the reception hall where Frank waited. The man's jaw fell open in surprise. The agape mouth seemed to be a favorite expression of his. Erik looked away. "I'll take possession now. I expect the paperwork to be drawn up tonight, and I'll be to your office first thing tomorrow to sign. The money will be wired to whichever account ya specify soon after. It will be paid all in cash, asking price minus ten thousand because ya didn't tell me about the other resident on the hill. Unless that isn't good for ya?"

"Ah, no, it's fine. Thank you, sir."

"And I'll need a complete list of available properties in town, including any downtown apartments and business fronts for the rest of my family to look over. If they're interested they'll contact ya. I'll need a street map of Green Vallis, numbers for all the city departments, a list of all local businesses and their owners, an aerial view photograph of this property and the names and phone numbers of all our neighbors." Erik held out his hand. It was a simple enough trick to get the realtor not to question his terms. Frank glanced at his palm, confused. "My keys."

"Oh, yes, yes, of course." The stunned realtor fumbled with his pocket before producing the keys.

"Good day, Mr. Fenton," Erik dismissed.

"Good day, sir," Frank answered, hurrying out of the house as if he was afraid Erik might change his mind.

Erik chuckled when he was alone. Frank would probably become a rich man off the MacGregor family. They could well afford the extra ten thousand for the house, but this man needed to understand no shady half-facts would be accepted. If he misled or neglected to reveal part of a situation again, one of his cousins would start a realty business and put him under. If Frank played his cards right, by the time they were done setting up businesses and investing in the town, he could retire off the commissions he made. No doubt the man had never had such an easy sell.

As a warlock, Erik knew to trust his gut. His magick told him this was the place that had been calling to his clan. There was something powerful about it, unlike the other houses they'd lived in over the centuries. Just standing in the hall made him feel stronger, more powerful. He couldn't ignore it. This was the place they were going to be living—at least until it was time to move on.

Erik walked out the front door, making a slight motion with his hand to lock it. He glanced around the long drive of the front yard. Green grass rolled over the property. It had been freshly cut—no doubt by Frank because of his coming. Taking his cell phone out of his pocket, he pressed redial.

"Erik?" the voice answered.

"Aye, it's me, da," Erik said in Gaelic. "This is the one."

"You're sure?" his father answered in the same language.

"Have I ever not been?"

"Don't get smart with me," his father answered. Erik grinned. "And wipe that look from your face."

Erik obliged, not at all surprised by his father's intuition. Angus MacGregor was a very powerful warlock. "My powers feel stronger here. Stronger than they've felt in a long time."

A tingle worked its way over Erik's body. Someone was watching him. Closing his eyes, he sniffed.

Mm, lavender and mint. Lydia.

"Da, I have to go."

"Aye. I know," his father answered. "I'll tell the others ya found it. Good job, laddie."

LYDIA BIT HER LIP, trying not to meet the accusation in Charlotte's gaze as they hid behind a giant shrub. She tilted her head to the side, trying to see what she could of Erik through the dense leaves. Charlotte poked her hard in the side with her finger, forcing Lydia to finally pay attention.

"He. Is. Fucking. Hot," Charlotte mouthed slowly, her eyes round with meaning.

Lydia nodded. What else could she do? Erik was sexier than anyone she'd ever seen before in her life. Considering him a second time didn't do a thing to harm her first impression of him. If anything, it made the longing inside her worse.

She motioned for Charlotte to be quiet as she continued to look at him through the thick shrub. It was hard, but she finally managed to get a great view of his tight ass beneath the gray pants. His back was to them as he talked on the phone. She couldn't make out his foreign words, but did detect the thick burr of his accent on the breeze.

"Damn, I would give anything to see that man naked," Charlotte whispered. "How could you only say he was 'all right'? Shit, hon, I'd love to see what you thought went into the 'sexy as sin' category."

"Shh," Lydia scolded. "I don't want him to hear us."

"Lydia Barratt." Erik said. "I can't see ya, love, but I know you're there."

Lydia froze. She made a motion to Charlotte to run seconds before she tried to herself. Charlotte giggled, grabbed Lydia's arm and pulled. Lydia tumbled out from behind the shrub.

"There ya are." Erik grinned, his eyes alighting with amusement as he looked at her on the ground.

"How'd you know I was here?" Lydia slowly picked herself up off the grass, doing her best not to make eye contact. Her cheeks heated in embarrassment.

"I know your smell. Lavender and mint."

"Oh." Embarrassment? Make that intense, flaming desire that flushed her face and made her whole body shake. Never had a man done this to her. And what exactly did he mean, he knew her smell?

His brow arched, incorrigibly sexy. "Spying on me?"

Say something incredibly smart. Don't let him see you're flustered.

"Ah, no," Lydia denied weakly, brushing off

her sleeves though they were clean. She'd never been a good liar.

Very suave, Lydia, she thought dryly. Movement caught her eye, and she peeked through the sides of her lashes to see Charlotte wiggling her fingers, grinning like a fool as she stayed hidden.

"No?"

"I was looking for…ah…Frank. I saw his car. I wanted to talk to him about this estate. I didn't realize he was showing it today or else I'd have called him."

Erik grinned. His look said he didn't believe her. "Sorry, love, but I already bought it. You're too late."

"Oh, I can't afford a place like this." The response was automatic. She shook her head. In her dreams, she could afford a place like this. Actually, growing up she'd often dreamed that this was her house.

She forced a calming breath. Knowing he was her new neighbor pretty much threw cold water on all her fantasies of him. The last thing she needed was to get involved with a rich, handsome Scotsman who lived in town. It wouldn't take him long to hear all the rumors about her family's past and get all freaked out. "Well, nice to see you again. Welcome to the neighborhood."

"Actually, ya want to poke around a wee bit? I

was going to walk the back gardens, see what I've gotten myself into."

"No, thank you. I've seen the house before." Lydia started to back away. "I own the place just down the hill and used to come up here as a child. I know every inch. Oh, which reminds me…"

She continued to back up as she pointed toward the mansion's back yard. When he looked, she motioned frantically for Charlotte to run. Charlotte stubbornly shook her head and indicated that Lydia should go back up to the main house with Erik.

"…there's a cellar window, three from the left on the back side that can be opened with a key hidden beneath the fifth stone out from the, ah," she motioned at Charlotte again when he wasn't looking, jerking her thumb down the hill, "second stone vase in the back. I don't think many people know the key's there, but it's a secret entrance into the house. You might want to check on it so there are no surprises."

Erik's grin widened, watching her retreat through narrowed eyes. He didn't look worried. "Ya know a lot about the house, then?"

"Yeah, I guess so. Kind of hard not to, living beneath it my whole life."

"I'd consider it a favor if ya walked the property with me." Erik made a motion toward Charlotte. "Your friend can join us if she likes."

Charlotte popped out from behind the shrub. "No, thank you, but no. I've got to be going to work. My boss is a real tyrant."

Lydia shot her friend a bemused glance. She was Charlotte's boss. Seeing the mischievous look on her friend's face, she mused that she might not be her boss for long. When this was over, Lydia just might fire the meddlesome woman.

"But Lydia would love to show you around." Charlotte appeared completely unconcerned by Lydia's expression of warning. "She knows everything about this estate. Don't you, Lyd? She even did a research paper about its history in high school. Got an A."

Kill me now, she thought. *This is going to be torture.*

"Wonderful," Erik exclaimed.

Lydia knew when she was beat. Charlotte pushed at her back. Erik's almost wicked smile drew her from the front. Before she knew what had happened, she stood alone with him on the mansion's front lawn.

"I don't know exactly what I can tell you that you don't already know about the place." Lydia weakly motioned in the direction of the back garden. She took a step, pausing until he moved to follow her. It was nerve-racking being so close to him, and she was having a really hard time concentrating. "It's been dormant my whole life. A few people have looked at it over the years, but there have been no takers."

"Hum," was all he said.

"Anyway, you might want to consider putting up a perimeter fence of some sort, not that we've had too many problems with the—what?" Lydia stopped. His grin had widened as if he laughed silently at her.

"The protection of the house is well in hand, lassie," he assured her. "My brother, Euann will take care of it as soon as he arrives. He always does."

"Oh," Lydia nodded, slightly irritated. "I only meant that we've had some vandalism around here as of late. I'd hate to see inverted pentagrams and whatnot spray painted on your walls, or carved into the oak molding around the doors. Honestly, many of us are surprised this house was never hit, being as it's so secluded and the sheriff hardly ever sends patrol cars up—well, unless I call and ask him to."

"I'll tell Euann to be on watch," Erik assured her, "but ya need not concern yourself."

What was the point of her showing him around if he wasn't going to listen to her? They strolled down the wide cobblestone path leading from the house to the main gardens. Grass poked from between the stones. Overgrown shrubbery and tree limbs blocked part of the walkway, forcing them onto the grass at times.

"So, are you…?" she began, only to let her voice taper off. Were his intentions really any of her business?

"Am I what?" Erik reached for her, brushing a small bug off her shoulder. His hand paused briefly in mid-action, barely touching her as he whispered something. She leaned closer, but couldn't understand what he said.

Tingling erupted on her shoulder, making a quick trip to her neck and chin. She dashed the back of her fingers over her jaw, trying to stop the mystical sensation with the firm press of reality. It didn't work. The electricity of it grew, traveling like a static charge down her arm and across her chest. Her body jerked. To her horror, she realized that she *still* didn't have a bra on. She'd been so frazzled earlier when Charlotte insisted they sneak up the hill to spy on Erik that she'd forgotten about it.

Lydia turned slightly under the pretense of glancing around so she could sneak a peek at her chest. It was as she feared. Her nipples poked against her shirt like two little traitors saluting the enemy. When she managed to finally look at his face, she admitted, "It's really none of my business, but I was going to ask if you were opening a business here with your brother."

"Why wouldn't that be your business?" he inquired, unconcerned. "Ya own land on the hill as well and ya have a business too."

"Ah, yeah, but..." Lydia quivered. The electricity had made its precarious way over her entire length.

"No. No business. This will be a family home."

"Oh, so you and the wife?" Disappointment threatened to unfurl in her stomach.

His eyes narrowed at that. "No. No wife. Just cousins, brothers, uncles, a sister, father... We tend to stick together. Call it a cultural thing."

"Oh." Okay, why did that little piece of information make her want to shout for joy? So what if he was single? She wasn't going to get involved with a neighbor. Besides, maybe he was just being nice. She didn't even want to think of how hellish it would be if all the MacGregors made her feel like this one did, all hot and shaky. She'd have to move to the Arctic Circle before the month was out just to cool off.

"Sorry, I'm prying." She forced her legs to move faster. The sooner they finished, the sooner she could run home and hide. "The house comes with about eighty acres, I believe."

"I'm more curious about the neighbors," he interrupted her. "One neighbor in particular."

Why was he looking at her like that? All liquid hot and sexy, like he could already picture her naked? Or was that her imagination running wild? She couldn't be sure.

The sparks of his initial touch intensified, seeming to jump off his flesh onto hers. These weren't the euphuistic sparks of romance novels, but real, sure as fire, sparks of pure sexual energy that incinerated her skin and made her so wickedly inclined that she became certain her knees might buckle. It was as if she could already feel him pressed to her skin, his naked body hovering at the point of entrance. Moisture gathered between her thighs, eagerly urging her to welcome him.

They'd come to a shaded part of the gardens. The unkempt trees blocked the late afternoon sun, illuminating them with dancing spots of orange-cast light. Birds called from the distance, adding music to their seclusion.

"Perhaps ya know her," Erik said softly, his tone so achingly seductive she couldn't speak. She swallowed in apprehension. The smoldering expression in his eyes said he felt it too. His words dropped an octave, as he continued, "About your height." Long fingers reached for her shoulder, touching her as before. Only this time, they stayed. "Very pretty."

Lydia gasped, turning her head to watch his fingers, the flesh of them dark compared to her paler skin. Heat hummed where he pressed against her shirt. She tried to tell herself not to fall for the gorgeous foreign guy. He probably used the accent all the time to get sex. His finger moved the tiniest measure. All rational thoughts left her. She didn't care that this was wrong, that this man was a stranger. She wanted him.

Obviously, after three years of being denied, her body was going to have its say. His fingers trailed along her neck, skimming across her rapid pulse to the bottom of the V in her shirt's neck-line. He reached her top button and she felt the material over her chest give as he unfastened it.

"Mm, aye," he continued, "big, sexy eyes. Silky, dark hair." Was he actually undressing her? Here? Now? Like this? "Incredible breasts that make my mouth water to suck on them. An ass so firm I've been thinking about sinking my teeth into a ripe cheek ever since first putting eyes on it."

At that her rounded gaze darted up to meet his. Was he serious? No man had ever dared to talk to her like that. She would've screeched in feigned outrage at him if she had a voice. His fingers popped open another button as he leaned forward. Lydia stayed grounded to her spot. Her heart hammered against the walls of her chest, and she breathed so hard and choppy she was sure she'd pass out soon.

Just as his lips were about to close on hers, she whispered, "No."

The protest came too late. His lips captured hers, sending a potent wave of unspeakable yearning from her mouth to her breasts, only to make its way down to her very core. He didn't grab her, didn't force her to stay against his kiss. He didn't have to. Lydia couldn't pull away. The wind seemed to pick up, whipping their hair around them.

This had to be a dream. Today had started so unmistakably normal. She was a good girl. She didn't kiss strange men, didn't let herself fall into an abyss of lust and confusion.

The devastating erotic feel of his closeness only made her all the hotter. She itched to be freed from her clothes. His firm mouth worked gently against hers, and when his warm, delicious tongue slipped past her lips, dancing and twirling in her mouth, she lost all willpower. He tasted good, like warm, sweet liquor.

Lydia gripped his shirt, feeling the hard, solid press of his muscles beneath. Damn, but he was in perfect shape! Moaning, she arched her chest, sucking his tongue like she suddenly wanted to suck the rest of him.

He was a drug, some potent, virile sexual drug that made her want to get on her knees and beg to give him pleasure. Lydia had never been particularly fond of giving oral pleasure, but suddenly it was like she craved it—as if her life depended on taking him between her lips.

He'd worked his fingers into her shirt and groaned as he found her naked breasts. The erect nipples were waiting for him, already puckered and sensitive. As if he knew their torment, he pinched them between his fingers, rolling the delicate buds before grasping the mounds in his strong, warm hands.

The power of him flooded her each time he touched her, driving her crazy with animalistic lust. Her hips jerked in response. She broke the kiss and aggressively pushed, forcing him against a tree trunk, hidden from the outside world by the branches.

Lydia had never been aggressive during sex— usually opting for a lights out, after dark kind of lovemaking. She gripped his waistband, pleased to feel the ready heat of his erection straining against the soft material. His hands roamed over her body as she worked his zipper. He ripped her shirt the rest of the way open. With a groan, he leaned over to take a mouthful of breast between his teeth. The way he devoured it, his low growl vibrating her flesh, was sinfully arousing. The dark silk of his long hair blew against her, just as much a caress as the rest of him.

She didn't want him to stop, but she had to wiggle free to reach his shaft. Her hand slipped down over his pants, and she was surprised to discover the full girth against her hands. Jerking his pants down, Lydia tensed, her eyes widening in surprise. The bulge only seemed to grow bigger beneath the tight fit of his cotton boxers.

"Don't stop, love," he murmured.

Almost in a daze, she clawed at his chest, trying to work the shirt up so she could feel his skin, even as she fell to her knees. Erik tossed the shirt aside. Lydia kneeled before him, her fingers shaking as she went to pull the tight black cotton down. Even as she was apprehensive of his size, her mouth watered for it. This was a man who could conquer every inch of her and suddenly she wanted to be conquered.

What was going on in her head? Why did she suddenly want him to overpower her?

She pulled the material, revealing the thick,

blunt tip of his arousal. Lydia lightly touched it, watching as he gasped and arched, his knees buckling slightly before he caught himself. When he looked at her, his eyes filled with a dark plea, she knew instinctively what he wanted. Her breath caught in the back of her throat. Lydia didn't stop to think as she flicked her tongue to taste the warm, salty essence of him.

There was something potently erotic to the intimate smell. Her gaze raked over his gorgeous body, before she looked up into his eyes. His expression was strained, caught between pleasure and awe. Shaking with her desire, she pulled his arousal free.

Erik groaned, his beautiful body leaning back against the tree as he bent his knees to better position himself. His pants were caught around his ankles, trapping them together. Lydia licked her lips.

"*Mo chreach!*" The foreign words left him like a curse.

Lydia wanted more. Running her hands over his tight stomach, she grabbed his hips and pulled. She wanted this, and she was going to take it.

ERIK GROANED, his entire body trembling. When he'd cast a small spell to loosen her inhibitions, he'd not expected her to do this. The spell should have made her act naturally toward him so that they may talk without the awkward newness of having just met.

Though, who was he to stop her?

Her big eyes had looked up at him, and he just knew she ached like he did. The sweet smell of her told him she was wet, so ready to be taken. Erik had lived too long not to trust his inner instincts. As he'd kissed her lips, he couldn't help thinking of how he wanted them intimately wrapped around his body. Almost instantly, she started sucking on his tongue, just as he would have her do his arousal.

As if by instinct, she knew what he wanted. It was like she read his desires. Her fingers gripped his hips, just as he liked. The animal inside him sought a woman who was aggressive and confident. Good thing he'd bound the creature until he could get the house secured for his family, or he'd not be able to control himself with her.

Her scent was in his head, calling to him. He wanted to lay her on the soft grass and spend hours worshipping her body, taking her until they came so many times they couldn't move. And then, he'd take her again. If she let him he'd spend the next several weeks, as he got the house ready, hopping in and out of her bed.

Oh, the things he wanted to do with her.

Her gorgeous eyes opened and looked up at him. She licked her lips, wetting them as she moved them closer. Erik tensed, not having realized what had happened until that moment. A light sheen of his power was in her gaze, mixing with her passion. Suddenly, it all made sense as the truth came crashing around him. She was an *inthrall*.

In a moment of painful sanity, he pushed her away. He wasn't sure how he managed with as weak as he was becoming. She growled low in her throat, her head bobbing possessively forward as if she'd continue. Erik was torn. It had been so long since he'd felt such longing and desire. Only the look in her eyes stopped him.

No. Not like this. Not with an *inthrall*. Already she'd taken too much from him, leaving his body weakened. Breathless he groaned. Half-teasing, half-serious, completely desperate to say anything to get her to back away until she could reclaim her senses, he said, "Aye, lass, it's a fine welcome ya give a man."

LYDIA STOPPED MOVING, completely stunned by what was happening. Her lips were still parted, on the verge of going forward to finish what she'd started. The strange euphoria that urged her to act on primal, carnal instinct—and nothing else—lightened its hold over her. Slowly, as if by not moving too fast she could disappear, she pulled away, drawing her hands to the ground for support as she pushed up.

Aye, lass, it's a fine welcome ya give a man.

Oh. My.

She took a deep breath.

Omigod!

Lydia couldn't look at him. What in the world had she done? She just got on her knees like some cheap slut and tried to give her new neighbor head like it was an everyday occurrence.

Bad. This is very, very bad. And wrong. So very wrong.

Horrified, she discovered her breasts were exposed for all to see. Well, for him to see anyway. Thankfully they were completely alone.

Lydia struggled to her feet, gripping her shirt. Her sex was so wet, ready to be ridden. Each pull of her body shot fire through her limbs. By the look of his remarkable, still erect shaft, he was willing to continue their tryst.

Lydia made a weak noise of dismay. If not for

his words bringing her back to reality, she would've still been on her hands and knees begging him to…

No. No. She couldn't even think it. She had to get out of there. This was too humiliating. Her mouth opened, but no sound came out. She shook her head, ready to run.

"Lydia," Erik said. "It isn't a bad thing to have a bit of fun now and again. I'll not think less of ya for staying and enjoying yourself if that is what ya chose to do. I know I would enjoy your company immensely."

She met his eyes for the briefest of seconds before taking off into a full sprint down the hill.

ERIK TRIED to run after her, grabbing his pants as he tripped. He couldn't stand the confused, hurt look in her eyes. Even more prevalent was a sense of utter humiliation. He knew instinctively that she'd never have done such a thing had he not cast the stupid spell. Usually the thing acted as a harmless icebreaker. With Lydia, it opened her up to him. He stumbled on a patch of grass, catching himself. With his size and strength, he could easily overtake her on foot. Suddenly, a gust of wind came from behind her, slamming him back into the tree. Feelings of horror, mortification and regret washed over him. The strength of them tore at his heart, making his entire being physically ache. They were her feelings.

Erik had sex aplenty in his long life and with many women. None of them made him feel like she did without even completing the act. None made him feel like he did at this moment—weak and powerful at the same time, dominant and protective, possessive and slightly obsessive. He took a deep breath, pinned to the tree with magick unable to move, still feeling the aftereffects of the pleasure she'd almost given him, now mixed with her repentance.

For a long moment, he stared, stunned that she'd absorbed so much of him from just a brief contact. They hadn't even had sex. If she absorbed so much of his magick from just thinking about him between her lips, as to keep him away, then what would happen if he would've actually slept with her? Would she drain his energies dry? Would such an act be the end of his powers? Would the act be the end of his life?

Remembering her sweet scent and the pleasure of her kiss, Erik groaned. He could tell by her reaction that she hadn't meant to go that far. Had she been herself, the best he could have hoped for this first day was the brush of her hand, or perhaps a chaste kiss. Ah, but would it matter if she was the end of him? If he was ever to surrender to a woman, he couldn't think of a better way to go than at the mercy of the most captivating Lydia Barratt.

Chapter Three

Lydia shivered from head to toe, letting the freezing cold water from the shower hit her skin. It helped to alleviate the full body throbbing, although barely.

"Omigod," she moaned. "What did I do? What did I do?"

How in the world could she even walk out of the house again? She barely left it as it was, except to walk around on the hill and down to the post office. Now she'd become a total recluse, the crazy lady with the scary house little children dared each other to knock on. And what was worse, the mansion gardens had been a favorite spot of hers. It looked like she wasn't going to be able to go there anymore. It wasn't like she could face Erik after the little "welcome gift" she'd almost given him.

"Omigod."

Just thinking of it made her tingle in a way she'd never experienced. Closing her eyes, all she could see was his firm body, the way his neck and face looked under the dancing lights of the shade. Lydia opened her mouth, letting the water hit inside. It was no use. She could still taste his lips and the damned warm, sweet liquor that flavored them.

Her body ached, despite the cold water. She couldn't calm her racing heart, couldn't temper back the desire in her belly. As she lathered soap over her skin, the sensations only became worse. The same thing happened as she washed her hair. Deciding the cold shower wasn't going to do the trick, she got out. Pulling a soft pink robe around her arms, she stumbled weakly from the bathroom.

Not bothering to brush her hair, she fell onto the soft feather mattress of her bed. Even the suppleness against her back was a caress, driving her senses over the edge. Before she could think to stop herself, she was wiggling, parting her thighs. Her robe fell open, exposing her body.

"Erik," she whispered, desperately wishing he was with her. Instantly her body heated, no longer cold from her long shower. It was as if she'd never taken it.

The scent of him came to mind. With one hand she pinched her nipples, running the other down her stomach to her sex. Parting her wet folds, she bit her lip. She never remembered being so aroused before. Her finger glided in the moist heat, and she found her swollen bud buried in the velvet folds.

What would his body feel like prying her open? At that she shivered. Maybe he would be too big.

"It's not like I'm ever going to find out," she promised herself, not daring to give credence to the disappointment the words caused her.

The early evening sky darkened considerably outside her window, as if a cloud passed over the setting sun. Lace curtains blew inward, carrying with them the smell of fresh air. She wondered what it would be like to have him there, strong hands gripping her hips to keep her from squirming, warm lips tasting and licking every inch of her.

Automatically, she knew he'd be demanding in bed, conquering her as he saw fit. He was so bold, so confident. And why not? He had the body of a god to back it up.

It was like Charlotte always said. Men weren't

confident anymore. There were no more warriors, no impossibly dominant males who fiercely protected their women. Society had driven fear into men, fear that they'd be arrested for allowing their base urges to roam free. Not that taking a woman against her will was acceptable. Somehow, Lydia doubted Erik would be the type to need to ask for permission to be a real man.

Whatever was going on inside her today was definitely working. Tension built where her fingers touched, spreading uncontrollably over her taut flesh. Her skin was so sensitive and firm, her breathing ragged. Lydia closed her eyes, arching back on the bed. Self-pleasure had never done this to her before.

"Erik," she cried softly, closing her eyes tight. Her hands flew back over her head. The sensations only continued. It was like she could feel his mouth on her. Lydia was too afraid to look down, afraid that if she saw no one was there that the feelings would stop.

Her thighs and stomach tightened. Tensing from head to toe, she met with release. A soft caress brushed her thigh, causing her to shiver in the aftermath. Gradually, she opened her eyes and looked down. She was alone in the bedroom.

Lydia took a deep breath, so numb she couldn't move. Her heart beat so fast she was scared it would explode. Closing her eyes, she whispered, "Oh, please let this dream end. I can't do this. I can't handle a man like Erik MacGregor."

ERIK!

Erik tensed, looking around the inside of his new mansion's foyer. He'd been trying to reason what happened with Lydia when he heard the sound of her voice echoing in his mind. Scanning the darkened corners, he found their empty shadows staring back at him.

The soft cry washed over him again and he licked his lips, tasting the unmistakable flavor of a woman's desire in his mouth. Even as it made his body jolt with perfect sexual awareness and torture, he couldn't help the satisfied grin that crossed his features. Lydia was fantasizing about him.

"Soon, *leannáin*, very soon."

LYDIA STARED at the mess of lotion that covered her kitchen. It glopped down the walls, over the floor, covering both her and Charlotte. The scent of lilies filled the air, heavy and unmistakable. For a long time, she didn't move. After the last four days filled with clumsy accidents, she was hardly surprised the thing exploded.

"What just happened?" Charlotte asked, her eyes wide. "How does a vat of lotion just blow up like that?"

"I…" Lydia shivered. Her grandmother's favorite scent was lilies.

"Gramma Annabelle?" Charlotte asked, as if reading her mind. She took a deep breath before covering her mouth and coughing.

"No, there has to be a reasonable explanation for this." Lydia flung her hands, trying to shake off some of the mess. Splats of lotion rained onto the floor around her. "Something logical. Something that is not my dead grandmother sending messages from beyond the grave."

"But she always said she'd come back if you needed her," Charlotte insisted. Lydia knew Charlotte had always been a little more open to the possibilities Annabelle had talked about. "And, well, you've been moping about the house for days. Is something going on that you aren't telling me about?"

"No, there's nothing," Lydia assured her. "I'm just overworked."

"Feels like a warning from Gramma to me,"

Charlotte said under her breath. "We didn't put lily oil in the batch. It should smell like mint."

"I was distracted. I could have grabbed the wrong scent." Lydia doubted it, but the denial made her feel better.

"Uh-huh." Charlotte picked up the mint oil and wiggled the nearly empty bottle, drawling sarcastically, "I'm sure that's it."

Just as Lydia was about to retort with another logical excuse, a knock sounded on the screen door. Both women jumped and yelped in surprise, turning to see who it was. Lydia's heart flip-flopped in her chest. Erik eyed them, smiling, his brow quirked in amusement. He looked extraordinarily striking in his button down black shirt and faded blue jeans. The shirttails hung loose about his hips blowing in the wind, causing her gaze to drift downward.

"Afternoon, ladies. I'm not interrupting, am I?" His words caused her gaze to dart back to his face. Why was it she ogled him like some depraved addict whenever he was near? She purposefully looked away.

Lydia didn't meet Charlotte's eyes. She hadn't told her friend what had happened that day in the mansion's gardens. How could she? In fact, she'd not seen Erik since it happened either. Her face heated with embarrassment. Weakly, she waved him in. Erik acted like he was about to move and then paused, glancing around the door frame.

"Ya going to invite me in, love?" he asked.

Lydia frowned. Isn't that what she just did with the universal hand gesture of "come on in"? Instead of repeating the offer, she said, "It's a little messy in here right now—not really a good time."

Charlotte made a weak noise, and Lydia could practically feel her friend's determined look. Charlotte had spent every second since she'd met Erik telling Lydia how perfect it would be if they got together. The handsome Scotsman neighbor and the local business lady, sharing the same hill overlooking town, romancing it up in the very mansion that had captured Lydia's girlhood fantasies.

If Charlotte only knew the half of it.

Oh, please, make him go away. This is too embarrassing.

"All right." Erik lifted a bouquet of lavender. "I found a bunch of this on the property and thought ya may be able to use it."

My lavender!

Lydia nodded weakly. He'd found her herb garden. She knew it might happen, but she'd hoped to be able to harvest and transplant the herbs to her own property before they saw it. It was just that the light and soil was so much better on his land than on hers. She'd already snuck onto his property the night before and had taken some of it back to her house. Since he'd bought the land, it was possible she'd have to buy her entire stock back from him now that he knew it was there. Or, maybe even have to pay to rent the small garden spot.

It was a sweet gesture, and Lydia could tell he was making an effort to be nice. She tried to smile, but it was hard with all the emotions rushing inside her. His expression seemed so open and kind, and also knee-weakeningly sexy. It was that last part that trapped her voice in her throat.

When she didn't take the flowers, Erik hooked the bouquet into the handle of the screen door.

Charlotte made a louder noise and motioned at the door.

"Ah, thanks," Lydia said. "That's very kind of you."

"There's nothing kind about it," he answered. "I'm lonely and it's a bribe to get ya to go out with me tonight."

Lydia's face colored. So what? He doesn't bother trying to talk to her for four days after what happened and now suddenly he wants a date? Sure, she knew what he wanted from her. He didn't want a date. He wanted them to finish what they'd started.

Could she really blame him for thinking she was a slut?

Could he really blame her for how pissed his assumption was making her?

"What I mean is, I'm new in town," he amended a little inelegantly.

Was he nervous? Maybe he wasn't just looking for a good time, but an honest date. Still, how could a man that looked like he did be nervous asking a woman out—especially a woman doused in lotion and not looking her exact best?

"Say you'll go out with me," he insisted. Then, almost as an afterthought, he added, "Please?"

"No, thank you, Mr. MacGregor. I don't date." Lydia felt like a fool. It was hard to look dignified when lotion stuck her shirt to her chest and plastered her hair to the side of her face. Thankfully, she wore a bra this time. That was something at least. Glancing down, she saw it didn't matter. Her shirt and bra were thin and she swore she saw the darker outlines of her nipples through the lotion-soaked material. She made a move to pull some towels from a drawer, dismissing him.

"She's free at eight," Charlotte said loudly.

"Great, I'll pick ya up at eight," Erik announced. "And we'll not call it a date."

Lydia gasped, spinning on her heels to face him. He was gone.

"So, nothing happened the other day, eh?" Charlotte chuckled.

"There's your warning from Gramma," Lydia said. "She's telling me to stay away."

"Annabelle would never tell you to stay away from a sexy piece of manmeat. She probably wanted to give you that wet T-shirt look before he got here." Charlotte laughed harder as Lydia pressed a towel to her chest. "So want to tell me the truth this time about what happened between you two on the garden walk? Or do I need to run after Mr. MacGregor and hear it from him?"

"No," Lydia grumbled, throwing a towel at her friend's head. She experienced a moment of satisfaction as it hit Charlotte's face. "I'll tell you, but I don't want to. I only come out looking bad."

"MM, didn't go so well, eh?"

Erik glared at Euann, but his brother merely smirked. Women seemed to think Euann looked like a thirty year old Latin movie star. Erik didn't see it. For one thing, he was a Scotsman—though how Euann could call himself part of the MacGregor clan and hate golf was beyond all of them. For another, he was just Euann—the pesky second oldest son of Angus and Margareta MacGregor and a pain in his older brother's ass.

"Ya do not have to look so smug," Erik grumbled. "I'm picking her up at eight."

Euann stretched on the dusty chair they'd uncovered in the downstairs library, his grin widening. Erik wondered why Euann hadn't started cleaning yet. "Would that be at sword point, brother? She didn't sound too willing to me."

"Ya were listening?" Erik growled. Euann's snicker of amusement was answer enough. "Where is it?"

Euann motioned to his neck. Erik frowned and searched under his collar, coming out with a small listening device no bigger than a ladybug. He flicked it at Euann, who jumped up, caught it and cradled it in his hand.

"Eh, now, that little thing cost me a pretty penny," Euann protested.

"Keep it off me, or else it'll be a squished penny, ya hear me?"

Euann grumbled, not looking at all sorry as he studied his little gadget. "Would ya mind giving me the one in your hair as well, then? I do not want anything to happen to it."

Erik grimaced and ran his fingers through his

hair, felt a tiny snag and yanked it out, taking a few strands with it. He flung it at Euann with a look of warning.

"Ah, I couldn't help it. Ya have been languishing about this place ever since I got here. I wanted to know what she was like, that's all."

"I have not been languishing," Erik denied. "My energies have been drained."

"Masturbating too much will do that." Euann nodded, trying to act serious but unable to hide his grin.

"I have not been masturbating," Erik denied with a growl.

Euann's grin widened, and he arched a disbelieving brow.

"Too much," Erik corrected, making his statement believable. "Ah, shut your mouth, little brother. Ya want to know what has happened? Lydia's my *inthrall*."

"No," Euann gasped, sitting forward. The smirk finally faded from his expression.

"Oh, aye."

"No."

"Aye, she is."

"Ya do not say!"

"Euann!"

"Sorry." Euann gave a sheepishly apologetic shrug. "Did she have to touch ya for a long time?

Does she know? What's it feel like? Being sucked of energy like that?"

Sucked?

Remembering her sweet lips, so close to wrapping around him, Erik wanted to groan.

"Ach." Erik waved his hand in dismissal. Absently, he drew his finger over the air, swirling up dust from the fireplace mantle and tossing it aside. It happened to land on his brother's shoes. Euann jerked, grumbling and cursing as he leaned over to dust them off. With his brother sufficiently distracted for the moment, Erik took a deep breath and shut his eyes. Every fiber of his being had been on edge for days, causing an ache to settle in his joints only to be outdone by the constant nagging of his lust.

As his *inthrall*, Lydia was susceptible to Erik's powers to the point she would be able to absorb them freely if he wasn't on his guard. Just one touch and she could leech his life force and leave him for dead. Usually it had to be just the right combination of warlock and human for the bond to work. Such a woman was rare, and she wouldn't be susceptible to just any warlock, though she would normally be quite sensitive and perceptive to the other warlocks' feelings.

"She have any of those dreams Uncle Raibeart goes on about?" Euann waggled his brows with meaning, finally giving up on dusting his shoes manually. He swiped his hand, whisking the dust aside with magick.

Erik's expression must have answered for him because Euann laughed. Lydia had been fantasizing about him to the point she nearly drove him insane with it. It had taken four days for his energy to weaken inside her enough that he could go and visit her without fear she would throw him across the town in a gust of wind, and thus cause a scene. Although, getting run out of town after one day would be a new MacGregor record.

"I don't know whether to feel pity or jealousy," Euann admitted. "She'll not use it against ya, will she?"

"My first instinct said no. But when I went to her house, it was protected by magick. I couldn't go in without verbal invitation. She didn't give me one."

"She practices?" Euann questioned, surprised. Not many humans practiced the old craft anymore, at least not in any way that actually worked.

"I don't know, but I'm going to find out," Erik responded. "If she's an *inthrall*, it's possible she cast a spell to become one. She's not of natural magick like us, but some things can be learned.

There could be a reason we've felt the pull to stay here."

"Be careful around her until we discover what she is about," Euann warned. "Ya want me to go check it out?"

"No." Erik experienced an almost selfishly dark urge inside himself. Lydia was his, and he didn't want his brother anywhere near her. What if it was a spell? What if she had the same effect on Euann? Erik didn't want to fight his brother over a woman. Under most circumstances, he wouldn't. But with Lydia, he felt an animalistic possessiveness. "I plan on doing another binding spell to keep my powers veiled."

Euann nodded, giving him a strange look. "Fine. But I'll leave myself open to ya tonight. If ya have need of me, I'll feel it."

"Aye, but no more of your gadgets," he warned.

"Och, ya are no fun," Euann pouted. Then, giving his brother a careless grin, he added, "I'll just have to entertain myself tonight by listening to the tapes I made of your brilliant performance. Did ya know I can email the audio file to the rest of the family?" Thickening his burr, he poked fun of Erik's earlier blunderings with Lydia, "It's a bribe to get ya to go out with me tonight, lassie.

No? Ya don't want to? Then, I'll have to make ya with my—"

Erik needed no more excuse. He lunged for his brother, fist pulled back to give him the fight he'd been searching for.

THIS IS CRAZY.

Lydia studied her reflection in the mirror as Charlotte watched. How in the world did she let her friend talk her into going on this non-date date with Erik, let alone putting on a dress for it?

"You are not going to change," Charlotte said from the bed, as if reading Lydia's mind.

Lydia's frowned deepened. The silk dress was simple, yet elegant. Small rhinestones accented the straps and a long sash tied around the waist, knotting in the front. The low bodice was tight with a looser skirt flowing out from the high V shaped waistline.

Lydia eyed the short black skirt before looking at her legs. They were bare. She didn't have pantyhose to put on. The night was warm, so maybe it was better if she didn't wear any. "I don't think this is the impression I want to make. I should wear a giant muumuu and call it good."

"Why?" Charlotte grimaced.

"Because, I thought we agreed that the idea was to show him I wasn't a whore. Under the circumstances, I'd say this dress screams hooker."

"Whatever." Charlotte rolled her eyes. "At the very most it says high-class call girl. Be sure you don't undercharge and get the cash up front."

"Ha, ha," Lydia responded, her tone dry, "very funny."

"So you almost gave the guy head," Charlotte said, as if it were no big deal. "You're an adult. He's an adult—"

"You're a—"

"Ah! No name-calling." Charlotte laughed, hugging a lacy pillow to her stomach. "Don't blame me because you can't keep your tongue in your mouth."

"I'm going to change," Lydia announced, heading for the closet.

Charlotte sprang to her feet and blocked the door. Spreading her arms wide, she said, "No, you're not."

"Uh, yeah, I am."

"No," Charlotte ordered, her voice stern. "You're not. In fact, you're going to put on Gramma Annabelle's pearls for good luck, you're going to let me curl your hair while you put on makeup, and you're going to go out with an incredibly delicious Scotsman to have a wonderfully good time tonight."

"*Char*," Lydia whined.

"*Lyd*," her friend mimicked her.

"Fine." Lydia backed away from the closet door and walked to the bathroom to get her makeup bag. It wasn't fair to get irritated with Charlotte, but the truth was she was nervous. Inside, she shook with a myriad of emotions—fear, desire, anticipation.

Did she mention the fear?

"Don't be like that." Charlotte followed right behind her. "Really, it's no big deal. Sure, it was a little…"

"Whorish? Slutty? Embarrassing?" Lydia offered, her cheeks a bright red as she looked in the bathroom mirror. Her grandmother would've been horrified to see how skinny she was. She was just too busy with the business that she sometimes forgot to eat. And now that she really looked, her skin was pale, maybe too pale.

"I was going to say fast." Charlotte sighed, coming to her side. "You said the first moment he touched you, you felt him all the way to your toes. Maybe it's love at—" Lydia shot her friend a hard look in the mirror, and Charlotte amended, "Maybe it's *like* at first sight."

"Do you think?" Lydia couldn't help the small

hope Charlotte's words gave her. Maybe her friend was right. Maybe Erik really did want to take her on a date and get to know her. Wasn't sexual chemistry something people wanted in a relationship? Just because she'd never felt desire so strongly didn't mean it wasn't normal. Maybe tonight he didn't expect her to have sex with him at all.

Lydia frowned. And maybe ghosts and leprechauns really did exist.

Chapter Four

Erik grinned, revving the engine of his 1968 Mustang, as he backed away from the mansion. Evening shaded the surrounding trees, casting shadows over his path. Eight o'clock hadn't come fast enough. After renewing the protective veil over his powers, he'd re-bound the beast inside him to keep it at bay. Sure, in many ways the precautions were overkill, but he decided he couldn't be too careful where Lydia was concerned. A very animalistic part of him determined that if she were to try and make love to him again, they would not be stopped by her use of his powers.

His grin widened and he felt almost giddy. Putting the car into drive, he hit the gas, speeding down the long gravel road. For four days he tried not to think of her and for four days that's all he'd done. Even the house preparations were behind schedule. With his energies down, they'd been unable to fix cracks in the plaster and a few antique portraits covered holes in the walls. At best he manually moved furniture around and cleaned. With as many rooms as the place had, it was a slow process. A night of sexual bliss in Lydia's arms would do just the trick to get him rejuvenated.

That is, if it doesn't kill me.

Erik's excitement wavered as he reminded himself to keep his wits about him. With an *inthrall* he had to be careful or his death could be a very real possibility. Even so, he couldn't wait for his date to start. He was going to wine and dine Lydia, romance and seduce her with every ounce of his MacGregor charm, and then he was going to thoroughly enjoy the fruits of his labor as he fucked her until sunrise.

It was all planned. Dinner at the best restaurant in town. A drive in his classic car—a vehicle women just loved. Then back to her house for an all-night love fest. He moved uncomfortably in his seat. Four days longing for her had definitely been too long a time. Shifting gears, he forced his foot to ease up on the gas as he drove down the hill to her house. It wouldn't do for her to know he was overeager.

LYDIA GLANCED over the dim silver and blue interior of the Mustang. Though a little on the loud side, the car suited a man like Erik. Notwithstanding the stereo system hidden in the opened glove box with the digital clock front, the car had been restored to classic condition.

Erik reached between them, grabbing the shifter as they came to the bottom of the hill. The car slowed to a stop. He looked over at her and confidently winked. She quickly turned away, focusing on the two thick white stripes painted down the center of the dark blue hood.

When the car started to move, she glanced back at him from the corner of her eyes. Erik rested his hand on his bare knee. Lydia took a deep breath. She could definitely say this was the first date she'd been on where the man was wearing a skirt.

Kilt, she corrected herself. *It's not a skirt, it's a kilt.*

And it was damned sexy on him.

On top he wore a basic white shirt, a black five button waistcoat, matching argyll jacket and a lighter wool tie. A black leather bag with silver studs wrapped his hips. Below the waist, the red and green plaid pattern fell to just above his bare knees. About three inches below the hem, longer kilt hose covered his calves.

"It's called a sporran," Erik said.

"Huh?" Lydia pried her eyes away from his waist, horrified to discover that she'd been staring at the man's crotch again. Almost defensively, she said, "I wasn't wondering what you wore under your kilt."

"Ah, well that would be nothing at all, lassie," Erik said, again winking at her, "but I was telling ya that the black bag you're looking at is called a sporran."

"Oh," Lydia turned to the window, rolling her eyes as she mocked herself.

Great going, Lydia! Way to make him think you're not a sex crazed whore. Wait. Did he just say he was naked under the kilt?

She peeked at him, trying to determine if he was teasing her or not.

Oh, great. It's bad enough I can't think straight around him, now he has to tell me he's not wearing any underwear.

Was it too late to fake an illness and back out? Probably.

How about jumping out of the car to run home screaming?

Argh! Make conversation. Say something.

"So, do you wear your kilt often?" Lydia instantly wanted to die. What an American thing to ask. He probably got asked dim-witted things every time he had one on. Mumbling, she said, "Never mind, that was stupid."

"I don't think it's a stupid question," Erik said. "Aye, I wear the short kilt for special occasions. It's just like putting on a pair of pants and can be a sight more comfortable on a warm night."

"So are these your family colors, then?" Lydia asked, motioning to the plaid.

"Aye." When he smiled at her, his whole face lit with pleasure. He really was handsome in a very arousing and rugged way. "Clan MacGregor has been wearing this same tartan since before the eighteen hundreds."

Erik pulled the Mustang in front of a restaurant and shut off the engine. "This is Perfection Restaurant, isn't it? I followed the directions they gave me, but it looks closed." Erik frowned at the tinted front windows. "I don't understand. I made reservations."

"No, it's open," Lydia assured him. "Alana Davis, the owner, moved here three years ago and created quite the stir with her culinary talent. So much so, that she put a couple of the other restaurants in town out of business. Now, as retaliation, the two restaurant owners have gotten together and are trying to sabotage her business with a combined effort of their own. It's turned into quite the legendary feud. Since the two owners were born and raised here in Green Vallis, a lot of the townsfolk stopped eating at Alana's out of loyalty to their own. It's too bad. She really is the better chef."

"Do ya want to go somewhere else?" Erik inquired. "I wouldn't want to get ya on bad terms with the townsfolk."

"No, I don't really care what everyone else in town is doing." Lydia smiled. "Besides, George, one of the rival owners used to tease me when we were in grade school together. I still haven't gotten over it."

Erik chuckled and stepped out of the car. The breeze whipped his kilt and she received an intimate peek at the back of his thigh. He hurried around the car and opened her door, offering his hand. Lydia hesitated before taking it. Warm, humming energy coursed through her veins. This time, the warmth was followed by the cold chill. She shivered, drawing her hand away.

"Are ya wearing…?" Erik leaned forward. "Is that lilies? Strange, I didn't notice it earlier."

"No." Lydia tensed. She was wearing lavender, her favorite.

"Hm, curious." Erik glanced around the dimly lit street. Just like the rest of the downtown area, the old buildings were squished closely together. Aside from a few parked cars, the streets were empty. He offered her his arm.

Lydia bit her lip. She didn't really have a choice but to take his arm. As her hand slid against him once more the tingling became palpable, feeding into her veins and pumping around her entire body. He led her to the front door and opened it for her. Inside, Perfection's lights were soft. The red and gold classic décor added an elegant charm that bespoke sophistication and class without being overly pretentious. Italian oil paintings and antiqued mirrors graced the walls. Rustic chandeliers hung overhead, matching the tall candelabras. Soft music created a lovely background. A grand piano was in one corner, but Lydia had never seen it played.

"Lydia, it's so nice to see you again."

Lydia smiled, turning to look at Alana as she spoke. The woman was thin, oddly so considering she was an Italian chef. Her red-brown hair had been pulled back into a high bun, and she wore a dark red apron that matched the restaurant. By the looks of the place, Alana was the only one working that night. Only three tables were filled with dining couples.

"Alana, this is Erik MacGregor. He just bought the old mansion," Lydia introduced, using the moment to pull her hand away in hopes of severing the sexual connection now running rampant over her body. It didn't work. "Erik, Chef Alana Davis."

Lydia turned to see Erik's eyes intently studying her ass, as he temporarily ignored Alana. She trembled, wondering what wicked thoughts danced through that brain of his. Drawing his gaze away with a sheepish grin, he gave the chef one of his most charming smiles.

"Pleasure," he said, grinning.

As Alana and Erik made small talk about being new to a small town and the current business economy of a place like Green Vallis, Lydia couldn't concentrate. Erik had smelled lilies. Even someone as skeptical as she was could admit when it was time to start paying attention to the signs around her. It was hard to admit though, since she'd spent most of her life trying to live down her grandmother's "witch on the hill" reputation. It had been difficult growing up as the granddaughter to a self-proclaimed eccentric, but she wasn't a child anymore. Maybe Gramma Annabelle knew a thing or two about what she'd always gone on about. There were a lot of unexplained things in the world.

Did her grandmother try to send her a message? The cold chills? The smell of lilies? The vat of lotion exploding moments before Erik came to the door. Was Gramma Annabelle really trying to warn her? Was there a reason why she'd acted so out of character with the handsome stranger in the mansion gardens? A spell, perhaps? She felt like she was under an enchantment just being near him.

That's lust, pure and simple lust. I'm overworked and have gone without for too long. When the vat exploded I was tired and not paying attention. I had lily lotion all over. The scent could have lingered in my hair. The breeze stirred the smell.

Symptoms of stress made more sense than her dead grandmother talking to her from beyond the grave.

Alana led the way to a small round table in the corner, away from the other guests. Erik stepped aside, letting Lydia walk in front of him. Her legs stiffened, and she imagined he once again stared at her ass. She wasn't surprised when he pulled out her seat for her. He did have the way of a gentleman about him.

Once seated, Erik ordered wine. Lydia didn't hear what kind. She was too busy trying not to gaze at his handsome face, while imagining the many ways she could discreetly drop something on the floor to see if what he said about the underside of his kilt was true. Lydia was glad the linen tablecloth fell low over her lap to hide the fact that her legs shook. She forcefully pressed her thighs together, trying to bury all thoughts of his body being so assessable and yet never more distant. It wasn't like she could really do anything to him right here.

Count my blessings, she thought wryly. *If we were alone, I'd be in trouble.*

"You're quiet, *a stóirín*." When Erik looked at her, she felt she was the only one in the room. The low light softened his features with a seductive contrast. His gaze held hers before slowly traveling down her throat to her breasts and back up again.

"Am I? I didn't mean to be?" Lydia forced her mind to something other than carnal pleasures, relieved when her racing thoughts found a safe topic. "How's the house coming along? Will you be hiring a maid service? I can imagine it was pretty dusty on the inside."

"No. No service. My family likes to tend to all the details ourselves."

Before she could inquire more Alana came back with the wine, poured their glasses and left the bottle. Lydia quickly took a sip, trying to hide the fact that she was again getting really hot and bothered by his steady gaze.

This is such a mistake. Whatever made me think that if this man came on to me, I'd be able to refuse him?

"So, where did ya learn magick?" Erik asked.

Lydia blinked in surprise, nearly choking on her wine. Trying to recover gracefully, she managed, "I'm sorry? Magick?"

"Aye, your Love Potions?" Erik grinned.

"Oh, Love Potions," Lydia repeated, wanting to slap the side of her head. For a moment she thought he meant real magick. Why was her heart beating so fast? They hadn't even ordered yet, and she was ready to run out of there—away from the very delectable Erik MacGregor.

He was looking at her expectantly. Lydia bit her lip. What had he asked?

"Ah, my grandmother was an, uh, herbalist, and she taught me everything I know about it. She started making lotions for tourists and locals and, before she died, I took the business over. Last year I put it on the internet."

"Hm, I would have thought she was a witch," Erik said.

Lydia stiffened, waiting for the ridicule and disdain that usually followed that statement. He must have gone into town and met up with some of the local busybodies. Or, knowing Mrs. Callister, the woman trekked up the hill to meet Erik for herself. Yet somehow, when Erik said the word

"witch" it was as if he mentioned the weather—
like having an eccentric in the family was an
everyday occurrence. Perhaps in his travels, it
wasn't as odd as it appeared to the sheltered small
town she grew up in. He watched her expectantly,
but his expression was straightforward. Faintly, she
said, "Some have called her that."

"Then, she wasn't?"

Thankfully Alana came back to take their
orders, and Lydia was saved from answering. It
took all of her willpower not to grab the woman's
hand and force her to join them. Without even
reading over her options, she handed the menu to
Alana. "You know what I like."

Alana chuckled. "Yes, but I keep hoping you'll
try something else."

"Why change what works? I like what I like."
Lydia grinned.

"I'll have the same." Erik handed his menu
over without looking.

"Very good," Alana answered, leaving them
alone.

"But you don't know what I'm getting," Lydia
protested.

"If ya like it that much, it can't be bad." Erik's
eyes sparkled, reflecting the candlelight in a way
that it appeared as if they glowed from within.

Lydia felt her cheeks heating. Was she actually

blushing—again? "For all you know, it could be snails."

Erik actually looked worried for a moment. Then, smiling, he said, "Doesn't matter."

Lydia quirked a brow, trying not to laugh.

Leaning forward in confidence, he whispered, "It isn't, is it?"

"No, it's not." Lydia giggled at his concerned look.

"I never did care for French cuisine." He relaxed, leaning back in his chair. "Ya have a pretty smile, lassie. I'm glad to see ya have finally decided to wear it for me."

Her giggling stopped. "Listen, I feel we should talk about the other day. I—"

"A gentleman doesn't expect a lady to talk about such things, unless of course ya want to?" He glanced around. "Though perhaps this is not the most opportune time."

Hell, no! I'd rather saw off my left arm than have the, "I'm sorry I almost gave you a blowjob like a whore" conversation.

Lydia merely shook her head in denial. By the time she got the apology out anyway, she'd probably be under the table trying to give him another one. She clamped her thighs shut. It didn't help calm the raging fire Erik lit in her sex with just his nearness.

"Ya never answered. Was your grandma a witch?"

Lydia thought about lying, but found herself saying, "Yes."

Wow. Did that actually come out of her mouth? It had to be the first time she actually admitted it out loud—well, to anyone who wasn't Charlotte. What was it about Erik that made her want to be honest, to bare all—including his gorgeous body—and act on instinct?

She watched his reaction, surprised when he still didn't look fazed by her words. "That doesn't shock you?"

"Why should it?" Erik asked. "Do ya practice?"

"No," Lydia shook her head. "I know some herbs have healing properties or can be used as aromatherapy, but my grandmother took it all a step further. She believed in the old magick and ghosts and... Well, I never did see anything that made me believe in actual magick. Now, magic tricks and illusions, yes, I believe those are possible on a Las Vegas stage, but true power?"

"And seeing is believing?"

"Yeah, it helps." Lydia laughed. "I'm one of those people who, when everyone else is looking at the stage, I watch the dark side of the theater to see the magician running along the aisle for his magic trick's grand reveal."

Alana came back carrying two plates full of fettuccine alfredo topped with parmesan and pine nuts. Lydia hummed softly in appreciation. The portions were way too big, but that had never stopped her from trying to finish her plate. Setting a basket of garlic bread in between them, the chef left them alone.

"And what would ya do if ya saw true power?" Erik picked up his fork.

"If I saw real magick?" Lydia shrugged. "I'd like to think I'd be brave, but the truth is I'd probably run screaming for the hills."

NIGHT CARESSED THE HILLSIDE, pressing into the little Victorian house nestled in its fold. Within the shadows, the air stirred differently as if pulling away from the threat of blue moonlight. They had waited for this moment, so long trapped in wraith-like form, mere lingering shadows of the powerful beings they so desperately wanted to be again. The shadow creatures had been waiting for the signs that it was time, able to read the age-old hints buried in the flow of the wind, divined in the falling leaves. It had only been a matter of time before the warlocks would be drawn to the great source of natural power. They were only two now, not the legion of millennia past. They had been conserving their powers, storing them for the energy it would take to create the army they needed.

Nothing could get past the barrier encircling the Victorian home. The spell was airtight, woven perfectly around each piece of siding, each pane of glass, each block of foundation. It didn't stop the shadow creatures from searching, poking and prodding every opening. For as all shadows knew, no spell was faultless, no enchantment lasted forever and no *inthrall* ever lived through what they had planned.

Chapter Five

Lydia wasn't sure how she did it, but she managed to make it through dinner without jumping over the table and attacking Erik with very indecent kisses. When she stopped fantasizing long enough to listen to him and have a real conversation, she found him exceedingly funny and remarkably charming. He told stories of his ancestors as if he'd actually lived beside them. Since most of them shared his name and the names of his brothers, it was easy to assume he grew up hearing the tales through oral storytelling until they became a very real part of his heritage. But when he talked of his living family, she could tell he held back.

"So you were saying, Euann the Ugly, Iain the Woman, and Niall the Stench fought over the same woman?" Lydia prompted, glancing across to the driver's seat only to pry her eyes away and stare forward. As long as she kept him talking she wouldn't have to be inside her own head, hearing her brain's naughty suggestions.

Erik smirked, chuckling. "Aye, but the beautiful Lady Julia was an English lassie and would take no notice of the lowly MacGregors. She hated the western highlands near Mount Sail Garbh where her father forced her to journey. However, her ill temper did not stop the three brothers from trying."

"So they fell in love with her beauty?" Lydia asked, imagining three very handsome, medieval versions of Erik running around the moors and mountains of Scotland in nothing but kilts. Julia must have been an amazing woman to capture the notice of men like that. Then, realizing she sat next to the real life Erik, she blushed. Lydia hardly considered herself amazing. However did she get his notice? Her blush deepened.

Oh, yeah, let's not think about that.

Again looking across to the driver's seat, she bit her lip and tried to adjust her hips without drawing attention to her aroused state. Outside the car, the slow drift of city buildings passed by, towering over the empty sidewalks. Yellow street-lights mingled with blue moonlight, casting a mesmerizing light over Erik's features.

"Not exactly. After her first rejection it became more of a wager." He laughed harder, as if able to picture what happened next. Again, if Lydia didn't know better, she would have thought he lived it. "None of the three brothers would give up wooing the English lady, until their antics escalated to the point they had to be punished by Lady Julia's father for embarrassing her. Iain tried to sing her a love ballad in the main hall of her home."

"That's romantic," Lydia inserted.

"The only song he knew wasn't about romantic love. It had more to do with the lady lifting her skirts about her head. As a punishment, he had to wear a lady's dress for a week." Erik laughed harder. "Niall went hunting to show her his prowess, but the unusually hot weather and her untimely absence caused the meat to rot before she saw it. So, he ordered the fur prepared instead, but the meat had rotted so badly that the fur reeked. He was forced to wear the thing as a robe for a sennight without washing it."

"And Euann the Ugly?"

"His mere presumption that she could look at him for more than a glance was offense enough to warrant being punished." Erik grinned. "But they took pity, believing his face was penance enough."

Lydia laughed, his good mood infectious. His

sexy accent only added to what he said until every fiber of her being jumped with giddy anticipation and hope. Her gaze traveled leisurely over him as he concentrated on the road, turning up the hill toward her house.

Let's face it, everything about him is damned sexy.

Without even looking at her, he said, "Ya know, *leannán*, ya look at me like that for much longer, and I'm bound to get ideas."

Lydia blushed, instantly drawing her gaze away. As the streetlights faded, left behind in town, the moon shone brightly over the car, penetrating Erik's window like a celestial spotlight. No matter how she tried, her eyes kept straying to the hem of his kilt. Her hand flexed, the fingers begging to discover if what he'd said about being naked beneath the plaid were true. She trembled with the knowledge of their privacy. No one else would be on the hill. They were completely alone.

In the isolation of night, she couldn't help but think that maybe being intimate with Erik wasn't such a bad thing. He was nice, funny, charismatic and polite. Just entertaining the idea of sex made the moisture dampening her thighs all the worse. What was it about this man that caused her body to become desperate with need?

Deep breaths, Lyd, she ordered herself. *Keep your*

head. Say goodnight and go into the house alone until you can rationalize what's happening.

Stopping the car in front of her house, Erik shut off the engine. Lydia smiled, her heart fluttering nervously in her chest. Every part of her aching body wanted to invite him up to her bedroom. Only her brain, and the staunch promise she'd made herself not to act like a whore, kept her from doing it.

"Thank you, I had a nice time." Lydia reached for the car door, ready to run if she had to. She was almost home free. If she could just get inside her door, she'd keep her dignity intact. His hand on her elbow stopped her. Her breath caught, feeling that light touch all the way to her toes.

Don't look into his eyes. You won't get lost if you don't look.

"You'd not be wanting company, would ya?" When she turned around, he winked audaciously. Damn, she looked. The sinfully dark eyes glistened with moonlight. How she wasn't sure, as his face had become shadowed by the long length of his black hair. Her heartbeat quickened. The low honeyed tone that had first stopped her on the street now washed seductively over her entire being. "Or we could go up to MacGregor Estate."

It was tempting. Lydia loved the view from the

top of the hill at night. From the mansion grounds, lights from town glittered over the valley like stars. Her house was a little too close to get the same effect.

Who was she kidding? If she said yes it wouldn't be because of the view.

"No, it's late." Lydia glanced at the stereo's clock in the opened glove box and again made a move to reach for the door. How she managed to grip the metal handle she'd never know.

"Och, I can take care of that." Erik reached for the clock and reset the time so it looked like it was three hours earlier. His strong arm brushed the tip of her breast, and she wondered if it was on purpose. She squirmed in her seat as the nipple hardened beneath her gown. Grinning, he said, "There, magic, now it's early."

Lydia dropped her hand to her lap and laughed. The subtle smell of his cologne wafted over her, causing her to breathe deeply. The man really was persistent. It was actually kind of cute, the way he blatantly tried to get her to stay the night with him. When he sat up, he didn't pull all the way back into his own seat. Heat radiated from his body into her, melting away all willpower.

She didn't want the date to be over quite yet. What she wanted was to kiss him. What she should do was try and preserve some of her self-respect, showing him she could actually control herself around him. Feeling the ache in her sex that had been there since their first meeting, she wasn't so sure that was possible. What if she couldn't control herself? What if a force greater than the both of them pulled them together?

"We both know what's happening here," Erik said, his voice dipping to an almost low growl. He pulled back, sighing.

"We do?" Lydia couldn't stop herself. She leaned over the seat, closer to him, reversing their positions. Her eyelashes fluttered, and she looked down to his lips. Already she could taste his kiss on her mouth, almost feel it. She'd imagined it enough over the last several nights.

"Aye, we do." Erik moved closer once more, stopping when he was only a hairsbreadth away. She felt his breath hitting her mouth, a teasingly light caress that made every thought she had focus on his lips. "I don't know why you're fighting the energy between us, *leannáin*."

Lydia's breath caught. She couldn't move. His lips drew closer, brushing lightly along her mouth as he continued. Her nerves reached out for his touch, and her mind focused on every breath, every sound.

"Aye, it's potent, hot, primitive. Since that first moment, I've wanted ya. My body's burned to possess ya, to finish what was started between us in the garden."

"No—" she began to protest, not liking the embarrassing reminder of her wantonness.

"Oh, aye, how can ya deny it, Lydia?" His strong, warm fingers hovered near her cheek, as whispering of a caress as his lips were. "I can feel your sexual energy calling to me right now. It has been all night. I know ya tried to cool it all evening by parting your thighs beneath the table, but it didn't work, did it? All it did was made your scent all the more potent to me until all I could think about was crawling beneath the table and sampling the sweet taste of your body."

"Erik, I…"

"I've accepted it, your body has accepted it, why won't your brain? Just look how hard your nipples are and I haven't even touched them. I'll bet your panties are soaked as well, so wet from the thoughts you've been having of me buried there."

He was right. Her nipples were hard. She didn't have to look down to see it. They'd been erect nearly all night.

Everything about this man was strange. Sure, thoughts could be arousing, but to this extent? To the point that her body was always in a constant state of lust?

Emotions like these didn't happen to regular, everyday people. They couldn't or else the entire world would be fornicating all the time. It didn't make any sense. Lydia couldn't stop the nagging idea that something was definitely off from normal with this situation, with Erik in general. It wasn't really anything he did or said, but just an overall feeling that he wasn't telling her something, that he had secrets.

Was she overanalyzing the situation because she was scared? Was she crazy to believe that maybe Gramma Annabelle had been trying to warn her about this man?

Her thighs parted and she closed her eyes, hoping he'd take it as an invitation to run his hand beneath her short skirt. She could practically feel the rough texture of his fingers to her sex.

"Just say the word and I'll have ya bent over with my dick shoved so deep inside your tight body, stretching ya so wide you'll never fit another man again." His voice was hoarse, thickening his accent. "In fact, I'll bet you're so tight you'll be begging me to stop, but I won't, *leannáin*. No, once inside ya, I won't stop—ever."

She gasped, taking in his bold words and unable to eke out an answer through her suddenly dry throat.

His sultry voice continued, fanning warm

breath over her cheek and neck as he drew closer to whisper directly into her ear. Still he didn't fully touch her, as if waiting for her permission. "You'll be crying out unsure if it's pain or pleasure you're feeling. Oh, but aye, you'll know as soon as ya come, covering me with that sweet body of yours."

Lydia couldn't have formed a sentence if she wanted to. Her lids drifted lazily over her eyes. At her lack of protest, Erik ran his hand down her throat, pushing the strap of her dress off her shoulder as he moved to liberate a breast from the bodice. She knew she should stop him, but she couldn't remember why. The heat of his palm felt too nice. His finger brushed over the lace of her black bra, giving relief to the taut nipple for a brief instant before gliding down over her hip to her thighs.

He kept talking, the naughty suggestions turning her on even more. "I'm going to fuck ya so good, ya won't ever want another man between those thighs. Say the words. Tell me to make ya mine. You'll belong to me completely and you'll never get away, *a stóirín.*"

When he stopped talking, she struggled on brink of dizziness, taking in hard, harsh pants of air. There was a long silence, and she knew he was waiting for her to say the words he longed to hear.

She couldn't, not because she didn't want it but because she couldn't form a coherent thought.

His eyes narrowed. "Kiss me."

Lydia automatically pressed her lips to his, opening her mouth and moaning lightly as his taste flooded her. Already his scent was in her head, until every sense became filled with him.

Erik's tongue rolled into her willing mouth, bringing a new flood of awareness and desperation. He touched her cheek, pressing up into her hair to draw her tighter into the kiss. A battle ensued between their lips. Lydia grabbed his face, turning her head to get a better angle along his mouth. He groaned in approval.

Her nerves actually erupted with sensation, sending a lively signal over her flesh. Lydia parted her legs wider and he ran his hand along her inner thigh. The first touch of his fingers along her clothed sex made her break the kiss in a rugged gasp for air. Desire pressed an electrical current directly onto the swollen bud of her clit.

"*A mhuirnín!* So ready for me," Erik moaned, drawing his lips along her neck and ear so that he could nip and bite her flesh. He pressed harder, rubbing her through her panties. "Let me ease the ache from us both. Invite me inside your house."

Lydia didn't answer as she reached for his leg. Proceeding under his kilt to eagerly explore, she discovered the truth about his being naked underneath. Her hand met with the hard flesh of his erection, and it was just as immense as she remembered.

"Oh, aye," Erik's hips jerked as she wrapped her fingers around the base. The air inside the Mustang snapped with their sexual energy, making her powerless to stop what was happening. "I've been dreaming of those sweet lips wrapping around me, sucking me."

Her own body ached with such need, and yet she was compelled by his words to aggressively push his chest back and lean across the gear shift. His hand fell from her panties. Lydia pulled the kilt up, revealing his beautiful cock. Instantly, her lips parted and she pulled him into her mouth. Erik groaned, jerking as she aggressively began bobbing up and down on his turgid shaft.

"*A ghrá!*" His words made no sense, but she understood the sound of his voice.

Lydia tried to pull away, but it was as if her lips were glued to him. She loved the taste and feel of him, loved the noises of pleasure he made in his thick accented voice. Her own body screamed in neglect. Erik touched her breast the best he could in the cramped interior of the car, but she wanted more.

"Ah, let's go inside," he insisted, working his hips beneath her. "Let me tend to ya as well."

Lydia wanted to say the words, but her mouth was full. She moaned instead, sucking harder and faster. Energy hummed inside her and she'd never felt so alive. A faint whisper filtered over her, urging her to keep going, to suck him dry, to take more than just his physical pleasure. Erik jerked, grunting as he came inside her mouth. She didn't stop right away, as she continued to move over his shaft, milking every last ounce. She swallowed, feeling incredibly empowered and strong. It was as if she could feel his life force inside of her, his vigor and strength.

Pulling back, she stared at him, roughly demanding, "More."

"Och, no, love." He whispered, eyeing her strangely. "Ya did it again, didn't ya?"

"More," she ground out. Erik fell fully against his seat, his shoulders pushed into the leather back. Unable to control herself, she looked at his eased cock and willed it to lift. It magickally obeyed, growing before her eyes with impossible speed.

"Lydia?"

The plea was lost as she once more leaned over his lap to suck him a second time. This time her actions were purposeful and demanding, taking more than giving. She'd suck him again and again until there was nothing left of him. As he came one of his arms broke free from her mind's hold and he pushed at her shoulder.

"Lydia, look at me. Let me see your eyes." The words were garbled, but she obeyed.

She opened her mouth, but no sound came out. A chill worked over her—stronger than before. Every emotion known to man hit her in full force at one time, wreaking havoc on her soul. She shivered, not wanting to be in the car anymore.

The succession of time made no sense. Blinking, she found herself on the side lawn, close to the kitchen door. She pulled at her dress, trying to cover her naked breast. The motion detector light didn't turn on. Only the moon lit the yard, and she stumbled over a shadowed rock, hitting hard upon the ground. Her hand landed near a closed flower and the green leaves rolled and wilted, instantly dying. The chill hit her again, stronger than before.

"What…?" She grunted, terrified as she jerked her hand away from the dead plant and pushed to her feet. What was happening to her? How did she get out of the car? What was the strange urge she had to throw out her arms and drain the life from everything around her?

Wind whipped through the night, making the tops of trees crash noisily together. Leaves rattled, the new growth turning brown before falling to the ground like it was fall and not spring. She heard a car door slam behind her, and she instinctively knew Erik was coming for her. Lydia scrambled to go inside, even as she looked over her shoulder at him.

Erik glanced around. "Lydia, invite me inside. Now. Something's out here."

Why did he want inside her house so badly?

"Lydia!" Erik demanded, a growl in his tone.

"Stay right there," Lydia whispered, edging away from him. The closer he came, the colder she felt. "I don't know what you're doing to me, but I want it to stop. Stay back!"

"Lydia?"

"Stay back, Erik." She made a move toward the kitchen door. Holding up her hand, she said, "I'm warning you."

"I won't—" Erik began only to stop and look around. Black hair blew wildly over his shoulders. With a look of determination on his face, he too held up his hand. It glowed softly. He turned his palm so it faced upward. A small gathering of light balled and hovered over his curled fingers. He lifted his hand, as if to throw the light into the trees.

Lydia screamed. Her arms automatically flew to her sides, as if controlled by a greater force. A burst of energy shot out of her at him, distorting the air like heat over a desert road, but otherwise invisible. The energy slammed him in the chest, throwing him back. The movement flung his hand to the side, causing the light to streak harmlessly across the lawn.

The Mustang jerked, the car seeming to come to life as the engine started and the headlights turned on, lighting up the dark night. Wind blew Erik's kilt up and she saw the evidence of his desire for her still standing proud. She screamed again, running inside the house.

The screen door slammed shut behind her. She heard him yelling, running after her. "Stop, Lydia!"

Lydia locked the door before running to the telephone to call the police. Through the window, she saw him lurch to come inside. A blue glow erupted over everything and he bounced back, grunting as if he'd hit an invisible wall. Angrily, he pounded his fists on the air, striking the blue barrier. He couldn't get in.

"Lydia, invite me in!" Erik's voice and face had changed. No longer did he look like a man, but some kind of mythical beast.

"This isn't happening," she whimpered, over

and over. Her hand shook so badly she kept pressing the wrong buttons and had to hang up to start again. "This isn't happening."

"Lydia!" Erik growled.

Lydia held the phone and stretched the cord as she crept closer to the window to see what was happening. She jolted in fear, trying not to look at his shockingly demonic appearance. Darkness swirled from his pupil to fill the whites of his eyes with black. The ridge above his nose had thickened, leading to long, sharp fangs that glinted in the combination of headlights and moonlight. He was the thing of nightmares—a demon, part cat, part man. The wind blew his kilt and she saw that his erection had lengthened, his cock so long and impossibly thick it was more weapon than a tool of pleasure. She hugged her body, even now tasting him in her mouth.

What was he doing to her? Who was he? What was he?

She felt drained, as if that energy blast she'd shot at him had sapped her reserves of strength completely. Lydia stumbled back. Her legs weakened and she dropped the phone, unable to hold on any longer. A tear slipped over her cheek. She'd never been so scared in her life. Falling to the floor, she drooped against the cabinets. It was all she could to keep her eyes open.

"Gramma?" The smell of lilies surrounded her, giving some comfort. Erik stopped hitting the house, and she could no longer see him from where she slumped. "Is that really you?"

There was no answer.

"What's going on, Gramma?" Lydia tried to fight the looming darkness, but the pull of oblivion became too strong. "What is he?"

ERIK FELT the beast inside him raging to the surface. With the last shred of common sense he possessed, he pulled away from Lydia's window. He knew his shifted appearance frightened her, but he couldn't help it. When she took his powers, she'd unleashed the hold he had on the animal within. Primal and unthinking, the creature he could become acted on pure instinct. It ate, drank, fought, fucked, whatever it needed to do to fulfill a desire.

It had taken a mortal lifetime for him to learn to control the beast and in short span she'd nearly broken all the barriers. Had that been all, there would have been a chance the creature would stay dormant. But, he sensed something evil lurking outside her house the second he stepped out of the car. It was an ancient evil whose very presence called the protective instinct forth.

He'd tried to illuminate the forest, to see who lurked in the shadows, but Lydia's uncontrolled use of his power had thrown him aside and stopped him. His muscles ached from his hard landing. Lydia had done it again. She sucked his power from him—quite literally. It wasn't her fault. They weren't her powers to control. Without direction, they simply became an extension of her emotions.

"Erik?" Euann yelled, running full tilt down the hill.

"Aye," Erik growled, recognizing the hoarse tone of his voice as that belonging to his shifted form. The beast was restless.

"What's happened? I felt a disturbance," Euann demanded before suddenly stopping. His brown hair blew wildly around his face. His dark eyes flashed with a golden light and he took a deep, long breath. Quietly, he whispered, "A *lidérc?*"

"Aye." Erik nodded grimly, the deduction making sense. He would have determined as much had he been able to focus. The *lidérc* were nasty creatures who feasted on the emotional energy of their victims. In myth, they took many forms—

man, woman, animal—but in truth they were more like shadows and light.

"There can't be that many of them left after the Hungary exterminations. Is it inside Lydia?"

"No," Erik shook his head, looking at the side door to her home. His heart squeezed with fear, possession, longing. The beast in him wanted to conquer, but thankfully the protection spell on the house was strong. To pass through the door, he'd have to either be invited or strip himself of his magick for all eternity. "Lydia used my power and called the winds. I can't get a good scent."

"Is she…?"

"Safe," Erik said. "I do not think she'll be coming out of that house any time soon."

Euann quirked a brow. "Not if she saw ya like that."

Erik frowned. He knew well enough how he looked.

Euann glanced over Erik's face before looking down. Giving a sardonic laugh, he said, "I mean, your legs never did look good in a short kilt."

"Ach." Erik's scowl deepened. His brother might appear to be taking the situation lightly, but Erik knew better. In a time of need, he'd be glad to have anyone of his siblings by his side. "Help me put our own protection spell around this place. If magick goes in or out, we'll know it. After, we'll get to work on securing MacGregor Estate with a perimeter."

"Ya want me to include this house in our perimeter, as well?"

"Aye," Erik said, torn between the need to find a way past Lydia's threshold and what he had to do. He struggled with the beast, using most of his strength to keep from shifting fully and running about the hillside like a feral animal. "Might as well. We'll most likely buy this property from her when Da gets here."

"We should get some of these dead flowers out of here." Euann studied alongside the house, ever vigilant to signs that magick had been used. "The flowerbed looks like a plague hit it."

Erik nodded and continued to stare at Lydia's kitchen door. Every part of him wanted to pound against the barrier and yell until she let him in. He took a step toward it.

"Erik," Euann said, his voice lowered with concern. "That's no way to win a lass. Come on. Let's just keep her safe until we know what we're dealing with."

"Aye." Erik nodded. Euann was right.

Calling forth the wind from inside her home, Erik forced the slightly opened windows of her kitchen to shut and latch. Just that little act took a lot of energy. He might not get his magick through her barrier, but he could propel the wind. Fortunately, he could sense no one was in the house with her. After the power surge she threw at him, it was no surprise she was drained enough to pass out. Undoubtedly, she'd be sore the next morning from being on the kitchen floor, but he couldn't get to her to carry her to a bed.

"Erik," his brother insisted. "I know it's hard, but until we can bind your beast, ya must try to focus on something other than that lady. Don't worry. We'll make her forget what she saw. It will be like tonight never happened."

"Aye, that we must." Erik clasped his brother's shoulder. "Go get what we need. I'll wait here until ya come back. I doubt the *lidérc* will return tonight. I don't feel it anymore."

Chapter Six

Lydia moaned, smacking her dry lips as she pushed herself up from the kitchen floor. Blinking, she looked around the room, trying to remember how she got there. Her head throbbed and her entire body ached as if she'd just run a marathon before getting beaten up by a gang of bikers.

"What the...?" she mumbled, gingerly touching the side of her face.

How did she get on the floor? She glanced around the room. Why was she wearing a dress? This didn't make sense. She never wore dresses.

She pushed her palm against her temple and slowly ambled to her feet with a groan. The world spun, and she wondered if maybe Charlotte had brought over a bottle of tequila again. Last time they'd gotten so drunk they'd somehow fallen asleep in the empty bathtub—fully clothed and facing opposite ways. Still, it had been cramped.

"Charlotte?" Lydia called, her voice hoarse. "Char, are you there? What the hell happened?"

A thought tried to unfurl in her mind. It was right on the edge of her consciousness, but she couldn't figure out what it tried to show her. Disoriented and a little creeped out, Lydia put on a pot of coffee in hopes a strong brew would clear her mind. As she waited for it to percolate, she hiked upstairs to take a quick shower.

The warm water didn't help. She was still confused.

Feeling the need for comfort, Lydia slid on a pair of stretchy gray exercise pants with a black stripe down the side and a knit tank top. She pulled her wet hair to the nape of her neck, twisting it up into a sloppy bun. It wasn't like she would have company today, and she really needed to replenish her lotion supply. Lavender mint and rosemary were both completely out of stock. And, after the lily lotion exploded all over her kitchen, she might need to redo that as well. Though, how she could have grabbed the lily lotion instead of an unscented base was beyond her.

Lilies. Gramma Annabelle.

Lydia stopped half way down the stairs. There

was something she was supposed to be remembering. What was it? The lotion had been everywhere in the kitchen. Charlotte was there and they cleaned it up. Wait, no. Erik had come by.

Shivers instantly racked her spine. Mm, Erik. Just thinking about him made her so hot she could barely stand it.

"He asked me out," Lydia said, smiling slightly. That is why she'd been in the dress. Her smile fell. Why couldn't she remember the date ending? She remembered the restaurant and the drive home. He'd been charming and so damned sexy she could barely take her eyes off his bare legs. The details were fuzzy, fragmented, like someone had taken an eraser to her brain and quickly swiped it, leaving behind crumbs.

She'd been hot for him in the car, so aroused she contemplated inviting him in for the night. The man was a walking aphrodisiac. Even now she was wet between the thighs and her body temperature rose above normal.

The rest of the date was a blank. They pulled up in front of her house. She thanked him for the date. He asked her if he could come in. And she said…

Lydia frowned. What had she said? By the gnawing insistence of unfilled desires, it was clear that they'd not had sex. A man Erik's size would've left her more than a little sore. Did he come in? Did she invite him and he'd refused? Did she send him on his way?

"Gramma, I know I said I wanted nothing to do with the beyond the grave stuff you talked about, but if you can hear me, I could use a little help." She continued down the stairs. "Something strange is going on here and for once it's not our family."

"I DON'T KNOW what to tell you, Lyd," Sheriff Johnson said, staring at the oblong patch of dead grass leading out from her door across the yard. His salt and pepper black hair was cut short and bore the line of the cowboy hat he carried in his hands. A displaced Southerner, he had a fair and evenhanded approach that drove some of the citizens a little crazy, especially Mrs. Callister who—he'd once let slip—called his office nearly daily to lodge complaints. "I'm guessing someone sprayed your lawn with weed kill."

Lydia stayed close to her front door. She crossed her arms over her stomach and hugged her waist. She gestured her finger toward the empty flower bed. "Whoever it was dug up all my flowers. Even Gramma Annabelle's rose bushes. Who steals rose bushes?"

"And you didn't hear or see anything?"

Lydia thought of waking that morning on the kitchen floor. "No, I don't remember anything unusual. Do you think it's the same people who've been vandalizing the other properties?"

"We're pretty sure those are just kids trying to stick their noses up at authority," Sheriff Johnson answered. "Nothing is missing besides the plants?"

"Not that I've seen. I checked the valuables. I don't think anyone was in the house." She felt somewhat safer with the police cruiser in her driveway.

"Did you get in a fight with anyone lately?"

Lydia shook her head in denial.

"No, I suppose you wouldn't have." He smiled kindly at her. "Honestly, there's not much we can do about this without more to go on, but I'll write up a report if you want to make an insurance claim for damages. I'm sorry about your grandmother's roses."

"Don't be. I think she hated those things. She'd always curse at the thorns whenever she had to prune them back."

"I always liked your grandmother. She was a spunky thing. When I moved here, oh, forty years back, she was the first person to give me a genuine welcome to office."

"She always liked you, too, sheriff. Sorry to have to call you out here for this." She went to the kitchen door and leaned inside to grab a bag off the counter. "I have your wife's order here if you'd like to take it with you. It'll save her a trip."

"Did she order the vanilla tea?" He took the gift bag and peeked inside.

"I might have slipped a few boxes in for her." She smiled, knowing the vanilla tea would never make it past the police station.

"You're one of the good ones." He smiled as he slipped on his hat and nodded at her. "Ma'am."

"Thank you, sheriff." Lydia turned her attention to her half-dead yard and waited until Sheriff Johnson was turned around and heading on his way. Memories tried to tug at her when she saw the lawn, but there was nothing beyond a wall of confusion.

"MALINA, I'm glad ya could come." Erik rushed to his sister as she strode through the front door.

Pulling sunglasses from her face, she glanced around the foyer and nodded. "This will do nicely for the family." Just like all the MacGregors she had dark hair and eyes. At the moment they were outlined in dark blue to match the streaks she'd dyed into her long bangs. However, she might look and act like a MacGregor, but her voice lacked the stronger accent of her brothers. When she was a child she'd been sent to England for refinement and now, even after hundreds of years, she sounded more Brit than Scot—unless her temper was raised or she was being playful. The jeans and T-shirt might have appeared casual, but Erik knew they were designer and that his sister's wardrobe would have cost the family a small fortune if not for Malina's power to materialize objects. Turning to her oldest brother, Malina eyed him warily. "Aye. I came because you asked, but don't think I don't know when something's up."

"Can't we miss our little sister?" Erik shot her a wide grin.

"That charming smile won't work on me, so you best just tell me why it is I had to leave New York like the city was burning to the ground." She thrust her backpack at him and he set it on the floor. "So help me if it's to help get this house in order, I'll brain you. I did the houses last century." She frowned, eyeing the dusty ceilings. "You haven't even started the clean. What are you boys up to?"

"Lassie," Erik wheedled, grinning wider.

"I knew it!" she growled. "Da told you to get me away from the city. This always happens. I meet a nice guy who wants to take me out and in rushes the MacGregor men, protecting my maidenhead like it was some prize. Bloody hell, Erik. Why do you think I left the family house in the first place?"

Erik furrowed his brow in confusion. "We always thought ya lost that thing to Lord Barrison back in the seventeen hundreds."

"Oh, you would have to mention him, wouldn't you?" Malina wrinkled up her face and hit him in the arm. Then, giving him a big hug, she said, "And I've missed ya too, laddie."

Erik lifted her off the ground and kissed her on the forehead. Unlike the men in her family, she was tiny and petite like their mother. It often made her brothers even more protective of her especially in the old days when women tended to act like delicate flowers. Her beauty reminded them of a fragile china doll, even if she insisted she could kick ass like the best of them. He knew she sometimes resented their overbearing protectiveness over the centuries. But she was a woman, in spite of being one powerful warlock, and it was a man's duty to protect the women of his clan.

Centuries might have passed but that didn't change biological facts.

"You better have an adventure for me or I'm leaving," Malina warned.

He turned serious, as he set her down. "How about a *lidérc*? Adventure enough for ya?"

"A *lidérc*? Here? And you called me, not Niall or Rory?" Malina grinned, as to say, *Finally!*

"It isn't a laughing matter."

"Who's laughing? I'm simply excited you called me." Malina bounced on the tips of her toes, looking like a little girl who just received her dream pony. "You're finally going to let me fight alongside you after all these—"

Erik lifted up his hand. Her expression fell.

"What?" she demanded. "Erik, I know what I'm doing. Do you think I never get into trouble in New York? I can take down ten grown men if I have to."

"I called ya because I need a woman to take care of some womanlike things." Then, grimacing, he added, "We'll discuss what you're doing in New York later."

"Oh!" She growled, reaching to pick up her backpack. "I knew it. Ya want me to decorate while ya play 'hunt the *lidérc*'."

Erik whirled past her with the aid of his

magick, blocking the door. "Easy now. Take that Scot out of your voice, English Rose."

"I willna hesitate to cast ya into another dimension, laddie," she warned. Erik swallowed. He knew she could do it. Once she sent their brother Kenneth to a spirit realm. It had taken him months to find his way back. "Call me an English Rose again, I dare ya."

"Her name is Lydia, and she's my *inthrall*." He drew his eyes away, unable to meet Malina's probing gaze. "Perhaps more."

"More?" She dropped her bag. Her tone softened, as did her expression. He felt the heat of her anger dissipating.

"I need ya to befriend her." Erik took a deep breath. "She keeps taking my powers every time I'm near her. I can't protect her and she won't trust me after…"

"After?"

"I had to erase her memory." He inhaled a deep breath. "And there were things in that memory. The *lidérc* was outside her home so I fear he's already set his sights on her."

"Aye, that is serious. If she's your *inthrall* and he uses his powers to drain her of yours." Malina swallowed, worried. "Aye, this is bad. For both of you."

He nodded. The *lidérc* could suck his power

from Lydia and then turn it against Erik and his family. When magick was more prevalent in the world, *inthralls* were made to do that very thing. In the end, he'd be dead and Lydia would be insane —if she were lucky. "It's been a week and she runs every time I try to go near her. I can't get an invite into her home. It's protected with natural magick. She won't see me and she won't talk to me on the phone. I've tried everything. She even threw out the flowers I sent her."

"Natural magick? She knows what she is? What we are?"

"No. She doesn't. The spell over the house is old. Her grandmother was human, but a practical witch. She must've put the spells over the house. They're pretty powerful for a mortal's work." Erik closed his eyes. "That's not all. I lost control of the beast and started to shift. She saw and it went over about as well as ya could imagine. I erased all memory of my shift and of her use of my magick, but she has to have questions about the missing time."

Malina took a deep breath and slowly nodded her head. "I'll stay, but no gallantries. If I'm here to help, you trust me to do what I do."

"Aye." He nodded, grateful.

She gave him a strange look. "You must really like her to agree to that."

"This is new territory for me. The *lidérc* I can deal with. Ya women are another story altogether."

"I can't believe it. The untouchable Erik MacGregor lovesick over a woman and a mortal one at that. This is one lassie I have to meet."

"Thank ya, Malina." Erik watched as she lifted her bag over her arm and began to climb the staircase. With everyone yet to arrive, she'd just take whatever room pleased her. When she was half way up, he added, "And while you're here, it would be great if ya could help get the house ready. The place could really use a woman's—"

Malina screamed, dropped her bag and practically flew down the steps at him. Erik laughed, whisking away from the tiny banshee of a woman.

THE COOL GLASS of her bedroom window pressed into Lydia's face as she stared out into his dark eyes. It was night, but the moon was full and she could see him clearly. He hovered above the ground, floating by her window. It should've scared her, but it didn't.

Her nipples were so hard she feared they might break the glass. A cool smile crossed his features, as if he knew what she was thinking, knew the fantasies she had in her head. His long hair whipped forward, the dark strands striking against the glass. It was the barest of brushes, wind on hair on glass, but she felt as if every strand pressed through her clothing and stroked her naked flesh.

Erik reached for her, but a blue light surrounding the house kept him from crossing the boundary between them. He opened his mouth, and she watched his tongue slowly travel the length of his firm bottom lip. Her body hummed, needy, aching, and she thought she might pass out from her desire. He wanted her to open the window, to break the spell and let him pass. But, she couldn't open the window. Didn't dare. The complications that came with a man like this were beyond anything she could comprehend. Not to mention the fact he was possibly evil—the very evil her cold chills had been warning her about. The evil her gramma was making herself known because of.

"Lydia," he mouthed, a look of intense longing and hunger on his face. But, also there was a sadness in his eyes, a pain that matched what she felt inside. Every part of her wanted to be with him, to say the words that would invite him in.

Gasping, Lydia sat up in bed. She was covered in sweat and her entire length hummed with life. Taking a deep breath, she threw the covers off her legs. She didn't have to look at the clock to know she'd only slept a couple hours. It was like this every night for the last week.

Every time she finally managed to sleep Erik would come to her in her dreams and each night she'd wake up worse off than before. Every inch of her flesh itched and every nerve ending tingled. She wanted him—desperately, completely. And she wanted him now.

"LYD, honey, why don't you come for a walk with me? We can take the packages down to the post office together." Charlotte leaned back on the floral-patterned couch in the living room and watched Lydia through veiled eyes. "I think the fresh air will do you some good."

Sunlight streamed into the picture window behind the couch. Boxes piled along one wall. The orders needed to ship or they'd not make their guaranteed delivery date. Lydia had been packaging and fulfilling orders like mad. Only problem was, she wasn't walking them down to the post office. She couldn't. Erik might be out there. Waiting. Lurking.

"No, no, I'll just call and see if someone can pick them up for me." Lydia stood, pacing the living room.

Energy coursed through her, and she felt like a caged animal. She barely slept, hardly ate. If she tried either she felt sick. The only time she felt close to normal was when she worked. So that's exactly what she did—cleaning the house, making lotions and soaps and teas. She'd even invented five new lines, designed their labels and uploaded them to her website, in addition to the full twenty she already had. They were selling like hot cakes. The strangest part is that she'd done all of this in one week. Despite the nervous energy, productivity had never been higher.

"I'm going to check the computer and see if any more orders came in," Lydia said.

"You checked three minutes ago and there weren't any. You've got them all done." Charlotte stood. "You're starting to scare me. What's going on with you? Why won't you tell me what happened on your date? Does this have something to do with Erik? Did he do something? You've been acting so—"

Lydia turned to her, cutting her off with a look. "No. Yes. No. I don't know."

"Did Erik do something? Did he...?" Charlotte gave a meaningful pause.

"No, I don't think we had sex."

"You don't think? You mean you don't remember?"

"I told you I don't know." Lydia tossed out her hands. She was so confused. Weird things had been happening to her—things that may or may not have anything to do with the handsome Scotsman. The dreams could be dreams, or maybe they were more. Were they a spell he put over her to make her want him? Well, no, just one look at him made her want him. Any woman would have to be dead not to be attracted to the walking mass of sexy that was Erik MacGregor. And if she accepted the spell scenario, that would mean she believed in real spells. After what had been happening to her, she kind of did. A thought danced alongside her brain, but she couldn't quite grab it.

"Do you think he drugged your wine or something?" Charlotte frowned.

"No." She shook her head. Erik was definitely not that type.

"Come on, let's go for a walk. If it helps, Erik never comes down from the mansion. No one in town has seen him. Some even say they've seen other cars drive up there, but no one else comes down either."

"He comes down," Lydia said. "And he calls. I don't answer the phone."

"If you don't answer then how do you know that it's Erik calling?" Charlotte crossed the living room, took Lydia by the arms and made her stand still to look at her. "With anyone else I'd know it was caller ID, but you still haven't advanced fully into the modern age. You don't even own a cell phone. If not for the business, I think you'd still use dial up to connect to the internet."

"I just do. I can't explain it. I just know. I feel it's him." Then frowning, she defended her corded phone, "And I like Gramma Annabelle's old phone. It works just fine."

"Whatever, keep your shrine," Charlotte dismissed.

"And I don't want to be one of those people that walk around with a phone attached to me all the time, avoiding life like—"

"Like the rest of modern society?" Charlotte laughed. "Yeah, you're a big go-out-and-live kind of gal, aren't you? You never leave the house. I think I'm going to buy you a smart phone for your birthday and get you addicted to social networking. I already put your profile on a dating site."

Lydia inhaled sharply, horrified. "You did what!"

"I'm teasing." Charlotte laughed, holding her stomach and flinching dramatically when Lydia swatted at her. "Though I should, you hermit. You say Erik's been here? What did he say?"

"I don't talk to him. I hide upstairs until he goes away. He leaves me flowers on the doorstep every day. I throw them out back." Lydia shivered. She felt cold again. Was it even possible to have cold flashes?

"Why won't you see him?" Charlotte slowly urged her to walk toward the kitchen. "You're starting to worry me a little, Lyd. I'll put on another pot of coffee, and you can tell me what really is going on."

"You really want to know?"

Charlotte nodded and gave the "of course I want to know" look.

"Okay, stand back." Lydia took a deep breath.

Charlotte stepped back, leaning against the kitchen counter. She watched her, waiting.

Lydia bit her lip. "Okay, here goes nothing."

"Lydia? You home?"

Lydia jumped, gasping as she turned to the side screen door. Charlotte must have left it open. Joe stood on the other side. Covering her heart, she forced a smile. "Yeah, come in."

"Hey, didn't mean to startle you," Joe said, smiling kindly. "We were at the post office and Mr. Baker mentioned you hadn't been down all week. Thought we'd check in on you and make sure everything's all right."

"We?" Lydia leaned over.

Joe's new best friend, Brad, had come with him. She hid her grimace and tried not to physically recoil to see the man at her house. She couldn't explain why the man always made her uncomfortable—he just did. He didn't act menacing, so much as socially awkward. After being made fun of for her "witch on the hill" upbringing, Lydia was too polite to point out another person's peculiarities. What could she say? Don't come in because your facial expressions make me uneasy?

Brad stood outside the door. Against her better judgment, she motioned him inside. "Do come in."

The squat Brad nodded. "We also need your help."

"Oh?" Lydia forced the smile to stay intact. She ignored her instinct to kick the man out.

"My wife's birthday," Brad said. "I need a gift for her and thought you might have something. She likes vanilla. At least I think that's what she's always putting on. Or I thought that stuff you wear. I think she'd like that."

When Lydia didn't answer, Charlotte said, "I think we can find something for you."

Charlotte left her alone in the kitchen with the two men.

"You been sick?" Joe asked. The laugh lines around his mouth shifted and he looked concerned.

"Yeah," she lied. Well, maybe it wasn't a lie. Could what was happening to her be considered sickness? "I haven't been feeling well. I think it was the stomach flu. I'm getting better though."

"Oh, sorry to hear that." Brad's eyes strayed downward to her chest only to sweep back up. "Though, I'm glad that you're better."

Lydia nodded. She liked Joe. Brad just made her feel awkward, like she was a piece of meat. Suddenly, the vision of him pleasuring himself to a stalker-like photo popped into her head. It was vividly real, but she shook it off. Where the hell did that come from?

Gross.

Beyond gross.

"Got it!" Charlotte called. She set a couple gift bags on the table. "This is vanilla rose, vanilla lavender and my favorite vanilla ginger. Plus, with purchase we'll throw in a small bottle of what Lydia wears."

Brad, still staring at Lydia, pulled out his wallet. "How much for that last one?"

"Thirty-six," Lydia answered.

Brad blinked in surprise. "Must be some good lotion."

"It's a whole gift bag," Charlotte explained.

Brad turned to look at it for the first time. "Oh, yeah. That's perfect, wrapped and everything." He handed the exact change to Lydia, letting his finger brush up along hers.

"So, do you need help with anything?" Joe asked.

"No, thank—"

"Actually," Charlotte interrupted, instantly smiling in a very un-Charlotte like way. It was a look she used when she wanted something. "We do have a giant load of packages to take down. I saw you drove your truck. Would you mind giving me a lift down the hill? Neither one of us owns a car. It would take several trips to get them all."

"No, of course not. It's on the way," Joe said.

"You're a lifesaver!" Charlotte gushed. She turned, secretly winking at Lydia as she led the men to where the boxes were stacked.

Lydia followed them, and they started carting boxes out to the truck. Brad worked the slowest, but with all four of them they managed to get it loaded fairly quickly. She handed Charlotte the company credit card to pay for the postage.

"Aren't you coming?" Brad asked, glancing over her.

"No," Charlotte said for her, "I don't want her out and about yet." To Lydia, she said, "Forget the coffee. Try the chamomile tea. Get some sleep. I'll be back later."

Lydia nodded, as Charlotte climbed into the truck. She had the urge to stop her, but there was no logical reason for it. She watched as the vehicle pulled out of the drive. Feeling a familiar vibration along her spine, she tensed. It felt like Erik. He must have been coming with flowers. Like a wimp, she turned and made ready to run for the kitchen door. He felt close.

"Hello, neighbor!" It wasn't Erik. The accent belonged to a female and sounded more British than Scottish.

Lydia turned. It was too late to run to the door anyway—well, too late not to look rude or insane doing it. A slender woman wearing all black lifted her hand in greeting as she came down a narrowly worn path in the trees. She grinned, an infectiously impish look.

"My brothers tell me this is the place for girly stuff. I'm Malina MacGregor. My family bought the place up the hill, but you know that already."

"Hi, Lydia Barratt."

"So I've been told." Malina grinned.

"Oh?" Lydia wondered at the pleasure that washed over her at the simple statement.

"Aye. Erik's smitten with you. We've been teasing him mercilessly about it." Malina's smile widened, as if she just loved revealing that piece of information about her brother. Lydia instantly liked the woman. There was something mischievous and carefree about her in a spunky, don't mess with me way. "So, got some time to sell me some stuff? I've got a ma, two aunts, my cousin Maura, a guestroom and myself to stock bathrooms for. Not to mention, if you carry stuff for men—a da, three uncles, five brothers, a pile of cousins and another guest room or two. Plus I have to stock the supply closet for when they run out. I swear invite them to a round of shinty and the men drop everything to run for the door with their sticks, but if one of them runs out of shampoo they're too busy to be bothered to go to the store. They resort to stealing each other's and when that runs out, I catch them in my shower smelling like a perfumed rose. Trust me when I tell you, you do not want a household of men using your shower."

"All of you are going to live up there?" Lydia asked in surprise. Erik mentioned he had family coming, but she never imagined so many.

"Aye. Why not? There's space enough for it. Our clan likes to stick together. Some of us come and go as we please, but we always end up back in the family home more often than not."

"Why don't you come in? I'll see if I have anything you might like." Lydia motioned to the door. "It must be nice coming from a large family who's so close."

"Oh, aye and then again no. Try having five brothers and a Da who thinks it's their duty to protect you—from everything." Malina's smile fell, and she rolled her eyes. "Men. You'd think they'd let me make my own decisions. On the plus side, they're always there when I need them to be. I'll tell you, the MacGregors fiercely guard what is theirs, especially their women."

Lydia wasn't sure what to say to that, so she didn't say anything. The chatty Malina didn't seem to mind her silence, as they walked into the living room.

"Tea?" Lydia asked.

"No, I'm good."

"So, what fragrances did you have in mind?" Lydia asked. "Or I can just cart everything out and let you pick and choose."

"Let's do that," Malina said. "It'll give us a chance to talk."

"About?" She blinked in surprise, suddenly a little nervous by Malina's visit. If she hadn't been so preoccupied about Erik, she might have suspected there was more to this than a shopping spree.

"About why you are hiding from my brother." The woman nodded slowly in understanding. "Don't worry, I'm not here to plead his case. It suits me just fine if you torture him a little. Pardon me for saying so, but he deserves it. "

Lydia laughed. How could she not? There was something honest and simple to the way Malina talked. She instantly sensed that whatever the woman said, the woman meant. "I think you may have the wrong idea. We've only gone out on one date and quite honestly it wasn't a very memorable one. No offense. I'm sure he's a nice guy."

"Hm." The woman nodded. "I have never heard anyone refer to any of my brothers as a nice guy. Usually girls try to be my friend to get closer to them. I'm going to assume you really meant he's a pain in the arse but you like him anyway against your better judgment."

"No, I…"

"You really can't remember how the date ended, can you?"

Weak, Lydia sat down on the chair, forgetting all about going to get the lotions. "How...? How did you know that?"

"Because I know what he did to you. I know that strange things have probably been happening to you. Don't worry, Erik and Euann only cast a little spell. In his own way, Erik was trying to protect what he thought was his. Only, I suspect you have it worse in some ways. I know what he is. You do not."

"Then, I'm not crazy." Lydia's whole body shook violently.

"No, darling, you are not crazy. But I have a feeling when I tell you what he's done, you are going to be rightfully mad."

"Cast a spell?" Lydia tried to comprehend all that Malina was saying. Erik considered her his? Erik cast a spell? "Tell me everything. Please, I have to know what's going on. There are the dreams. And so many strange things have been happening since I met him."

"Like?"

"Like this," Lydia said softly. She took a deep breath, put out her arms and instantly the air in the room sped up like a fan had switched on. Only she was the fan. A piece of paper blew across the floor and the curtains fluttered along the picture windows edges. Malina didn't look at all shocked by the display. Dropping her arms, the wind slowly stopped. "What's happening to me? What did he do to me?"

"Well you see, lassie. It's like this. The men would tiptoe around this part, but at my age I can't be bothered. We MacGregors are a clan of ancient warlocks and you are my brother's *inthrall*. You are connected to him and can borrow his powers with a single touch. That thing you just did, calling the wind, that's Erik's power you are using. It's different for everyone. His gift came in the form of weather. It may sound neat, but try being weatherman's sister. He used to make it flood when I had a date so they'd cancel."

"But I don't want to be his *inthrall*." She sat down on the chair, fidgeting.

"In this case, it wasn't a choice. Unless you cast a spell to become one?"

Lydia shook her head in denial. "I wouldn't know how."

"Then you come by it naturally." The woman shrugged as if it were no big deal. "If things get passionate, more power will be absorbed. I'm not sure all you have done with him, but if you were to have sex it would only make the powers you absorbed all the more potent. In fact, knowing Erik, he probably cast a spell on you the first time you were alone with him. Something small to relax you so you would be yourself around him without the awkwardness of having first met. He was never a very patient man."

"You mean...?" Lydia stood and began to pace. She was getting a little irritated. It was bizarre that she could talk to a complete stranger like this, especially since that stranger was Erik's sister. Something inside her told her she could trust Malina, even if she couldn't completely trust the woman's brother. "If I am what you say and he is...then, that means...? If he cast a spell to relax me, could it possibly make me do things I would never normally do?"

"I suppose." Malina nodded, her brow furrowed in thought. "If inside you really wanted to do it but would never normally act on the instinct. Erik would never force you to like him or be with him against your will, but such a spell might speed up the course of nature."

Lydia didn't know whether to feel relief that she had an excuse for acting the way she did, or anger at Erik for making her act the way she did. It didn't matter that she had enjoyed it. Not every impulse she had was meant to be followed. "I don't know what to say."

"I'll let you think about what I've told you, but I'm sure you'll have questions later." Malina grinned, changing subjects. "Now, about these lotions."

Lydia slowly nodded, going to get the samples. Was she crazy for believing Malina so readily? Maybe, but in truth it was the only explanation that made sense.

Grabbing a sample box out of the kitchen, Lydia carried it back to the living room. She had a feeling she and Malina were going to be friends— just as soon as she strangled the woman's brother.

Chapter Seven

Time did not cool Lydia's anger toward Erik over his little spell. In fact, all it did was give her an opportunity to plan ways to pay him back. With Malina's help, she was able to make a special fragrance just for him. Her nervousness over Erik dissipated with the more time Lydia spent with his sister. Malina helped her channel some of the left over power flowing through her blood, controlling it.

Hugging the special gift basket close to her chest, while trying to carry the bags of lotions and soaps Malina had ordered, she waited at the MacGregor mansion's front door. "We should have split this into two treks up the hill. My arms are killing me."

"I still say this is strange." Charlotte, her arms

also laden with product, adjusted her weight, lifting her knees to inelegantly steady the bottom of her bag. "Yesterday you wouldn't leave the house and today we're delivering half our inventory to the very man you've been avoiding."

Loud footsteps sounded on the other side of the door and Lydia gave her friend a slight smile. "Yesterday was a very interesting day."

"I suppose," Charlotte drawled. "Then again, you weren't standing in line at the post office with pervert Brad staring at your ass while he slurped on a slushy. I told him he could go after they helped me carry the load inside, but he insisted on keeping me company. Apparently, I needed help watching my ass. He kept asking about you. Think he was angling for a threesome."

"Gross, Char." Lydia gave a small laugh. "I'm very proud of you for not stringing him from a flag pole like Buck Mitchell."

"Buck *grabbed* my ass." Charlotte said. "Big difference."

"He was eight."

"Old enough to know better. And he still asked me to prom in high school."

Lively footsteps neared and the door was pulled open. By the look of the man, he was undoubtedly another MacGregor. This one had short dark hair. His bangs fell over brown eyes flecked with green. Damn, but the whole clan of them were undoubtedly attractive specimens of male perfection. This one was no Erik, but his cute, devil-may-care smile and sparkling eyes were just as charming.

"Iain, who is it?" came a voice.

Another MacGregor man poked his head around the corner. His hair was longer and his eyes were solid brown. He glanced first at Lydia, before stopping to stare at Charlotte. His mouth fell open, and he didn't say another word.

Iain, the one with short hair who held the door, grimaced and pushed the second man back. "Forgive my brother, Euann, he has no manners. We only keep him around because every family needs an idiot."

Euann grunted as he was shoved behind the door. Suddenly, his fist reappeared, slamming Iain in the shoulder with a loud pop.

Iain grinned. "Ladies, excuse me."

Iain dove behind the thick oak door and the sounds of a scuffle ensued. Lydia shared a glance with Charlotte before they both rushed to peek at the fight. The two men growled at each other in a gruff foreign language as they wrestled around the floor.

"Och, not again!" A third MacGregor paused at the top of the stairs. His brown hair was tipped with blond. His green eyes filtered to Lydia and Charlotte, their arms still laden with packages. He quickened his pace, hurrying down the stairs. "What's all this?"

"Hi, I'm Lydia Barratt. I live just down the hill. Malina ordered these products from my store yesterday, and I told her I'd deliver them this evening." Lydia glanced at the two brothers, who paused in their fight to stare at her. Euann's face was squished against the floor under Iain's hand. "If this is a bad time, we can come back."

"Och, no lassie, do not pay attention to my cousins. Every family needs a couple idiots and we keep them around for entertainment." The man came to the end of the steps. "I'm Rory. Let me take those for ya."

Rory took Lydia's bags and set them on a long decorative oak table near the bottom of the stairs before doing the same for Charlotte.

"You're Lydia?" Euann asked from the floor, sounding surprised. His words were muffled from Iain's hand against his cheek, as his brother kept him pinned. "I didn't recognize you —*mururphum…*"

Iain pushed his fingers over Euann's mouth.

"Erik's Lydia?" Iain asked, as if his position was the most natural in the world. At that moment, Euann grunted and bucked up, tossing his brother off him. Iain slid a few inches across the marble floor on his back.

Lydia didn't know how to answer.

"Why don't ya two go see if ya can unpack some manners?" Rory shook his head at his cousins. "There are plenty of boxes to look in."

"Wow," Charlotte said. "You've really cleaned this place up fast. It looks wonderful."

"Aye," Rory said. "Then again, there are a lot of us to attend to it."

"If ya think this house is impressive, wait until I get the golf course put in. That will be a thing of beauty." Iain picked himself up off the floor. "And shinty field."

"Och, not again with the sports. I'm sure these ladies don't want to hear about that," Euann muttered.

"I love golf," Charlotte stated. Lydia wondered at the challenging stare she gave Euann.

"Do ya now?" Iain grinned. He slapped Euann on the shoulder. "Maybe Lydia will let us trade ya for this one."

"Actually, I'm rather partial to Charlotte," Lydia answered.

"Och, ouch!" Euann grabbed his heart.

"Oh, no, I didn't mean it like…" Lydia shut her mouth. Iain pushed Euann as he moved past him. Euann laughed.

"Though, I don't know what shinty is," Charlotte admitted.

"Oh, lass, ya don't know what you're missing!" Iain exclaimed.

"It's only the best sport in the world," Rory added. "Ya should come around next spring. We'll have a shinty tournament and caber tossing."

"It's glorified Scottish field hockey," Euann stated dryly. He met Charlotte's stare as he righted himself. Lydia actually felt sorry for the guy. Two seconds into seeing Charlotte, he looked like a love-sick pup. With Charlotte's complete oblivion to a man's attraction, her friend would never even notice.

"This one hates sports," Iain announced, nodding at Euann as if that was the worst offense of all. "We can't understand how he can call himself a MacGregor and hate the two best sports in the world. I'll tell ya what, as soon as the course is finished, ya can come play golf with us."

"I'd love to." Charlotte grinned.

"Ya wouldn't happen to like whiskey as well, would ya?" Rory asked, offering his arm to Charlotte.

"I might," she said.

"A lassie after our own hearts," Iain proclaimed. He hooked his arm through Lydia's.

"Where—?" Lydia tried to ask. She looked

about, helpless as he tried to lead her from the room.

"Well, of course we expect Erik's Lydia to stay for dinner," Iain said. "Ya did not think we'd let ya escape once we had ya in our grasp, did ya? Malina was very clever to invite ya here tonight. She knew we'd be here to greet ya."

Erik's Lydia?

Lydia shivered, all too aware of the power these men had. She looked helplessly at Charlotte's back as they were led deeper into the house. What had she done? Was it a mistake coming here? Should she have told Charlotte about the warlock's powers? Lydia had tried, but everything she came up with sounded insane, and Charlotte had already been worried. She'd been so angry with Erik and intent on delivering his present that she hadn't stopped to think about what would happen if she couldn't leave the MacGregor mansion.

"Do not look so worried, lassie," Iain said softly. "We'll not bite ya."

"Erik might," Euann winked at her, grinning widely.

Not knowing what was coming over her, she couldn't help herself as she said, "He'd better be careful. I bite back."

LAVENDER AND MINT.

Erik's heart quickened as he hurried down-stairs. He'd been painting the far wing, expecting someone to bring him dinner. When no one did, he'd been forced to venture to the dining room.

The large pile of packages on the table near the bottom of the stairwell caught his attention. Lydia's scent lingered in the front hall. She'd been there. Automatically he moved toward the front door, hoping he could find her and stop her before she had a chance to hide in her house again.

"She even drinks like a Scot!" Iain's laughter stopped him. "That settles it. We're selling ya, Euann, and giving this one your room."

Erik froze. He could tell by the tone in his brother's voice that they had visitors. He looked at the packages, this time seeing one labeled with his name. A small smile curled his mouth. Lydia was still there, and she forgave him. Why else would she bring a present? Erik excitedly glanced down at his clothes, before looking to make sure no one saw. He brushed his hand over his shirt, magically knocking off the dried paint stains from his old T-shirt and jeans. Yes, they could have magically painted the home, but they enjoyed old fashioned labor—at least for a few weeks until one of them grew tired of the chore and cast a spell to bring the paintbrushes to militant life. However, spells took energy and it would be a shame to sacrifice some of the old oak trees in the yard for such a purpose. Better they survey the gardens and protect the landscape they wished to keep first.

Next he ran his fingers through his hair to be sure it was clean, then over his face and arms. Satisfied he didn't look too much like a mess, he turned his feet toward the dining room, eager to save Lydia from whatever playful torment his family had planned. Jokes and insults were being traded between his brothers and cousin when he entered. Instantly he smelled the old whiskey. They'd gotten into the liquor.

"Erik!" Iain proclaimed. He sat next to Charlotte at the oversized dining table. The poor woman tried to smile at him, but he could tell by the tightness in her face she was still trying to breathe over the hard fumes still burning in her throat.

Erik nodded at her before finding Lydia in the chair next to Charlotte. Rory sat on the other side of her. Lydia met his eyes briefly before turning them to the plate in front of her. There much he wanted to say, yet with his family around he wouldn't be able to. Love them as he did, they'd not help the situation—especially with an open bottle of whiskey in front of them.

"Looks like ya started without me. Or did ya forget ya left me holding the paintbrush?" Erik asked. He jerked his head at Rory, silently gesturing that the man should move and let him take the seat next to Lydia. Rory grinned and didn't stand. Instead, his cousin placed his hand on the back of Lydia's chair and kicked his feet out in easy repose.

"I didn't forget," Iain assured him. "But we gave your Bridie pies to the ladies."

Lydia looked at her plate and then him. He read the apology on her features before she could get it out.

"A worthy enough cause," Erik put forth, stopping her words. "Where's the banshee?"

"Malina's in town placing orders with the locals," Iain said. "She said something about towels, sheets, robes..." He waved a dismissing hand.

Erik winked at Euann as he made his way toward Lydia. "Told ya she'd take over if we invited her down."

Euann lifted his whiskey shot in acknowledgement before tossing it back.

Then, grabbing Rory by the shirt collar, he forced the man to his feet and tossed him aside.

He took the now empty chair next to Lydia. She looked at him, stunned. He smiled, took her hand and lifted it to his mouth. He kissed the back of her fingers. Softly, he said, "I'm glad ya came."

Lydia pulled away from him and folded her hands in her lap. "Malina ordered supplies and asked me to deliver them. I'd be foolish to turn away such a big new client."

Rory gasped suddenly and pointed toward the ceiling. "I have golf balls in the attic!"

"No ya don't," Euann said.

"I do," Rory insisted. "We can hit them off the roof."

Iain instantly rose to his feet. He grabbed the whiskey with one hand and Charlotte's arm with the other. He pulled the slightly inebriated woman to her feet. "Come on then, love."

"Wait," Lydia said, standing, "she doesn't know about…"

Iain smiled knowingly. "Don't ya worry, Lydia, I promise not to let her fall off."

Charlotte laughed. "I think I know enough not to fall off a roof." Then to Iain, she said, "We should cut Lyd off. I think she's had too much to drink."

Lydia didn't look like she'd had anything to drink. The wine glass in front of her was untouched.

"I don't think we've had enough," Iain answered.

"Right you are!" Charlotte agreed. "To the roof!"

"To the roof!" Iain and Rory repeated in unison.

"Aye," Euann drawled without enthusiasm, not as excited but undoubtedly going to flirt with Charlotte and drink whiskey, "to the roof."

"I should go keep an eye on Charlotte." Lydia tried to follow Euann. "You all probably enchanted the clubs or something."

"Och, no!" Euann said. "No magick when it comes to sports."

"Some things are sacred," Erik added. "And we don't enchant objects. It never goes right."

Before he left the room, Euann grinned and mumbled to himself, "Besides, I hid all of the golf balls. Good luck trying to find them."

"I should still go keep an eye on her," Lydia stepped toward the door.

"No, wait, I want to talk to ya." Erik made a move to grab her arm, but stopped himself.

"But Charlotte doesn't know about your family," Lydia answered. She met his eyes briefly and then looked away.

"And ya do know?"

"Malina came to see me. She had a lot of

interesting things to say." Lydia crossed her arms over her chest.

Mo chreach! She was lovely even when she was mad at him. Let her be upset, at least she was talking to him.

Erik grimaced. "Did she?"

"Oh, yeah. And you should be worried. I know all about your little memory erasing spell. I spent days trying to figure out what happened to me. I almost checked myself into a mental institution at one point."

"Did ya now?"

"No," she admitted before declaring, "But I could easily well have."

"You're angry," he stated.

"Yes, I'm angry!" Lydia yelled. "You whammied my head."

"Whammied?"

"Hexed, cursed, erased," she answered. "Not to mention the fact I walked around my house like a freaking ceiling fan turned on high."

"A ceiling fan?"

Lydia glared at him. "If you keep repeating everything I say I'll touch you and suck all your power out and...and....and then I'll—"

"I handled it badly," he interrupted, trying to show her he understood.

"Badly?" She scoffed.

"Admittedly, very badly," he amended.

"Very badly?"

"Are ya now going to repeat everything *I* say?"

She placed her hands on her hips. "You call that an apology?"

"No, I call the flowers ya kept throwing on your lawn an apology."

"I hate that you're sounding reasonable." She stubbornly arched a brow. "I want an apology."

"I did apologize," he said, exasperated. Why wouldn't she calm down and let him kiss her? So what if kissing her made no logical sense? He'd missed her while she kept him away. He wanted to touch her. Surely the binding spell he put on himself would work this time. It had to. He willed it to be so with the sheer desperation of his lust for her.

"No, you dug up my roses and killed my lawn. Who does that?" She stalked the long way around the table, going the opposite way from him, and made a move to the door. "I need to check on Charlotte."

"My brothers won't hurt her." He went the short way to follow her. "Lydia—"

"But *I* very well may hurt *you*." She thrust out her hand. A tiny breeze hit his chest. The last of his power fizzled out of her. It tickled and he laughed. By the expression in her face, it was evident that the sound of his humor only irritated her more. Lydia shook her hand a few times, frowning at it. She gestured to hit him with wind, but nothing happened.

"For the record, ya killed your lawn," he said.

"Well, I wouldn't know that. *Someone* erased my memory." Lydia reached for his hand, held it tight for a few seconds before letting go. She tried to hit him again. A slightly stronger breeze knocked into his chest, and he stumbled back one step. She smiled in satisfaction as if she'd thrown him across the manor into the wall. The power transfer it took to perform that trick left her breathing heavy.

Erik sighed, growing more frustrated by the passing moment. Apparently, Malina hadn't done a good job explaining things on his behalf. He wasn't sure how to handle an irate female. Habit told him to cast a spell and make her emotions go away. Instinct warned that such a thing might not be his best course of action.

She paused on her way up the stairs. "Which way to the roof?"

"Mo chreach!" he swore under his breath. Never mind logic. He was casting a spell to calm her down. Erik narrowed his eyes and whispered an incantation.

Lydia arched a brow, cocked her head to the

side and gave him a superior smile. "Nice try. Your sister helped me with that too."

That little meddlesome banshee! he thought, ready to find his sister and throw magick at her.

"Oh, wonderful, my order is here!" Malina announced coming in the door with impeccable timing. She spoke before she could have visibly seen Lydia's delivery on the table and Lydia on the stairwell. After a lifetime of being related to his sister, Erik recognized the fake concern in her tone as she exclaimed, "Erik! Why ever are you stalking our poor lotion supplier?"

LYDIA WAS VERY happy to see Malina. She'd been seconds away from leaping down the stairwell to wrap her body around Erik's. Oh, but he was frustratingly sexy as sin. Even when she wanted to yell at him, she wanted to kiss him. When she'd touched his hand, purposefully trying to pull power out of him to wipe that smirk off his face, she hadn't counted on the tingling aftermath of contact to remain in her fingers. It radiated up her arm and neck, adding sensitivity to her skin.

"Wonderful to see you again, Lydia," Malina said, walking past her brother up the stairs to where Lydia stood. The woman hooked her arm through Lydia's and led her away from Erik. "Care to investigate something with me? I think a couple members of my dear family tried to douse me with whiskey on my way in. We'll see how funny they think it is when I knock them out of the attic window."

Lydia glanced back at Erik, but let Malina pull her along. The woman did smell of hard liquor.

"Malina." Erik sounded exasperated as he tried to stop his sister. "I was speaking to Lydia privately."

"Hm, I don't think she wants to talk to you," Malina answered for her.

"I'll paint your room first," Erik said.

Malina stopped and smiled as they reached the top of the stairs. "Perhaps you should listen to him, Lydia." She let go of her arm. "Just make sure he grovels before you forgive him."

It didn't take a genius to discover that it was difficult to get a word in when two members of the MacGregor family were in the same room. They seemed to fill up a place with their personalities.

"Lydia," Erik began, coming up the stairs as his sister left them.

"So, first, don't ya be mad," Rory said, coming toward them. "Second, she's alive. Third, it wasn't me."

"What wasn't ya?" Erik demanded.

Euann and Iain appeared carrying an unmoving Charlotte between them. Malina trailed right behind them shaking her head in disapproval.

"What happened?" Lydia asked, rushing to her friend. "You said you'd take care of her."

"She's alive," Euann offered. "Just…sleeping."

"Her eyes are open!" Lydia reached for her friends face. The men gave Charlotte a small bounce, readjusting her in their arms. "And why is her hand all stiff like that?" The woman looked like she was mid-drink.

"Now, love, it's only a small petrifying spell," Iain tried to explain. "She may not look like it, but we did put her to sleep."

"Put her to sleep!" Lydia looked at the crazy lot of them and held out her arms. "Give her to me."

"That means you killed her, moron," Malina said, before correcting, "They helped her to fall sleep."

Lydia had understood what the men meant, but she still worried about her friend. Charlotte didn't know about real magick. "I'm taking her home. I should never have brought her with me."

"Don't say that," Rory tried to soothe.

"We should get her to a bed," Iain said.

"She's getting heavier," Euann agreed. "My room is this way."

"A *guest* bed," Malina ordered. The brothers ignored her as they hurried down the hall to a door. Malina placed a hand on Lydia's shoulder, stopping her from following. "She'll sleep like a rock, almost literally. She won't remember anything in the morning. At least, nothing that can't be explained away with a hangover."

Lydia shrugged the woman off, going to follow her friend. She found the men maneuvering her onto a bed. Though she fully intended to yell at them if even one of Charlotte's hairs was pulled wrong she found they were quite gentle with the woman, even taking the time to cover her up.

"Euann tried to spike my drink," Iain explained.

"Only after ya spiked mine," Euann retorted.

"Charlotte grabbed the wrong one. We tried to stop her and..." Iain gave a light shrug. "A petrifying spell came out on instinct."

"It's better than shifting into a rat." Euann gave her an unconvinced smile.

"Ya were going to turn me into a rat?" Iain grumbled. "Had I known that I wouldn't have tried to turn ya into a snake."

"You used the last of my snake potion to prank each other?" Malina pushed her way into the room. "The next batch won't be ready for nearly two decades."

Lydia stumbled out of her way only to bump into warm flesh. She quickly turned, finding Erik right behind her. Rory had not joined them.

"Ya smell like a bar," Euann said, sniffing Malina. "Miss your mouth?"

"You threw whiskey out the window at me, moron," Malina hissed.

"We couldn't leave the potions lying around," Iain said. "A glass of whiskey around here is free reign to anyone walking by."

"Iain threw it." Euann pointed at his brother.

Malina glared at them in warning.

Iain didn't try to deny it. "At least I didn't toss out a match?"

An argument started about snake potions and stealing and a bunch of things she couldn't understand because they were shouted in Gaelic. Very calmly, she looked at Erik. He smiled at her, ignoring his siblings as he brushed a piece of hair from her cheek. The man actually looked like he wanted to kiss her—right there in the middle of the chaos.

"If you want me to forgive you, Erik," Lydia began. He nodded eagerly, clearly willing to please her any way he could. Leaning up to his ear, she whispered, "Then take your brothers out into the hall and petrify them."

His grin only widened. "Easily done." He kissed the tip of her nose before pushing his brothers' backs toward the door. "Leave our guests in peace."

Unsuspecting of their fates, the men mumbled apologies to Lydia, sheepishly unable to meet her gaze. When they cleared the door, she shut it behind them and turned the lock. She doubted the lock would do any good, but it made her feel better. She heard their muffled voices. Along the bottom edge of the door a yellow light shone briefly and all sound stopped.

Lydia crawled into bed next to Charlotte. She touched the woman's cheek, but the skin was hard. Charlotte stared at the ceiling over the foot of the bed. It was too creepy to look at so Lydia rolled onto her back and shut her eyes.

Lydia heard the doorknob rattle and instinctively knew Erik was outside trying to come in. Obviously, these crazy people meant no harm, and yet her friend was still turned into a statue. It was clear that Erik's family loved each other very much. She saw that in the way Erik talked about them, the way they looked at each other, and even in the way they mercilessly teased each other. Aside from Charlotte, she didn't really have anyone. She couldn't help but feel it would be nice to belong to such a big family.

Lydia held her breath, not moving, listening to see what Erik would do outside the door. The soft sound of tapping disappeared into silence.

ERIK PRESSED the pads of his fingers to the door a couple times in thought, wondering if he should call out. Then, thinking enough damage had been done and progress had been made in his relationship with Lydia, he let her be. Tomorrow he'd start fresh. She was here. She was talking to him. And, he grinned, she said she would forgive him.

Erik glanced at his brothers stuck like two sculptures. Euann's mouth hung open mid-sentence, his hands on his hips. Iain's finger was lifted mid-point. Their eyes followed him.

"Sorry, lads, but ya had it coming," he whispered. "At least it's only a little one and ya will thaw out in the morning."

Chapter Eight

"You should call someone about your tree," Lydia said, not taking her eyes off the branches of the large oak in the MacGregor's front lawn. Large brown spots dotted the leaves. The sun still rose, casting a brilliant orange light over the landscape. She never remembered a sunrise looking quite so pretty before. She felt Erik behind her before she bothered to look. "I know a lady in town. She belongs to the same women's business interest group that Chef Alana and I are part of. She tested the soil for me when I had problems with my lavender crop."

"How is Charlotte?"

"Supple," Lydia answered before chuckling as she thought of the two human statues in the upstairs hall. "Her arm finally came down, her eyes are closed, and her skin feels like skin."

"I can't stop thinking about ya. I'm crazy about ya," he said.

The confession caused a wave of pleasure inside her. She turned to him, smiling...until the very distinct scent of the special lotion she'd made for him with Malina drifted on the breeze. She looked at his face. His pupils were wide, too wide for the bright light of morning.

"I see you found my gift," Lydia answered. She walked past him in an arc, keeping distance between them.

"Wait," Erik darted forward, grabbing her arm. Without much warning, he kissed her. His lips pressed tightly to hers. A rush of pleasure and excitement filled her. She loved the taste of him, the smell.

Smell? Crap, the spell-tainted lotion.

She tried to pull back.

When their lips parted, his words came out in a rush. "I think I want to marry ya, Lydia. I love ya. I don't know why I confessed that." Confusion passed over him for a brief moment before instantly replaced by insistence. "I think we should marry. Tonight. No, right now. By this tree."

"Oh, crap," Lydia whispered, trying to pry her arms from him. Malina had said this potion would amplify Erik's feelings for her, perfect payback for when he had cast a spell on Lydia to make her relax around him. Lydia wasn't sure what she'd expected, but a marriage proposal wasn't it. Did Erik actually want to marry her? Was that the amplification of his feelings?

"We belong together. Can't ya feel it?"

Lydia didn't know what to feel. The attraction between them was palpable, but love? Marriage? She said the only thing she could think of, deflecting the conversation over to the one who helped her make the lotion to begin with. "You should tell your sister."

"Malina?" He frowned. "I don't think…well, if ya think, *fíorghrá?*"

"Oh, I do. You should tell her in full detail what you're planning." Lydia managed to pry his hands off her arms. She quickly led the way inside.

"Malina," Erik yelled, taking the stairs two at a time.

Lydia rushed to where Charlotte slept. Iain and Euann still stood, but Euann's mouth had closed and Iain's arms had fallen to his sides. They were coming out of it. Their eyes followed her as she passed them. She found Charlotte sitting on the side of the bed holding her head.

"Oh, good, you're awake. Come on, we have

to go." Lydia slipped a hand around Charlotte's back, under her arms. She hefted her to her feet.

"Lydia?" the woman mumbled. "What's going on?"

"We have to hurry," Lydia insisted. She didn't know how long Erik would be preoccupied with Malina. Surely the woman would get some enjoyment out of the chaos she wrought and would entertain herself with her brother for a long while. And Malina had seemed so nice and helpful when she came to place the lotion order. She said the spell would make him feel bad about what he'd done, give him a dose of understanding. Instead, he proposed marriage. It didn't take a genius to figure out Malina had used her. "That will teach me to trust a MacGregor."

"Lyd?" Charlotte mumbled.

"We have to go. I need to replenish the stock." Lydia forced Charlotte to walk.

"Is it time for work?" The woman lifted her arm looking at her watch, though Lydia doubted the woman could read it by the way her arm swayed in front of her face.

"Yes, hon, it's time for work."

"Oh, ok then." Charlotte didn't protest. She sounded a little drunk. In the hall, she stopped, looking at the two frozen men. "What the…?"

"They have a bet going," Lydia lied. "Been at

it for hours. Come on, we have to hurry."

"You work too much," Charlotte protested. "And I work too much. We need lives. Nothing interesting ever happens to us."

"We have lives," Lydia assured her, trying not to drop her down the stairs as they stumbled their way to the main floor. "And trust me, they're more interesting than you think."

"Does that mean you finally slept with the sexy Scotsman?" Charlotte asked loudly, too loudly for Lydia's liking. "You talk about him enough. I demand to know details."

Lydia grimaced. "Grab that red bag."

She led Charlotte past the table. Charlotte obeyed. "Hey, this is Erik's present." Her eyes rounding as they went out the still-open front door, she mourned, "Oh, no, Lydia, I'm so sorry. Was Erik's little Erik really that bad in bed you have to run away?" Then trying to stop, she asked, "Am I on your walk of shame? You did sleep with the right MacGregor, didn't you? Though, I have to say the others aren't bad to look at. I'd get frisky with—"

"Char?"

"Yes?"

"I love you, but shut up." Lydia practically dragged her all the way down the hill to her home.

ERIK THREW his arms open to express the full depths of what he was feeling as he finished his impromptu love ballad. He grinned happily at his sister.

Malina laughed heartily, clapping her hands. "Perfect," she snickered, "I think she'll love it. Especially the part about how you like staring at her ass when she walks, and think of fucking her when she talks. That's," Malina covered her mouth and took several deep breaths to quell the merriment choking her, "that's truly beautiful, brother, truly. And it all rhymed." She tapped her chest as another snort of laughter escaped her. "You got me a little choked up inside."

Erik watched his sister, not really paying attention to her reaction as much as her words that Lydia would love his ballad. It was as if a dam had been broken inside him, letting all his hidden feelings out to play. They surged through him. The moment he looked into her eyes that morning, at her beautiful face caressed by orange sunrise, he knew she was his destiny. All his centuries had been leading to one thing— marrying Lydia, making her his, possessing her.

"You should go and sing it to her," Malina encouraged.

"Then ya think she'll marry me?"

"How," Malina snorted, barely managing to get out, "could any girl resist?"

Erik ran to her for a hug. She stiffened, putting up her arms in defense at the un-Erik-like gesture. He kissed the top of her head before letting go. "I owe ya, sister."

"No, no, you really don't. Your happiness is enough for me," she assured him.

"LY-DI-AH! I sit beneath your window, laaaass, singing 'cause I loooove your a—"

"For the love of St. Francis of Assisi, someone call a vet. There is an injured animal screaming in pain outside," Charlotte interrupted the flow of music in ill-humor.

Lydia lifted her forehead from the kitchen table. Her windows and doors were all locked, and yet Erik's endlessly verbose singing penetrated the barrier of glass and wood with ease.

Charlotte held her head and blinked heavily. Her red-rimmed eyes were filled with the all too poignant look of a hangover. She took a seat at the table and laid her head down. Her moan sounded something like, "I'm never moving again."

"You need fluids," Lydia prescribed, getting up to pour unsweetened herbal tea from the pitcher in the fridge. She'd mixed it especially for her friend. It was Gramma Annabelle's hangover recipe of willow bark, peppermint, carrot, and ginger. The old lady always had a fresh supply of it in the house while she was alive. Apparently, being a natural witch also meant in partaking in natural liquors. Annabelle had kept a steady supply of moonshine stashed in the basement. If the concert didn't stop soon she might try to find an old bottle.

"Ly-di-ah!"

"Omigod. Kill me," Charlotte moaned. "No. Kill him. Then kill me."

"Ly-di-ah!"

Erik had been singing for over an hour. At first, he'd tried to come inside. She'd not invited him and the barrier spell sent him sprawling back into the yard. He didn't seem to mind as he found a seat on some landscaping timbers and began his serenade. The last time she'd asked him to be quiet, he'd gotten louder and overly enthusiastic. In fact, she'd been too scared to pull back the curtains for a clearer look, but she was pretty sure he'd been dancing on her lawn, shaking his kilt.

"Omigod," Charlotte muttered, pushing up

and angrily going to a window. Then grimacing, she said, "Is he wearing a tux jacket with his kilt?"

"Don't let him see you," Lydia cried out in a panic. It was too late. The song began with renewed force.

"He's..." Charlotte frowned. "I think it's dancing."

Since the damage was done, Lydia joined Charlotte at the window. Erik grinned. He lifted his arms to the side and kicked his legs, bouncing around the yard like a kid on too much sugar. "Maybe it's a traditional Scottish dance?"

Both women tilted their heads in unison as his kilt kicked up to show his perfectly formed ass.

"He's not wearing..." Charlotte began.

"I know. He doesn't," Lydia answered. Damn, the man had a fine body. Too bad Malina's trick had turned him insane.

"Let's not call the police quite yet," Charlotte said just as the kilt kicked up to show the back of his thighs. "Maybe he'll tire first and go home." They watched, suppressing giggles and looks of admiration. When the song became winded, Charlotte asked, "Is he drunk?"

"Kind of." Lydia avoided her friend's probing gaze and went to the tea glass she'd left on the counter. Thrusting it at Charlotte, she said, "Hold your nose and drink it."

"What do you mean, kind of? He's not on drugs, is he?" Charlotte sniffed the tea and grimaced. She wrinkled her nose, closed her eyes and tried to take a long drink. The liquid went down, but barely. She coughed, unable to finish all of it.

"Not really." Lydia moved to put the pitcher back in the fridge before hurrying to check the computer for orders...and to avoid answering. Since the MacGregors purchased most of her supplies on hand, she had her work cut out for her making more. "Can you grab lotion base from the basement and make sure we have enough labels for everything?"

"What do you mean, not really?" Charlotte arched a brow.

"He's under a spell," Lydia tried to explain.

"Obviously a *love* spell." Charlotte laughed, and then moaned as she held her head.

"Can you grab the lotion base from the basement and make sure—"

"No," Charlotte said, moving instead to go upstairs. "I'm calling in sick."

Lydia thought she might be joking until Charlotte didn't stop walking. Instead, she heard a door close and the shower turn on.

"Ly-di-ah! Ya smell just like a, uh, la-ven-der-ah mint, and I think I like your scent."

It would have been funny if she wasn't trapped inside her house unable to leave the protection of Gramma Annabelle's spells. She marched to the door and pulled it open. Yelling through the screen, she said, "Erik!"

He was standing before her almost instantly, his body blurred as if carried by magic. With a daydreaming expression, he answered, "Yes, my lavender."

"Don't call me lavender," she stated firmly.

"Yes, my rose."

"Don't call me rose."

"Yes, my—"

"Erik, could you find me lavender like you did the other day? I have a lot of work to do and I could really use a…" He was running off into the hills before she could finish. "…a bushel."

She closed the door, sighing in relief that the singing stopped. Really, how long could magickal lotion last? She'd grabbed the remainder in the gift bag and brought it home. It was covered in old ash, hidden inside the broken wood furnace in the basement. There was no way he was getting into it again.

"Malina better run the next time I see her," Lydia threatened, though no one could hear her. It was just as well. She wasn't sure how she'd go up against a powerful warlock family.

Chapter Nine

"Gramma Annabelle, I love you and your hangover cure," Charlotte announced, coming down the stairs two at a time. She wore a long sleeve T-shirt and yoga pants. Her wet hair was piled on the top of her head. She paused in the kitchen doorway to do a couple random, overly dramatic karate punches to illustrate how much better she was feeling. Then straightening, she said, "Oh, hey, don't forget to send in your business license renewal to the city. I forgot to tell you I ran into Mrs. Callister at the post office when Joe gave me a ride yesterday. She wanted me to remind you that you're due."

"I swear that woman is something else. She gave a threatening warning to Chef Alana and then had the gall to ask for a food discount.

Callister is not even on the board. Ah, but it doesn't matter, I already mailed it." Lydia glanced up from where she was counting drops of essential oils over warmed lotion. "Feeling better?"

"Much. As long as Erik doesn't start singing again." She chuckled. "That poor man cannot hold his liquor. I say we let it slip this one time because he's cute and your neighbor and I got some funny footage on my cell phone, but if it happens again we call the cops and post the video online. I don't care if he is your boyfriend, Lyd, that was noise pollution." Lifting her arms wide, she belted, *"Ly-di-ah! I want to have your kid-ie-ah! Please sit-ie-ah on my fac—"*

Lydia lifted her stirring spoon and flung warm lotion at Charlotte from across the kitchen.

"Hey stop!" The woman dodged the attack, laughing even as it glopped on her sleeve. Sniffing her arm, she said, "Lilies?"

"What? No, I'm…" Lydia held up the bottle she had just set down so she could stir. "It's mint. Smell."

Charlotte took the bottle, even as she held up her arm. "Lilies. Smell. And this shirt was clean. I stole it from the back of your closet."

Her grandmother's scent was unmistakable on Charlotte's sleeve. Lydia breathed deeply. After what she'd seen with Erik and his family, she couldn't deny the possibility.

"Lilies." Lydia whispered. "Gramma?"

"I know you don't believe," Charlotte held up her arm as it was undeniable proof of ghosts, "but…"

"I believe," Lydia said. "What would you say if I told you Erik is under a spell and that is why he is acting like that?"

"I'm being serious," Charlotte said, dropping her arm.

"So am I. What if I told you I cast the spell with the lotion I gave him?" Lydia bit her lip and waited, not sure what to expect. "And that his entire family is magickal, not magic tricks as in illusionists in Las Vegas, but real magick, the kind Gramma Annabelle used to talk about."

"You want me to believe that Erik and his family are witches?" Charlotte barely moved. She slowly looked at her lotioned sleeve.

"Um," Lydia gave a slight lift of her hands and corrected weakly, "Warlocks."

"Erik's a warlock?"

Lydia nodded.

"And you cast spells?"

Lydia nodded again. "A spell. One."

"And you believe that Gramma Annabelle is here, in this house, as a lily smelling ghost?"

Lydia started to nod.

"Finally!"

Lydia and Charlotte screamed at the loud boom of a sound. The kitchen vibrated all around them to punctuate the word, silverware clinking in the drawers, cups chiming in the cupboards. They grabbed each other's arms and ran from the kitchen to the living room, still screeching in fright. They huddled together behind the arm of the couch, the farthest they could get from the unearthly voice.

"Crap. Oh my fucking crap," Charlotte cursed, trembling. "Did you hear that?"

"What the hell was that?" Lydia whispered, as if her friend might actually have an answer. "Oh, crap."

"Crap," Charlotte agreed. They gasped for breath, refusing to let go.

"Crap?" a voice demanded sounding far away and in the room at the same time. "I pull off the spell of the century and all you can say to me is crap?"

"Is that…?" Charlotte began.

"Gramma Annabelle," Lydia answered with a halfhearted nod. That voice she would remember for the rest of her life.

"What do we do?" Charlotte asked. "Should we tell her to go to the light?"

Lydia shrugged helplessly. "Why are you asking me? I don't know."

"Well, that's what they always say on those ghost hunting shows and movies." Charlotte gripped Lydia's arm tighter, cutting off the blood flow, as the sound of tapping came from the kitchen. She forced Lydia in front of her and gave her a shove. "You're the spell caster. Go talk to it."

Lydia's entire body shook. She swatted the air at her friend.

"Go!" Charlotte gestured frantically, backing herself into the corner.

Lydia took a small step.

"I'm waiting," Annabelle's voice said, sounding less demonic than before.

"Um, Gramma?" Lydia asked, her voice tiny. She tried to speak up, but the sound was locked in her throat.

"Do you know how long I've been trying to get through to you? I cast every spell in the book to make the transition easy, and to ensure I remained tied to this house. If I knew you'd ignore me I would have hidden spell bags of my hair and blood all over town instead. Then I could at least go haunt someone who paid attention. I thought concentrating them here would help ground my essence."

Yeah, that sounded like her grandmother.

"Gramma, where are you?" Lydia didn't step into the kitchen but stayed just outside the door frame.

"Can't you see me?" The question was followed by a long sigh.

Lydia shook her head in denial and took one step into the kitchen. The air smelled of lilies. A wave of sadness hit her. She'd missed her grand-mother so much. Then, she noticed the spoon handle moving in the lotion. Someone stirred it. The image was faint, more of a distortion, like heat rising off a desert road during the midday sun. She gasped, covering her mouth as tears threatened. Not daring to move lest the spirit go away, she stared at her grandmother's ghost in wonder.

"I left you tons of potions and clues." The spoon paused in its stirring, only to start again. "You didn't do a damn thing with them, and I've been stuck in limbo for the last ten years."

"It's only been two years." Lydia whispered. A tear slipped down her cheek. Could it really be Gramma Annabelle? She wanted to run and hug the woman, but she still couldn't see more than a vague impression of where the ghost stood.

"Oh, has it? Well, still. It was a very long and boring two years. You think this place is boring when you're alive, you should see the afterlife. Let me tell you, the spirits floating around the yard are no party."

"Potions?"

"My moonshine in the basement. I thought for sure you'd at least get rip roaring drunk at the funeral. You didn't even touch the stuff. And this house. I thought for sure you'd redecorate not keep it like some old lady shrine. I left you enough money. The remodeling would have stirred me out of limbo, but no. You couldn't be bothered to knock down a few walls. I tried leaving scent trails—you don't know how hard those are to make, young lady. I moved objects, well, an object. I knocked your key ring on the floor a couple times. You ignored all my signs. I just needed you to believe in me to give me enough power to appear. Finally, you ripped out those damned rose bushes. It wasn't much, but it was something."

"I'm, uh, sorry I didn't get drunk and redecorate your home?" Lydia wasn't sure what to think. "Is that what you wanted to tell me from beyond? Drink more and change the curtains?"

"It wouldn't hurt," Annabelle mumbled. Her voice became clearer with each passing moment, but her body did not. "And it would be nice if you found my spell bags and hid them around town so I can finally leave this place."

"Lyd?" Charlotte asked from the door. "Is it…?"

"Charlotte, darling," Annabelle exclaimed happily, then, disapproval heavy in her tone she added, "You're letting yourself go. You're never going to catch a man dressed like a hobo."

Charlotte looked down at her borrowed clothes and reached for her drying bun. She turned wide eyes to Lydia. Weakly, she answered, "They're hangover clothes."

"Oh!" Annabelle said in full approval. "Well done, child, well done."

Charlotte moved slowly toward Lydia and grabbed her arm. They stared at the lotion pot.

"How've you, uh, been, Gramma?" Charlotte asked.

"Dead," Annabelle answered wryly.

"You, ah, look like you lost weight," Charlotte answered.

The spirit laughed. The spoon suddenly dropped and the apparition disappeared leaving the kitchen as it was before she appeared.

"What the…?" Charlotte whispered.

"Gramma," Lydia said, lifting her arm to try and stop the ghost. It did no good.

"Lydia, my darling," Erik called from outside the home. "I have brought ya lavender."

Lydia let loose a long breath and swiped at her

teary eyes. She walked toward the door, closely passing by the stove where the spirit had appeared. She reached out her hand to touch the air where Annabelle had been.

"Don't go," Lydia whispered.

"Lydia, my *fíorghrá*," Erik insisted from outside, sounding very pleased. "I thought of your beauty and I could not stop at lavender."

Lydia frowned as his words. She reached for the door, intent on dealing with the love monster her spell had created. Her first view was of Erik bending over toward the ground, his backside to her. The length of his kilt lifted in the breeze to show his ass. A small laugh of surprise left her, not expecting to be greeted in such a way.

Charlotte joined her. Yelling at him, she said, "Good to see the rumors about Scots and their kilts are true."

Erik quickly stood and turned, pushing the material down. He'd taken off the formal jacket and wore a looser white shirt with the sleeves rolled. Dirt smudged his chest. Behind him was a giant heart drawn on the yard with lavender stocks. In the middle of the heart were other green herbs. The creation wasn't complete, but there was enough of it there to know what he'd been attempting. If the smell was any indication, she'd say the green plants were various strains of peppermints and mints. Then, realizing where he would have gotten various strains of peppermints and mints, she groaned.

"He picked my whole garden," Lydia whispered. Though, technically, that garden was on his land now.

"For ya, my love," Erik gestured to the side, grinning widely.

In unison, Charlotte and Lydia leaned out of the door to look where he pointed. A giant pile of herbs and picked plants were stacked on her lawn. Before she could comment, a van appeared on her drive coming up to the house.

Erik clapped, still very pleased with what he'd done. When he spoke this time, she couldn't understand the foreign words, so she instead watched as the van stopped.

To Charlotte, she said, "This is getting ridiculous. Later, I'm going to stand here and distract him. I need you to crawl out the back window by the stairs like when we were kids, sneak up to the mansion and tell Malina to come and fetch her brother. Just, don't go inside with the MacGregors. They have a way of distracting a situation."

"I'm not leaving you alone," Charlotte denied. She may have been chuckling at Erik's antics, but she put a protective hand on Lydia's arm and squeezed. "If you're worried, I'm not leaving."

"Malina caused this. She can end it before it gets much worse. Someone is bound to call the sheriff. The last thing I need is some crazy warlock on my lawn casting spells at the local police. Any way you spin that story, it's not good." Lydia flinched as Erik took to a knee and dramatically lifted his voice. She still didn't understand a damn thing he was saying.

"Done," Charlotte agreed.

Jane Turner, the nursery owner, hopped out the front seat of the van. The woman's brown hair was pulled into a curly ponytail at the nape of her neck and held down with a red cap with her company logo on it. Lydia knew her from the women's business association, but the woman never had much to say unless someone asked her about gardening tips.

Jane glanced questioningly to the Scotsman reciting some strange foreign limerick before reaching to grab her clipboard out of the vehicle. She lifted it to Lydia as she walked to the house. "I have a delivery and install. Can you sign?"

"Delivery? I didn't order..." Lydia reached to take the clipboard, not daring to step out into the yard where Erik could grab her. She wasn't sure what he'd do, but her guess was smother her with affection until it killed her. "Never mind, I have an idea where they came from."

Jane glanced to where Erik kneeled on the ground and chuckled. Then, nodding toward the side of the house where the roses used to be, she said, "I guess I know where you want them."

Between Erik's very emotional declarations of crazy, her dead grandmother's visit, and Charlotte tugging on her arm, Lydia didn't have the energy to ask Jane what she was planning on planting. So, Lydia simply nodded. "Wherever you think is best."

Chapter Ten

Erik's throat was sore from a day full of singing and reciting ancient love poems—poems he hadn't bothered thinking about for nearly four hundred years but now seemed to remember in full clarity. He didn't care if he lost his voice. There was so much emotion inside him that it just had to come out somehow. With each second it built higher. He didn't want food, or air, or sleep. He just wanted his love, his Lydia.

He stared at Lydia's house bathed in moon-light, the windows dark from within. Thinking of her sleeping, he smiled. She would be so beautiful, so soft and warm, so touchable. His feet carried him to the house as he stared up to the second floor, to the last window to go dark. Without thought he reached for the kitchen door. The barrier spell zapped him and sent him flying back into the yard. He landed with a hard thud. The smile began to fade. Why couldn't he get to her? Why was the world keeping them apart? The wind stirred over him. If she didn't come out soon, he'd have to blow the house down. There was no other way. It made perfect sense. No house, no barrier spell, nothing keeping him and Lydia apart.

"Erik?"

Erik had sensed his sister's approach, but had chosen to ignore her. He stayed on his back, looking at Lydia's window.

"Erik?" Malina insisted. She moved slowly to look down at him, leaning over to block his view of the house. He grimaced and tried to shuffle to the side to regain his connection with Lydia's window. Malina leaned again to force him to look at her. "Erik, I need you to drink something for me."

"Later," he dismissed, again wiggling over the ground to look to where his beloved slept. He wanted to be ready when she awoke.

"Da is going to brain you for ruining that shirt." Malina again stepped in his way. "It's not easy to find a tailor who sews barrel cuffs the way they used to. You know magickal repairs aren't the same quality as the real thing."

Erik gave a small growl and waved his arm. The wind burst from the trees to knock Malina to the side. She skidded across the yard, her arms flailing. Around him, the grass died in the general shape of his body. He felt his powers suck the life from the blades.

"Erik," Malina warned, her accent slipping in her irritation. "I need ya to stop that, laddie. I have something for ya to drink and ya are gonna to drink it."

Erik pushed to his feet and growled at her. Why was she still talking? He lifted his hand to magickally toss her away from him so he could stare at Lydia's window.

Malina lifted her arms, making her expression less fierce. In a rush, she said, "Lydia wants you to."

Instantly, he dropped his arms and smiled. "Why didn't ya say so?"

"I thought you knew?" It was more of a question than a statement.

Erik held out his hand, turning his attention back up to the window. He yelled, "Lydia, my sweet tulip, I drink this for ya!"

The curtain stirred. She'd heard him. His grin widened. Not paying attention to what his sister handed him, he tossed back the contents of the vial. He glanced at Malina only long enough to give the vial back to her. Malina waved up at Lydia and stepped back, watching him. Erik's body tingled and he shivered violently. His senses became stronger. The air smelled of dead grass and picked lavender. Everywhere he looked became brighter, as if someone turned a flashlight on inside his eyes. Then the sensation was gone. He smiled up at the window.

"I drank it for ya, my ginger blossom, I drank it!" Erik yelled as loud as he could, trying to let Lydia see all the love he felt inside him.

"Shite." Malina made a weak noise beside him. "Bloody hell, Da is going to kill me for this." The faint sound of a cellphone was followed by his sister, saying, "Um, hi, Da, I'm going to need you to come out to Wisconsin earlier than planned. There's a slight situation—no, no, no emergency, just hurry." She paused moving in a wide arc around him to study his face. "Hurry really fast."

WHAT? No! Where was Malina going? Why wasn't she taking Erik with her?

Lydia tapped frantically on the window to get Malina's attention. Erik waved, as if she couldn't see him hopping up and down on her lawn.

Malina looked up at her and gave a helpless shrug as she hung up her cellphone and continued to back away toward the mansion.

Lydia opened her window and yelled through the screen, "Don't go!"

"I am here, my love!" Erik called.

"Shut up, Sir Galahad," she told him, irritated. Then, pressing her face to the screen, she said, "Malina, get back here right now. Undo this."

"I will get her for ya, my dear heart." Erik instantly charged at his sister.

Malina screamed in surprise at the aggressive attack. She threw a ball of crackling light at him. It hit his arm, knocking his shoulder back and sending tiny flashes of lightning down his arm to immobilize his hand. He kept advancing on his sister with single-minded purpose.

Lydia knew he tried to please her so she said, "Erik, stop."

He didn't listen.

"Um, ah, dear heart, stop. I..." She frowned and closed her eyes tight. "I love you, ah, crazy dear, um, heart guy."

He turned to the house and lifted his arms to her like an actor in a Shakespearean play. One of his hands fell limp at the wrist. Lydia grimaced. Malina was safe from his attack.

"I'll be back," Malina shouted as she disappeared.

"We will be one, my mountain bearberry," Erik assured her. "Soon, very soon. We are like the rare twinflower in the pinewoods, two blossoms to one vine."

Lydia quickly closed the window and backed away. What the heck was a mountain bearberry? Seconds later a soft blue light shone around the house as Erik tried to breach the barrier. She took a deep breath. Then, the sound of shuffling came from below. Panicked, Lydia grabbed a nearby brass lamp and held it like a weapon. She wasn't sure if Erik would try to harm her with his affections or would simply sonnet her to death. These types of situations never seemed to end well in horror-suspense type movies. Her heart began to thump wildly with fear. Her mind raced with outrageous ideas as anxiety overtook her thoughts. What if he tried to lock her in the mansion's basement as some kind of possession? He did say they would be one. His clear obsession could cause him to try to eat her so they could join essences and then he'd put her on like a—

"Lyd?" Charlotte whispered.

Lydia gasped sharply in surprise and dropped the lamp. The bulb broke. She hopped over the broken glass and hurried down the hall. Seeing

Charlotte at the bottom of the stairs she ran to her and wrapped her arms around her. "I'm so glad it's you."

Charlotte shivered violently and was cold to the touch.

Lydia pulled back and grabbed her face. She turned her friend's eyes to better see them in the dim moonlight streaming through the window. "What happened?"

"Did...?" Charlotte blinked. "Did you see?"

"Malina and Erik fighting?" Lydia asked.

"It's real. Magick is real." Charlotte blinked. "You said it was, but spells are one thing. They..." She lifted her hand to hold an imaginary light ball and gestured a weak throw.

"Yes." Lydia hugged Charlotte, leading her to the couch. Grabbing a throw blanket, she wrapped it around the woman's shoulders and pulled her close. "It's okay. We're safe in here."

"Your house was glowing blue. Why is your house glowing blue?" Charlotte grabbed Lydia's arm tight and shook it insistently.

"That's how I know we're safe. It's Gramma's barrier spell. He can't get in unless I invite him."

"Like a vampire," Charlotte made a weak, hysterical noise. "Great. Maybe we should throw garlic cloves at him."

Lydia didn't answer. Her grandmother always

said myths were based in reality. It's possible barrier spells were how the Victorians really kept out magickal creatures.

"Nothing is ever going to be normal again, is it?" Charlotte whispered. "How can we do anything anymore, knowing what we know? Vampires? Warlocks? What else? We can't leave the house."

Lydia didn't have an answer for her. The barrier again lit up as Erik tried to get inside. Charlotte made a small squeak of fear and hid her face in the couch. Lydia stayed beside her, praying that it would soon be over.

"WHY HASN'T anyone called the police?" Charlotte asked. "Someone had to of seen the lights flashing last night. At the very least a UFO hunter should have shown up with a video camera." Then stiffening, she whispered, "Do you think UFOs are real too?"

"I don't think you can see the barrier lights unless you know magick is real. It must be some kind of protection clause or something." Lydia ignored the last question. She'd just seen her dead grandmother and had a lovesick warlock on her lawn. The last thing she needed was to worry about extraterrestrial probing.

"And the magick hand ball?" Charlotte made a weak throwing gesture.

"This is my fault. I mixed the potion and gave it to him. I trusted Malina. I can't call the police. The phone lines stopped working yesterday after you left and the Internet is down. Besides, Sheriff Johnson is too nice of a man. He won't be able to help, and Erik is not himself right now. You saw what he started to do to his sister. No, right now, we just stay inside and wait it out."

Trusting Malina a second time wasn't exactly her best plan, but it was the only one she had.

Lightning flashed overhead and several seconds later thunder cracked. Guilt filled her. Even as she feared what Erik might do, feared the crazed look on his face, she knew it was her fault this was happening. She should never have dabbled in what she didn't understand.

"You don't have to stay, Charlotte. I'll understand if you want to go home."

"I'm not leaving you." Charlotte slowly walked to the stove and whispered. "Gramma Annabelle? Are you here?"

"I've been trying to talk to her all night. She won't appear, and I don't know how to make her." Lydia glanced down at the basement.

As if reading her thoughts, Charlotte inquired, "Moonshine?"

"I don't know if that will work, and I really don't want to be drunk right now." Then turning to the curtains, she hesitated before yanking them off the window. The rod broke as they crashed to the floor. "Let's try redecorating. Remodeling is supposed to stir spirits because it changes the environment."

"Doesn't that mean knocking down walls and major renovations?" Charlotte asked.

"Do you have a better plan?" Lydia pushed the kitchen table across the floor, knocking the chairs aside in her haste.

The women continued to pull the curtains off the windows and push furniture haphazardly around the house to change the layout. Lotion bottles were swept off the display shelf onto the floor—not that there was much left after Malina bought the majority of her stock. Breathing hard, they stopped and looked around the mess they had made of the living room and kitchen. Outside the storm grew worse. They watched, listened, smelled, but there was no sign of Annabelle.

"Fine, go grab the moonshine," Lydia said, desperate. If anyone knew what to do about Erik, her grandmother would. "If anything will séance her back, it will be that stuff. That, or drinking it will kill us first."

"You're coming with me," Charlotte said. "I'm not going in the basement alone."

Lydia glanced outside. Erik stood in front of the curtain-less window, looking in. She gasped and jumped back. He frowned at them and lightning streaked across the sky followed almost instantly by thunder. Violent storm clouds rolled over the landscape, darkening the day.

"Is he doing that?" Charlotte tried to tug Lydia through the mess they'd made. She tripped, falling over the arm of an inconveniently placed chair. "What's happening to his face?"

Lydia inhaled deep breaths. Lightning flashed but she saw headlights. She stiffened, unable to move. A rush of memories flooded over her, as the man in the window changed. Erik's eyes glinted with an inner light. His nose thickened and spread. Fur sprouted over his features. His mouth pulled forward, making room for the long, deadly fangs stretching from his gums. His hands lifted, as if it would touch the glass but held back. Claws stretched from fattening fingertips. Slowly, the sharp points tapped forward, striking the blue glowing barrier with steady thumps.

"What...the fuck...is that?" Charlotte panted. "Where's Gramma's gun?"

Lydia had seen this before. Is this why they erased her memory? Because she saw Erik change? She tried to step closer, but her body shook too forcefully. His eyes had become dark, feral pits. This was not the Erik she knew. Nothing about this creature reminded her of the man.

"I don't have any bullets," Lydia said. She never felt the need to use the old shotgun and it sat collecting dust in the attic.

The sky had become dark and, had she not seen it change for herself, she would have thought it evening. Her yard light turned on, the motion sensor activated on the side of the home. A soft glow radiated around the edge of the house and fell over Erik's changed face. The sound of wind whined through the windows and rattled pieces of the house's exterior. Though old, the Victorian was well maintained. The windows did not normally leak and the house did not rattle in storms. Another crack sounded and she saw a heavy tree limb fall behind him and roll toward her home. Leaves fiercely danced on the trees before falling like snowflakes in a blizzard toward Erik. The window panes vibrated. Erik's hair blew around his head in violent patterns. The tree limb slammed against the house's siding causing her to jump at the loud thud.

Lydia and Charlotte screamed in unison, huddling together against the wall.

"I should have made you leave," Lydia said, though she was glad she wasn't alone.

Charlotte screamed again as another limb hit the house. "He's trying to tear it down."

Lydia looked at her home, the inside destroyed, the outside being pummeled by magick. Tears slid down her face. This couldn't be real. How could it be real?

"He doesn't want the house. He wants me." Lydia whispered.

"What?" Charlotte cried, unable to hear her.

Lydia turned to her friend and pushed her slightly away. Yelling over the now high whine and heavy slams from outside, she said, "I love you!"

"What?" Charlotte reached to cover her ears to indicate she didn't understand.

"Get to the basement." Lydia took the moment to run. Charlotte removed her hands from her ears and tried to grab her, but Lydia hurried to the kitchen door before her friend could stop her. Her heart beat heavily. This was her doing. Charlotte was not part of it.

She turned the knob on the kitchen door. The wind whipped it open, ripping it out of her hand. The screen door was gone, lost to the storm.

"Lydia, no," Charlotte yelled. She turned to

see her friend gripping the interior door frame as she tried to enter from the living room. A gust of wind blew everything from the counter onto the floor. She heard the ceramic jars shatter. Charlotte turned her head into her arms as pieces flew past her.

"Erik?" Lydia called, not sure he'd be able to hear him. "Stop. I'm coming out."

She used the door frame to pull herself out of the house. Her heart felt as if it was stuck in her throat. She tried to breathe but it was hard. The wind hit her body, forcing her up against the side of the house. The newly planted bushes were uprooted. One went rolling away. The other clung to the earth but flapped to the side.

"Erik?" she called again. Her shirt snagged on a displaced nail. She felt the jagged metal cut into her skin. Lightning hit again, and she saw the outline of a giant branch rolling straight for her. Lydia screamed, but running in this weather was impossible. Her limbs felt like they were in sludge. She curled onto the ground and covered her head, braced for impact.

It never came. She blinked, looking up to see Erik standing over her, his hand stretched behind him to hold the heavy tree back without actually touching it. He slid his arm to the side, magickally tossing the branch away from them. It rolled away down the hillside.

The wind calmed by small degrees, but still whipped heavily around her and pushed her tears back into her hair to keep them from falling down her cheeks. She kept her back to the house. His dark eyes watched her intensely. He breathed hard, like an animal about to attack.

"Erik, this isn't you," Lydia said. She wasn't sure he could hear her over the elements but fear kept her voice soft and she barely managed to get the trembling words out. "Erik, please, stop."

The wind instantly died down though the storm clouds remained. A few drops of rain sprinkled from the sky. Erik didn't move.

"Erik, it's okay. I'm here. It's okay." She tried to touch his chest but he twitched, and she stopped with her hand in midair. "Try to calm down."

The rain fell harder.

"You're under a spell. This isn't you." She kept her eyes on his, hoping Charlotte would have the sense to stay inside. She forced her words to be soothing and calm. "You've been waiting for me to come out. I'm here."

His clawed hand lifted toward her face. She flinched, expecting him to strike. He didn't.

Instead, he touched the sideways trail of her tears along her temple. The rain hit harder still, thundering against the ground. She couldn't be certain, but she thought she saw concern in his eyes. They lightened by the tiniest degree. She took a deep breath, on guard, but suspecting that he didn't want to hurt her. He tilted his head and stroked her face. An uneasy smile formed on her features as she nodded gently, as if to coerce herself into believing that everything would be fine.

"Get away from him lassie. Run!" Lydia didn't recognize the voice but the Scottish accent gave her a few clues.

Erik's eyes darkened once more, and he growled. He turned, shielding her with his body as he pressed his back toward her. She was forced to remain against the house. His arms spread, as if protecting her from whoever yelled.

She reached for his side, trying to comfort him, trying to bring back the calm she'd succeeded in drawing out of him. The second her fingers touched he darted forward. He leapt into the air, arms wide, claws wielded, fangs bared. A roaring screech left his mouth. In the lightning she saw five figures waiting to fight him. They held guns pointed at Erik.

"No," Lydia yelled. "Don't hurt him."

She moved to stop them. Something hit her

from the side, throwing her to the ground. She felt a body pressing into hers and struggled to be free.

"No, you don't understand. I can stop him. He won't hurt me." Lydia tried to wiggle out of the tight hold on her body. She watched Erik's arm strike forward. Three shots sounded in quick succession, *pop, pop, pop*. Erik flung back as if shoved before dropping to the ground in an unmoving heap. "No!"

"Easy, lass, we got him." The grip on her body loosened. The sky lightened by small degrees making it easier to see. Iain laid over her. When he confirmed his brother was down, he stood and offered her a hand. "Did he harm ya?"

"No," she cried weakly. Pushing Iain aside, she half-crawled, half-ran to where Erik lay on the ground. She turned him on his back. His face was partially distorted but not as badly as before. The fangs had receded into his mouth, and his claws were gone. She touched his face, a strange combination of fur and flesh. "He was stopping."

"Are ya alright, lassie?"

Lydia leaned over Erik and looked up at the man who spoke. He appeared older than the MacGregors she'd met, but she saw the resemblance in his face and heard it in his voice. His accent was a little thicker than Erik's.

"This is my fault. He wasn't going to hurt

me." Seeing that they weren't aggressively holding their weapons, she turned to feel Erik's chest for a heartbeat. The steady thump hit her fingers. Darts stuck out of his arm, shoulder and leg. "What did you do to him?"

"I'd never harm my boy," the man said. Then, frowning, he gestured behind him to three men. "Come on, laddies, lift your brother." He reached a hand to help Lydia up.

Iain and Euann she knew. They wore jeans and T-shirts. The other two men were in kilts.

Iain gestured to the third man. "Lydia, this is our brother, Niall."

"Sorry to be meeting ya under these circumstances," Niall said. His eyes were green and lacked the playful light his brothers normally carried. Brown hair fell in a shag around his face, as if haircuts were the last thing on his mind. His kilt looked like it'd seen better days.

"This is our da, Angus." Iain motioned to the older man. The guy hardly looked old enough to have so many grown sons.

Lydia merely nodded at them.

"Malina," Angus growled. "Ya caused this mess, ya help this young lady clean it up."

She hadn't noticed Malina standing in the background away from the others. The woman gave her a guilty look and then turned her attention to the ground.

"Who's that?" Niall asked, nodding toward the house. He frowned.

Lydia turned to find Charlotte peeking out with wide eyes at them.

"Take him," Niall told his brothers, thrusting Erik's weight at Iain and Euann without giving them a choice. "She'll have to be dealt with."

"No, she's…" Lydia reached to touch the warlock's arm to stop him. Niall turned hard eyes to her, and she instantly pulled back. This man wasn't like his brothers. "She's Charlotte. She's my friend. I won't let you hurt her."

"It won't hurt, lass," Niall said, reaching for the sporran at his waist and pulled a small bag out of the pouch. "She won't remember a thing."

"Don't erase her memory," Lydia demanded. She automatically turned to Angus as their father. "She won't tell anyone. Who would believe her?"

"She's not one of us, lass," Angus answered softly. He reached to touch her. "Trust me, ya don't want to leave her in that condition. Let her think it all a bad dream and a bad storm. Look at her face."

Lydia obeyed. Charlotte was pale. Her lips worked but no sound came out. Tears ran over her cheeks. How could she agree to erase Charlotte's memory? Then she remembered what Charlotte had said, *Nothing is ever going to be normal again, is it?*

"Just, only tonight. Nothing else." Lydia looked from Angus to Niall.

"He's good at what he does," Angus assured her. "A wise decision, lassie."

Lydia had a feeling it was the only decision they would have given her.

Niall lifted his hand toward Charlotte. The woman began to shake her head violently, mumbling, "No, no, no, no…"

Niall blew against his palm. Sparkling dust floated. Charlotte swatted her hands but within a couple seconds her body went limp. Niall tried to catch the woman but only managed to grab an arm. His shoulder hit the barrier spell, lighting up the house. He jerked as it tried to toss him but held his footing. "Malina, ya help me work the spell."

Malina joined her brother, stepping into the kitchen to help shift Charlotte's fallen weight. She could go inside because Lydia had already invited her, but the others could not.

"Get Erik up to the house," Angus ordered. Then to Lydia, he asked, "This will go easier if ya have the original potion."

Lydia nodded and walked toward the house.

She ran downstairs and dug the lotion from the old furnace. When she came back up, Angus was standing outside her door, looking around at the frame.

"Pretty powerful natural magick," Angus said, as if admiring Gramma Annabelle's work. Then frowning he looked inside and sniffed. "Ya got ghosts, lass."

"What about me? Are you going to erase my memory?" Lydia handed him the bottle. He shoved it in his sporran.

"Is that what ya want?" Angus asked. Lydia shook her head in denial. The man nodded in understanding. "Then that will be up to Erik. Ya have magick, but ya don't come by it naturally."

Behind him, Malina and Niall hovered their hands over Charlotte whispering an incantation. Their eyes were three shades too light as they stared at each other. Tiny sparks danced over Charlotte's face, combining to give the slightest impressions of a memory before bursting into nothingness. Lydia watched the likeness of her own worried face explode and fade before having to look away.

The storm clouds had lightened considerably now that Erik was unconscious. Daylight peeked through the clouds, showing the full extent of her damaged home and lawn. She was too tired to do anything about it now.

"Will they be all right?" She looked at Charlotte on the ground and then Erik being carried away.

"Ya can check on him tomorrow," Angus said. "As for your friend, she'll be fine after a long sleep. Malina will stay and help ya put your house to order. It took a magical beating. There are cracks in—"

"Not now." Lydia shook her head. To Malina, she added, "Just help me get Charlotte upstairs so I can take care of her. I'll deal with everything else later."

The light faded from Malina's eyes as the color darkened to normal. She broke eye contact with her brother. Niall helped her lift Charlotte and carry her to the door. He looked at Lydia to let him in. Out of all the brothers, he'd be the last one she'd invite into her home. There was a coldness to his expression. Instead, Lydia went toward him and slipped her arm around her friend. Malina helped her carry Charlotte inside, the unconscious woman's feet dragging behind them. They laid Charlotte on the couch.

"Lydia, I'm sorry," Malina said. "I thought it would be funny."

Lydia simply looked at her. No part of what happened felt like a joke. Her home was wrecked.

Her best friend had the crap scared out of her and her mind wiped. The guy she'd been interested in turned into a monster. How exactly were they supposed to build any kind of relationship after that trip to Crazytown? Every time she looked at him she'd see the beast he could become. And Malina "thought it would be funny".

"Just go. You've done enough." Lydia went to the small closet door and pulled out a couple of blankets. When she turned back around, Malina was gone. She laid one blanket over Charlotte and then looked out the window to see Malina disappear into the trees. The MacGregors were gone. Wearily she wrapped the second blanket around her shoulders and sunk into a chair. Mumbling to herself because no one else was there to listen, she said, "I knew dating the sexy new neighbor was a bad idea. Lesson learned, universe, lesson learned."

Chapter Eleven

"A woman with clearly enough training in the old magick to be a natural witch, even if she only makes lotions like ya say, and Erik's *inthrall* after she'd recently fed on your brother's powers?" Margareta MacGregor's voice was low and soft. That was a bad sign. Whenever her tone dropped like that someone was in serious trouble. "It's bad enough ya chased Kenneth away, but now ya are trying to kill the rest of my sons?"

Kenneth? Why was she lecturing him about Kenneth? Erik's brother had been gone for nearly two decades and didn't want to be found, even though the family had tried, were still trying. Erik pushed through the fog in his brain to concentrate on what was being said.

"Kenneth left on his own. That's not my

fault," Malina answered. "I didn't try to kill Erik. It was a simple love potion, that's all. We pull pranks on each other all the time and nothing serious ever happens. He put moss growing potion in my soap and made me look like a swamp monster before a date last year. I hit him back with a mild love potion spell. It should have worn off naturally when the lotion scent wore off, or when I gave him the antidote. A few badly recited love sonnets and then done."

His mother wasn't yelling at him, but at his sister. That made more sense.

"How could I resist, Da?" Malina insisted. "Her store is called Love Potions. And you know how hard it is to find a practicing kitchen witch in these times who is also the romantic interest of someone you owe for causing frogs to jump out of your hair during your coming out party. With the man you wanted to marry standing right there." Her voice became a little pouty. "You might have done the same, Da?"

His father chuckled briefly only to stop as a loud thump sounded. Most likely he'd been hit against his arm—no doubt Margareta's doing. He answered with a very unconvincing, "No."

"Malina, ya want us to treat ya like an adult, but ya continually act like a child," Margareta scolded. "She's an *inthrall*. There is a *lidérc*. What were ya thinking? I knew it was a mistake sending ya to live with the English, but I didn't want ya getting swept up in the witch trials. They were examining babies for marks."

"Good thing yours is on your bum and not your face," Iain teased, clearly trying to break the tension.

Margareta's voice softened in warning, "Don't think I don't know about ya petrifying a poor human in our home."

"I'll just, ah, go check the news for the weather report," Iain said.

"I'll help ya," their da added. A door opened and shut. Erik tried to move, but his body was too heavy.

"I knew sending ya to live with the British was a mistake." Margareta repeated wistfully, as if her daughter might have missed them the first time she said it. The words were followed by a long sigh.

"That was over four hundred years ago," Malina retorted. "And I was a baby. You act as if I had a say in the matter."

"And ya still sound like them," Margareta countered.

"Then maybe ya shoulda handed me over to the authorities in the North Berwick witch trials, Ma. One look at the mark on me arse and they coulda drowned me for ya!" Malina's Scottish accent was incredibly thick and sarcastic. This was an argument he'd heard many times.

Erik groaned, trying to break into their fight but unable to form coherent words. His tongue was thick in his mouth. His head pounded, and straining to hear the hushed family argument wasn't helping. He felt sorry for Malina. She often received the brunt of their mother's lectures— probably because she was the only daughter and a strong-willed one at that.

"Erik," Malina gasped.

"Son," Margareta said.

He felt hands on his face and neck. Blinking open his eyes, he looked from one worried face to one very guilty expression and frowned.

"Did the lads petrify me for freezing them in the hallway?" Erik asked, trying to recollect the last thing he remembered clearly. He recalled Lydia outside on his lawn by a tree. She'd locked him out of her room the night before. He couldn't blame her for choosing to take care of her petrified friend, or if she was angry at him for what his family had done to Charlotte. A feeling of pure pleasure had rushed over him when he looked at her in the sunlight. Then things started to get a little hazy, and quite frankly a little sparkly.

His mother and sister leaned over him, their

faces a little too close to his. They were the only three left in the room. Their breathing hit his cheeks, and he smelled cinnamon rolls. He stretched his body, inhaling a deep yawn to gently force them back.

"I am so sorry, Erik. I didn't know she truly cared for you that much." Malina bit the corner of her lip and gave a sorrowful glance to their mother.

"What did ya do?" He furrowed his brow. He'd been around long enough to know when his powers had been used, let alone used to a great extent. The almost relaxed feeling in his limbs worried him. Automatically, he felt his face and teeth. "Did I…?"

Malina nodded. "Aye, you shifted."

"Is anyone hurt?" he demanded. Erik looked around the room as if he could make Lydia appear by sheer willpower. If he'd shifted, that is the first appetite his animal would want to sate— his unfulfilled lust for Lydia. The memory of darkness and the smell of fear slammed over him. He saw Lydia's face in his clawed hand. Lightning flashed over her features. "What the hell did I do? I used magick in my shifted form? But how did the binds slip?" Then remembering Malina's apology, he glared at her. "What did ya do? Why would ya unleash me?"

"The young woman is unharmed," Margareta soothed. "Her friend's mind has been erased so she won't remember. The situation is contained. All that matters is that ya are well, my son."

"Malina?" Erik demanded, ignoring his mother's attempts at comfort.

"She was so mad at you for erasing her thoughts. She already suspected something wasn't right. I thought it would be funny to help her cast a little revenge. I told her it would make you remorseful for what you'd done to her. It was supposed to be a simple love potion. We mixed it into the lotion she gave you."

"Ya don't mix a love potion with an *inthrall*," Margareta stated, as if such was commonly known.

"How was I to remember that? The family hasn't seen a natural *inthrall* since Uncle Raibeart's lover nearly drained him and left him a broken, crazy bachelor." Malina crossed her arms over her chest. Erik knew that stubborn look. A full blown fight was about to start. His sister did not like being attacked, and she really didn't like having to humble herself to apologize—especially when she was wrong.

"Ma, leave us a moment?" Erik asked.

Margareta studied both of them before nodding. She kissed Erik's forehead, just like she'd done whenever they were sick as children and left the room.

"Is Lydia harmed?" Erik pushed out of the large bed and swung his feet to the floor. He felt weak, but that hardly mattered at the moment. "I remembered the beast touched her. Did I...?"

"No. It was..." Malina gave a long disbelieving sigh. "It was actually quite remarkable. You didn't hurt her at all. It almost looked like you tried to protect her. Of course, this was after you tried to blow her house down with a storm, which was after you sang."

"I sang?" Erik flinched. Now there was some damage he might not be able to undo.

Malina nodded. "Aye."

"What?"

"Mostly songs you made up." Malina scrunched her face as if bracing for a blow. "And a few of the old ballads."

"Stop looking at me like I'm going to attack." Erik stood and brushed past her. His formal kilt hung around his hips but he wore no shirt. He sang made up ballads in his formal wear? Faint whispers of doing just that echoed in his mind. "I know ya didn't mean to cause this much damage. Had the roles been reversed I would have probably done the same and taken advantage of a prime situation. But we're even for the moss and the inked teeth and the pink horse."

Malina nodded in agreement. She had been yelled at enough by their mother, and he could see the age-old hurt in her eyes. In many ways she was different than her siblings. Her English mannerisms and speech were as ingrained into her as their Scottish manners were. She'd spent a human lifetime away from the clan in her younger years. Then grimacing, she said, "The pink horse was you? I've blamed Iain for the last hundred years."

"Even," Erik put forth.

She nodded, still frowning. "Da wants to erase Lydia's memory and move her and her business to one of the other cities where our people can keep an eye on her. I convinced him not to cast a spell until he spoke to you. I know she's your *inthrall*, but for the potion to work as strongly as it did, there has to be more there. I know our parents found their *fíorghrá* long ago. It was a different time for them. People lived with magick every day and accepted it. After all these centuries, none of us have come this close to love. Perhaps it's our ways. We send away anyone who might get close to discovering the truth of who we are."

"It's for the clan's protection," Erik said. "The family must come first. It is the only way we've survived the witch trials and inquisition."

"I know that. But you have a chance here, a rare chance that may never happen again." Malina patted his arm. "I think you really do love her. And I think she could come to love you. The spell I used should not have gotten that out of control so fast. The only explanation is that there is a natural chemistry between you, a destiny whose magick transcends simple spells and potions. There is true power in that kind of love."

Erik wasn't sure what to believe. What if his sister was wrong? What if he loved Lydia, but she could never forgive him for what he'd done? What if she couldn't accept him? Perhaps their da was right. They should erase him from her mind and send her on her way.

"And perhaps ya did nothing wrong," Erik disagreed. "Perhaps the *lidérc* has already cast a spell over her, and it interfered with your prank."

"You think that is how your binding slipped? She pulled it from you? Is that why your beast didn't hurt her? She was pulling your power out of you?" Malina frowned. "I hadn't thought of that. I wanted it so much to be love."

Erik wanted it to be love too, but he couldn't trust that what he was feeling wasn't the residual effects of the love potion gone wrong. "I'll shower first and then go down the hill to see the damage

I've done. Then I'll decide how best to handle Lydia."

"OH, did the meteorologists get it wrong, Chuck. In what was supposed to be a mild sunny day was hit by a freak storm over the middle of Wisconsin. Several towns are reporting wind damage. Insurance companies expect well over an estimated million dollars' worth of small damage claims will be filed within the next week."

Charlotte made a weak noise as she turned off the news. She rubbed her forehead. "I can't believe I was passed out for the entire thing."

Lydia hated lying. "Yeah, you scared the crap out of me when that branch hit you. Dr. West's office said to keep an eye on you."

"That's so strange they didn't want me to come in and get scanned or something." Charlotte felt the back of her head. "I don't feel any bumps."

"That's why they didn't say to bring you in. They said the light knock was probably nothing. You did drink a lot the night before at the mansion, and you didn't really have much to eat." Lydia couldn't look at her. Instead, she busied herself picking up the curtains and rods off the floor. She attempted to rehang them the best she could but some of the rods were broken and would have to be replaced.

"Must have been one hell of a wind storm to blow the furniture around like this. You're lucky the windows aren't broken." Charlotte pushed the couch back to where it belonged. "You want to know something strange. I could have sworn we saw Gramma Annabelle's ghost in the kitchen stirring a lotion batch."

Lydia stiffened and was unable to come up with a quick enough lie for that one.

"You mean that part was true?" Charlotte demanded, smiling. She hurried to the kitchen to look in as if Annabelle would still be there. "How awesome is that!"

"I think it was part of the reason you passed out. I didn't want to say anything in case you didn't remember."

Charlotte looked down at the mess. A small branch was on the floor. She tried to reason what might have happened. "And that's when the branch flew in and hit me?"

"Um, yeah," Lydia nodded.

"We're lucky to be alive," Charlotte said. "I'll bet that's why Gramma appeared. She wanted to warn us the storm was coming. Heck, even the weather guys didn't get it right on television."

"Yeah." Lydia nodded again, letting Charlotte create her own timeline. She felt guilty for letting the MacGregors mess with her friend's memories, but it was too late to change now. She'd seen how scared Charlotte had been.

"Oh, hey, look, it's Erik." Charlotte hurried out the door before Lydia could stop her. She rushed behind her, ready to pull her back behind the protective barrier if she needed to. "Hey, Erik. Crazy storm, right? Did you all suffer much damage?"

"No," Erik said, sounding completely sane. He gave a hesitant look to Lydia before saying to Charlotte. "I just came down to make sure ya ladies were unharmed."

"Aw, that's so sweet of you." Charlotte turned, winking at Lydia so Erik couldn't see the playful teasing. She pursed her lips in a kiss. Then, when Lydia didn't speak, she turned back and said, "We're unharmed, but the house took quite a beating. I was actually on my way out to check if there was any damage to my apartment. Maybe, if you're feeling charitable, you and your brothers wouldn't mind helping Lyd haul these branches down so the sanitation department can grab them from the curb when they do clean up. The city is usually pretty good about that after a bad storm."

"Of course," Erik agreed. "We'd be happy to help."

Charlotte turned again to Lydia and hugged her, whispering, "A bunch of sexy men in kilts lifting heavy tree branches? I'll be back later for the show. And we'll talk more about that Gramma thing later, too. That is so awesome. A ghost. I'll find some ghost hunting equipment or a spirit board so we can try to communicate with her."

Charlotte took off down the hill, her steps light.

"It's good to see she is well," Erik said.

Lydia crossed her arms over her chest. "Her mind's been erased. I'm not sure that classifies as well."

"I just meant it could have gone so much worse," he explained.

"Worse?" She gave a disbelieving nod and looked at her damaged home. "My garden is gone so I have no herbs to work with to make product so I can make money to pay for repairs. My insurance deductible is insane, if they'll even cover this kind of thing. I'm not sure my policy covers magickal storms and crazy boyfriends."

"Boyfriend?" He smiled slightly, his eyes widening playfully as if encouraging her to return the look.

"What would you call it? Manfriend?" Lydia

gestured helplessly. His grin widened. Damn, but he was sexy even as she tried to keep emotional distance between them. "Listen, I know this is partially my fault. I should never have dabbled in whatever this was, and I take responsibility for..." She looked around her battered yard and stepped out of the kitchen doorway. "You can rest assured I'll not be doing anything like this again. Ever. I'm done with magick."

"Done?" He tried to close some of the distance between them but her look must have stopped him.

"Yes, done." She sighed. "I can't do this Erik. I should have stopped us before we even started. I want to go back to making my lotions and living like a hermit. The most magick I want is the town whispering about how my grandmother was the 'witch on the hill' and that's it."

"Ya want me to erase myself from your thoughts?"

Lydia shook her head in denial. Yes, that would make things easier but she didn't want to forget him. "No, I don't want anyone else messing with my brain. Or Charlotte's brain. Ever again."

"We can buy this house," he offered. "We have property all over the country. Wherever ya would like to go, we'll set ya up. It's the least I can do."

"No. I'm not asking for anything. This is my

home, my grandmother's home. It's not for sale, and I can take care of myself."

He glanced around before stopping to stare at where he'd drawn the large heart in lavender. The heart was no longer there, having been blown away. "I remember…that was your garden I picked?"

She nodded. "Technically I was trespassing, so I guess I can't really complain that you picked it. You had every right. It was on your land."

"I did not mean to upset your life like this," he said, the words quiet and a little sad.

"I didn't get a chance to thank you for reordering shrubs planted after I stole your powers and killed my roses. It was very thoughtful though it wasn't entirely your fault."

He frowned. "I didn't order shrubs."

"You were a little out of it. You'd just picked the garden." She waved her hand in dismissal. "It doesn't matter. Please don't reorder the plants. I'm thinking of doing something different here anyway. It's time I redecorated and made a few changes. It's what my Gramma would want."

"I didn't mean to harm your livelihood or wreck your home. I'm sorry, Lydia. I just wanted to get to know ya. I like ya."

"I like you too, Erik, but let's face facts. We're too different." It took all of her control to keep her expression calm. Inside tiny voices were yelling at her, trying to shut her up. She told herself if she just got through this, didn't waver, didn't give in to his beautifully pleading eyes or his charming ways, then the hard part would be over. "We might be neighbors, but I don't see our paths crossing. We live such different lives."

"If this is what ya wish?" He looked as if he might cross to her and touch her. She couldn't let him. One touch and she'd be lost. The burn of tears threatened her eyes, she held them back.

"It is." She nodded.

"Then, I'll…" He looked up the hill and then down. "I'll go. But I would like to help ya clean up the mess. It's the least I can do after calling the winds. Neighbors can do that for neighbors, right?"

She wasn't that foolish. There was no way she was lifting the giant uprooted trees or oversized branches scattered all over the place. And she sure as heck wasn't going to try wielding a chainsaw to cut them. One miscalculated swing of the heavy power tool and she'd take off her own legs. "I'd appreciate that. Although, I do have a question."

"Aye?"

"How is it no one from town saw all the magick sparks and lights going on up here? I expected a flood of people and not one person has come up. Well, Sheriff Johnson made the rounds, but he was just checking to make sure everyone was all right."

"We cast protective spells around our homes to hide any hints of magickal mishaps as a precaution. Your home is included in all of our security measures. Normally we buy up all the surrounding property such as yours." He looked guilty as he admitted, "My original intention was to get ya to move, after we had our fling of course. I would have erased myself from your mind."

Wow. Honesty. She tried to ignore the slight sting of discovering his intentions, but respected that he'd told her the truth. "I told you, I'm not selling."

"I know. I'll make sure my family doesn't interfere with your life any more than is necessary. I promise I won't let them drive ya out of your grandmother's home."

Lydia nodded. "And I promise to keep the MacGregor secret."

She closed the door on him and sunk to the kitchen floor. She felt him walk away. Now, alone, she let the tears of heartache fall down her cheeks. "Goodbye, Erik."

"WELL?" Euann demanded as Erik stepped up the drive to their house.

Erik stopped walking and said nothing.

"Does she forgive ya?" Iain chimed in, pushing past Euann who blocked the front door.

"Aye," Erik nodded. "I need ya to come down and help me clear her yard of trees later. It looks like a warlock battlefield down there."

"Of course," Iain agreed. "I'll get the lads together."

"This is great news," Euann said, grinning. "She forgives ya. All is well. Little harm done."

"I said she forgives me." Erik kept his eyes on the ground, unable to look at his siblings. All he wanted was to crawl into a bottle of whiskey and be alone. "But I didn't say she wanted anything more to do with me."

"But it was only a little harmless magick," Iain said. He quickly stepped out of Erik's way as the man moved to go inside.

Erik walked faster, trying to get to the privacy of the study where he could lock his brothers out —or at least try.

"Did ya apologize?" Iain asked.

"Aye," Erik grumbled.

"He probably did it in song," Euann said with a snicker.

To answer the jibe, Erik turned, pushing his magick at his brother to toss him across the floor.

Euann laughed harder as he braced his feet and skidded to a stop. He began crooning, "*Ly-di-ah! Let me sing to ya my song so crass. Baby, how I loooove your a—*"

"You're dead!" Erik turned and ran at his brother, forgetting the whiskey.

Euann ran, singing all the louder. "*Ly-di-ah! Ly-di-ah!*"

Chapter Twelve

"This is not exactly what I had in mind when I said to redecorate."

Lydia gasped sharply. Startled, she lifted her head and pressed her back hard into the kitchen door. Tears stained her cheeks but she'd stopped crying several minutes before, at which time she started to wallow in self-pity. With Charlotte's memories altered and her break up—if one could call it that—with Erik, Lydia had never felt more alone. The world was full of magick and secrets and she had no one to share the burden of that knowledge with.

"Breathe, dear." Annabelle's transparent figure stood before her, hands on hips. The ghost looked down at her, seeming completely aware of what was happening.

Lydia's mouth opened. Annabelle was much more visible than before.

"Close your mouth or the flies will get in," Annabelle said.

Lydia snapped her lips shut.

"Not even a hug?" Annabelle shook her head. "Tsk, tsk."

Lydia pushed to her feet and lifted her arms, wanting nothing more than to have a comforting hug from her gramma. When she stepped forward, she went through Annabelle's body. A cold chill caused goose bumps to rise on her flesh and a pant of mist to come out of her mouth. The smell of lilies clung to her clothes. The coldness of her grandmother's spirit left her shivering, and feeling a little empty inside.

"Oh, poo." Annabelle pouted. "I thought I was corporeal this time."

"Where did you go?" Lydia sniffed.

"I'm not sure. Think of it as swooning. Something powerful sucked the energy right out of me." Annabelle floated more than walked to the window. She wore the same fancy, sparkling green ball gown she'd been buried in. "Did you drink all the moonshine and then trash the house? Is that what's wrong with you? You're hung over?"

"Ah, not exactly." Lydia wasn't sure how to explain everything that was going on. She had promised to keep the MacGregor secret, but did talking to your dead gramma count? Most people would say she was hallucinating right now anyway, so really she was probably talking to a figment of her imagination.

"Too bad. It would have made one helluva story. Ah, well. Sit, I'll make you some tea." Annabelle flitted to the stove and ran her hand through the tea kettle. "Uh, dear, make yourself some tea and we'll talk."

Lydia nodded and obeyed, slowly crossing to the stove. Under her breath, she whispered, "So this is what crazy feels like."

"DID ya have to chase your brother up a tree?" Margareta sighed heavily staring at Erik as he tried to ignore her. With a whiskey in one hand and an absent stirring of dust floating over the other, he swirled both. The library had been quiet and dark until his mother opened the heavy brocade curtains. "Well?"

"Aye," he mumbled. Even as he chased him, Erik knew his brother had only been trying to distract him from his misery. It worked for a short time. Now he just wanted to be alone.

"Euann showed me the security footage he could find."

Erik arched a brow, not following her topic choice. "Good?" Then dropping the dust, he pushed up from his chair in alarm. "Wait, do ya mean the *lidérc*? Ya saw him?"

"Not all threats are male," Margareta scolded.

"Ya saw it?" Erik corrected.

"No." Margareta sighed again, not taking her eyes off of him.

Erik frowned and fell back into the chair. "I have no idea what we're talking about. If you'd like to drink, you're welcome to close the curtains and pull up a chair. If you're only here to say ominous things that make no sense in order to make me feel as if I am drunker than I am because I cannot follow them, then I'll gladly take my misery elsewhere."

"Ya are a bumbling idiot," Margareta stated. At that, he again sat straight only this time in surprise. She continued, "God knows I love my boys, but ya are all idiots when it comes to women. No wonder I have yet to be made a grandmother after nearly five hundred years of waiting. I'm lucky we're not mere humans or my line would have ended."

"Uh, thanks?" he mumbled sarcastically.

"I blame your da. He's an idiot too. When I

met him he was tied to a tree limb half-trans-
formed into a bird because he used one of your
Uncle Fergus's spells." Margareta slowly crossed
over to her son and then snatched the drink from
his hand. Tossing it back, she finished it for him.
She brushed her hand through the air to slide the
bottle across the rug out of his reach. "I had to
rescue him. He bumbled after me for a year until I
finally caved and married him."

His parents adored each other. He knew that.
Sure, during the course of hundreds of years of
marriage there were bound to be some powerful
fights, but they always came back together.

"That's not how Da tells it." Erik tried to pull
the bottle back but his mother slid it hard into the
wall and shattered it. Liquor ran over the floor. He
grimaced.

"My point is that ya tricked her into agreeing
to a date. Ya crooned at the poor woman, and
God knows ya can't sing. Ya attacked her with
magick. Ya attacked her with your beast. Ya
erased her memories and her friend's memories.
I'm betting ya cast a few little spells here and there
to avoid the true work of a relationship."

Erik thought of that first day when she'd
nearly drained him of all his magick because he'd
wanted her to relax around him. Luckily, with his
mother staring at him, his mind didn't try to relive

the full extent of what had happened. He looked guiltily to the ground.

"I thought as much." She pulled at his chin, forcing him to look at her. "Sober up. Shower. And go win me a daughter so that I can have a grandbaby. Do it, or your sister's love potions will be the least of your worries."

"It's a little soon to be talking marriage," Erik said. "She doesn't want anything to do with me."

"Do ya blame her?" Margareta laughed. "She probably thinks you're psychotic."

Was this a pep talk? Erik wasn't sure.

"Ya haven't made your intentions clear, son. I don't care what all those talk show hocus pocus hosts say. Courtships have been around since the beginning of time. There is a reason they worked in my youth and are so messy today. State your intentions clearly and then woo her. It is a simple concept. Forget those horribly misguided rules of waiting three days before ya call. Oh, and forget that tweeting text nonsense. Charm is what a woman wants. She wants ya to charm her with thoughtful gifts and—"

"Bumbling around after her for a year?" Erik supplied with an insolent snicker, cutting off his mother's unsolicited dating advice.

"I heard Euann's recording. Ya actually told her ya weren't going to call your first date a date?

That is not stating your intentions. And ya bribed her?" His mother laughed harder. "And I thought ya were the charming one. Now Niall, I can see him clubbing a woman over the head. Euann would study her to death from afar. Iain, well, I'm not sure he'll ever marry. But, ya? Erik, ya can do better."

"And Malina?"

"Your sister is not ready for the serious commitment of marriage." The words were final and very serious.

Erik stood and swayed. Maybe he was drunker than he'd first thought.

"Or, we can always chase her away from here for the good of the clan." She moved to leave. "Ya know our laws. No outsiders can know our secrets. It risks too much and too many."

"WARLOCKS, AS I LIVE AND BREATHE." Annabelle declared as Lydia looked out the window. "Well, warlocks anyway. I thought they died out centuries ago."

Lydia shivered at the ghost's nearness, not used to the cold chill her grandmother radiated. Erik stayed true to his word, bringing all the MacGregor males down with him to clean up her yard. Iain pulled brand new chainsaws out of the back of a truck and laid them in a row on the ground as Euann carried a gas can to each and began filling them.

"That's not very magickal of them," her gramma said in disappointment.

"I think there have been enough supernatural things happening around here." Lydia's eyes strayed to Erik. His hair was wet and pushed back from his face. He smiled toward the house, finding her spying at them through the window. Her hand trembled, but there was no curtain to hide behind.

"You should put this in the grimmie."

Lydia arched a brow. "The grimmie?"

"My great-grandmothers grimoire." Annabelle frowned. The sound of chainsaws started up outside, forcing her to raise her voice, "Oh, that's right. I didn't give it to you."

"We have a family grimoire?" Why wasn't Lydia surprised?

"Where do you think I found all the protection spells? You didn't think I made them up, did you?" Annabelle laughed and her figure became more transparent before disappearing. Lydia slowly crept to look in the living room. It was empty. That was going to take some getting used to.

Living with a ghost inside. Trapped by warlocks outside. Could life get any stranger?

Though there was comfort in hearing her grandmother's voice.

Lydia crossed to the window and again looked for Erik. The men were busy slicing up a giant tree. Euann paused about half way through his cut, glanced around and then pointed his finger at the log, splitting it the rest of the way. Iain slugged him in the shoulder and then pointed for him to get back to work. There was a slight argument before Erik smacked them both on the backs of their heads.

He turned instantly to look at her window as he withdrew his hands, as if to judge what she would think of such a thing. Then, slowly, he made his way toward the kitchen. Lydia hurried to the counter and began pulling out glasses and a plastic pitcher to look like she'd been busy doing anything other than staring at him. Her good pitcher had flown off the countertop during the storm and now resided in the trash. A knock sounded, and she nearly jumped out of her skin though she'd known it had been coming.

Pasting a pleasant smile on her face she tried to force her heart to slow. It did little good. She took a deep breath, fussed with her hair, glanced at her reflection in the dented toaster and tapped at her under-eye makeup though it did little good in hiding her tired appearance.

"I was just making you lemonade," she said as she opened the door. Her smile fell and she gave a slight gasp. It wasn't Erik.

Brad grinned at her. "Well, don't mind if I do." He used the vague offer as an excuse to step inside her home. She glanced for Joe, but the man wasn't with him.

"I'm sorry, but I'm officially closed until further notice. A lot of my stock was damaged in the storm." She tried to smile, reminding herself that though this man gave her the chills he was a customer and lived in the same town. When she glanced out the door she saw Erik frowning slightly in their direction. She let it hang open, hoping Brad would take the hint and leave.

"Oh, pity, my wife liked that stuff you sent for her." Brad smiled. "Not the vanilla, but the other stuff. The bottle of lotion that you wear."

For some awful un-nameable reason she received a flash of him screwing his wife while the woman wore the lotion. He grunted out Lydia's name. Lydia gagged and tried to cover it with a cough.

"Is something wrong?" Brad asked.

Lydia cleared her throat and took a conscious step away from him. "No. It's just been a very long couple of days."

"Ah, the storms," he glanced outside. "I came

to help you clean up but I see the cross dressers beat me to it."

It was obvious he meant the slight to be charming and funny, but it only caused Lydia to frown. Only Niall wore a kilt today. The rest were in jeans. "Thank you for checking on me. I'll be sure to send your wife a flyer when I have my stock rebuilt."

Brad looked around. "I can help you in here." He moved past her to go the living room and kicked at one of the stray lotion bottles she'd yet to pick up. It rolled under the couch. He glanced around at the rehung curtains before making a move to go to the stairs.

"No, thank you," Lydia said, raising her arm to herd him back toward the kitchen door.

"Hey, Lyd, ya in there?"

"One moment," she called, giving Brad an expectant look. He again glanced around, as if considering his options before finally giving up and going back to the kitchen. She didn't stop, forcing Brad to come outside with her. Unable to help it, she smiled at Erik. "Hi. I was just about to bring you guys some drinks."

Erik stood, arms crossed as he eyed the smaller man. He didn't speak. For a moment, Brad stared back, as if he didn't plan on leaving.

Lydia turned to Brad, faked a pleasant look

and said, "Thanks for checking in, Brad. I'll be sure to mail that flyer."

"Hm." Brad nodded. He reluctantly left.

They didn't speak as they watched him near the end of the drive. Lydia took a deep breath and sighed. "Thank you."

"What did he want?" Erik asked, still watching the man's back.

Was Erik jealous? A small thrill erupted inside her even as the very idea of anything happening with Brad was ridiculous. "General lechery and creepiness."

"Did he try to…?" Erik stiffened and began to turn as if he'd go after the man.

"No, wait," Lydia gave a small surprised laugh at the very alpha prince charming move. She reached to touch his arm, stopping him. "He's just a creepy customer. Nothing happened."

"Oh." Erik relaxed some. "I just wanted to tell ya we should have this done by the end of the day." He looked down at her hand on him.

A warm tingling erupted beneath her fingers, and she quickly pulled her hand away. "Sorry, I didn't mean to take more power from you." She shook her fingers, but the heat of his body still worked its way up her arm. Once it started, there was no stopping the sensations.

"I thought about what ya said, and I have an

answer." Erik cleared his throat and glanced back at his family. Iain and Euann quickly turned and pretended they'd been working, not watching. With a heavy sigh, Erik began scratching through his hair and feeling around his T-shirt. With a tiny growl, he pinched a small black object out of his hair. Lydia thought it might have been a bug, but he turned, lifted his arm to his brothers and then squished whatever it was.

"No, don't!" Euann yelled, almost desperate. Rory grabbed his shirt and gestured that he should keep sawing.

"As I was saying, love, I thought about what ya said and my answer is no."

"No?" Lydia repeated. She furrowed her brow. "No, what? I didn't ask anything."

"Ya told me we could avoid each other and not be together. The answer is no. I'm going to woo ya, lass."

"Woo me?" Lydia started to chuckle, but the man looked so sincere she didn't dare. Instead, she stared at his handsome face, a little shocked.

"Aye. I'm making my intentions known."

"What about what I want?" she asked. "No offense, but I noticed things tend to get crazy with your family around."

"No offense taken. You're right." Erik's smile stayed intact. "We're a wild bunch."

"I like my life calm." Lydia crossed her arms over her chest.

"Give us a chance, love, the clan will grow on ya. Promise."

"Erik, I don't…"

"All I'm asking for is a chance. If ya tell me that ya honestly don't feel there is anything worth exploring between us, I'll respect your wishes and leave ya be. But if there is even a tiny part of ya that knows what I know, then…" His grin was incorrigible as he let his words taper off.

She couldn't keep a straight face. Giving a small laugh, she said. "Fine. Okay. You can woo me."

"We're going to finish cleaning this up. Then I'll be back tonight to woo ya." He leaned forward, his tone dropping by small degrees to the liquid warm sound that melted her insides and made her heart flutter in her chest. "Then, if you're lucky, I'll let ya invite me inside to play out those little dreams ya have of me."

"If *I'm* lucky?" She pulled back and arched a brow.

"Aye, love, I already know how good I am in bed. You'd be lucky indeed to get me between your sheets." He winked at her to let her know he was teasing and then turned to join his family as they began hauling the tree limbs down the hill to the curb for city pickup.

"I really hope that doesn't mean you're going to sing again," Lydia said to herself with a small laugh. He turned, his grin still intact. She bit her lip, having not intended the comment to be heard. When he reached his brothers, Euann began gesturing frantically. Erik held up his hand to stop him.

"Woo me," Lydia whispered. A small chill worked over her, and she looked at her hand where she'd touched Erik. The breeze picked up ever so slightly, seeming to stir around her feet and caress her skin. She wasn't sure if she was doing it, or if she was suddenly super sensitive to the movement. Licking her lips, she felt a flush rise over her cheeks. There was something alluring about the man that drew her from that first moment. How did she ever think she could push him away or resist him? Even now, with him working across the lawn, the nerves in her body tingled and pulled in his direction. As the feelings inside her grew stronger he looked at her as if he knew what she was thinking. "God help me for I doubt any woman could resist a MacGregor man bent on seduction."

~

GO AHEAD AND WORK. Clean up your mess.

No amount of cleaning could undo what the warlocks had done. So careless they were with magick, so aimlessly destructive and to no grand purpose. They did not deserve their powers. Ah, but their carelessness would serve the shadows well. The protection around the old Victorian had been chipped just enough to slip through. The day kept them back within the trees, but soon, very soon night would come and it would be time to play. The barrier spell was fading, it now had faults, and the enchantment would soon be gone. The *inthrall's* days were few.

Chapter Thirteen

"Where's Charlotte when I need her?" Lydia whispered, frowning at her reflection. She couldn't decide if the long white and cream-colored dress she wore said casual fun or virginal sacrifice. She'd bought it at a renaissance festival she'd gone to with her grandmother, and then never had the occasion to wear it again. Maybe date night with the sexily confident Erik wasn't the best time to resurrect what should probably be used only for a Halloween costume. She turned to the mound of dresses on the bed that came before the one she now wore.

She'd tried calling Charlotte after the phone lines came back on but her friend wouldn't pick up. It was possible Charlotte had her own storm damage to contend with, or downed phone lines, or simply had crawled into her own bed to sleep. Lydia would make a point of going over there in the morning to check on her. Since her memory of true events had been erased it was highly unlikely Charlotte was in a state of panic.

A shiver worked over her and she shook off the first reaction of chills to look around the room. "Gramma?"

There was no answer so she turned her attention back to the pile. Movement appeared out of the corner of her eye and she spun to the side. Nothing was there. Lydia gave a short laugh, trying to dismiss her apprehension as nerves about the upcoming date and her grandmother's ghostly presence lingering around.

She leaned over and flipped the pile of dresses to study the first two she'd tried on. To herself, she asked, "Sexy vixen," she lifted a red and then a black, "or seductively understated?" Then, louder, she asked, "What do you think, Gramma? Should I just wear the Halloween princess gown?"

She felt a light yank on her hair and dropped both garments. Spinning, she was caught between a startled scream and a scolding. Nothing was there. Her heart beat a little faster.

"That's not funny," she whispered, taking deep breaths.

The temperature of the room dropped

dramatically, so that she could see the pants of air coming from her mouth. Her grandmother's ghost never made the entire room this cold. Lydia shivered violently, feeling sick to her stomach. Another tug pulled her hair, harder this time. She spun around only to have her hair pulled again from behind. She turned again and again, seeing nothing. She swatted her arms, trying to push back whatever it was, yet her arms fell through air.

"What do you want?" she yelled.

A light humming answered, sounding very much like a child singing in play.

Lydia cried out, "Stop!"

Instantly, whatever it was obeyed. The temperature rose to normal yet she still shivered.

Lydia weakly made her way to the stairs, needing to get away from the room. She stumbled down the hall in her haste. Her long skirt tangled around her legs and she pulled it up to take the steps two at a time. The sound of footsteps ran down the upstairs hall. She trembled in fear, turning to look up the stairs. A shadow came forward with no figure attached to it before disappearing back down the hall, taking its footsteps with it.

Trying to watch where she was going, while keeping an eye on the stairs, she staggered toward the kitchen door. The footsteps came back and skidded to stop at the top of the stairs. A shadowy figure loomed above her. The same voice from before began to sing, louder and clearer, "You can't hide. You can't seek. You can't find the will to speak."

A giggle sounded by the couch. Lydia screamed as another shadow appeared in the living room. Then, suddenly, the roots of her hair were pulled from behind. She reached to fight free from her attacker, but there was nothing there. Whatever held her hair was an intangible force she couldn't escape. It flung her backwards and dragged her across the floor. Her feet kicked violently in an effort to stop the attacker's progress. Her shoes flung from her feet.

The force lifted her up, dangling her above the kitchen floor. Her scalp burned from where the full weight of her hanging body pulled at her hair. A loud whirl blew around her as she was rotated through the air. The living room laughter grew louder as new voices joined the first. More footsteps sounded upstairs, as if a child army ran through all the rooms.

A loud shriek sounded, and she was whipped forward. The force let go and she flew face first into the wall by the outside door. Lydia smacked the side of her face. Dizzy, she fell.

"Run!" her grandmother's voice ordered.

Lydia tasted blood in her mouth as she scrambled to her feet. Her grandmother's spirit hovered over the kitchen next to a dark shadow. Lydia hesitated, not wanting to leave Annabelle, ghost or not. She looked for something to throw at the shadow, knowing even as she launched the toaster it wouldn't do any good. Cold air blasted her. The toaster smacked into the far wall.

"Run!" Gramma Annabelle screeched. A sudden bright light radiated from the spirit, throwing back the shadows. Lydia reached for the door knob. The light didn't last long. Shadows converged on her grandmother's ghost. Annabelle commanded hoarsely, "Lydia, run!"

Tears streamed down her cheeks as she obeyed. Lydia's first instinct was to find Erik. She stumbled backwards out of the door and then turned to run up the hill. The long skirt of the dress caught on something and she leaned to pull it free. Her eyes met with a foot standing on the material. Lydia opened her mouth to yell but a hood was thrust over her head. She threw an elbow back, hitting a stomach. A loud grunt sounded and she ran. Just as she managed to grab the bag on her head to pull it off someone tripped her. She fell onto the ground.

Instantly hands were on her, pinning her legs and arms. Then ropes were wound around the length of her body. She heard tape rip seconds before someone pressed it around her neck to hold the sack in place. She writhed against her captors, trying desperately to be free. She screamed as loud as she could but the sack was dusty and caused her to inhale particles into her lungs. Lydia coughed, losing some of her fight as she struggled to breathe.

Her captors spoke but the words were muffled as they lifted her off the ground. She tried squirming, but it only caused them to hold her tighter. A hand gripped into her breast, the gesture not feeling completely accidental. Another hand pressed the hood to her mouth, cutting off her air. She stopped fighting and they released the pressure, letting her have whatever dirty air she could find in the bag.

Without her struggling, the captors were able to run. Her body angled downward toward the road. Then, tossing her to a hard surface she felt the rumble of an engine as they drove her away.

"YA SERIOUSLY ARE NOT GOING to wear that, are ya son?"

Erik looked down at his blue button down shirt and black slacks. He couldn't keep the smile off his face. Tonight he was going to woo Lydia, and this time he was going to do it right. He'd tried to do it right on their first non-date date, but the *lidérc* had ruined his plans. Glancing at his father's reflection in his mirror, he answered, "Aye. What's wrong with what I'm wearing, Da?"

"We Scots have great legs, ya should show them off." Angus kicked his legs, showing off his exposed calves. "If I know one thing, it's that women can't resist a man in a kilt."

"Careful, lest ma hears ya," Erik warned.

Angus glanced around fearfully for his wife and stated loudly, "Not as if I would know from firsthand experience. I love your mother very much. Fergus told me."

Erik started to laugh, only to stop as a cold wave of dread washed over him. It nearly stopped his heart from beating.

"What is it?" his da asked.

"Lydia." Erik ran out of his room, pushing past his father. He felt Angus behind him. "She's in trouble. I have to get to her."

"I thought her home was protected. She should be safe." Angus calmly followed him down the hall.

After hundreds of years of threats and possible doom it took a lot for the MacGregors to react with a sense of urgency. It was a family fault, one that Erik was suddenly sorry for. Why hadn't he focused more on the threat and less on his feelings for Lydia? They'd known there was a *lidérc* in the area and they'd taken the necessary precautions, but he should have made that more of a priority.

"Something's wrong." Erik gasped as another cold chill ran down his body.

"Wait, I'll get the others," Angus ordered. "If it's the *lidérc* ya can't go alone. He'll use her to get your powers. As much as ya hate it, she'll live so long as they have a purpose for her. Iain and Rory are walking the town searching for signs. I'll call them back. Niall is working on potions."

"There's no time," Erik answered, leaping more than walking down the stairs. "I can't wait. With everything that happened I didn't get a chance to warn her about the *lidérc* and what it is. I thought we'd have more time before it made its move. I was going to tell her everything tonight."

"But Euann assured me ya protected all within her home while ya cleaned her yard. It shouldn't be…" Angus's words trailed off as Erik ran out of the door. "Be careful, son!"

As the late afternoon air hit him Erik felt Lydia's fear more clearly. He slowed as the full force of her emotions bound his legs and glued his arms to his sides. It took some focus, but he managed to push past the sensation and again run down the hill toward her home.

All within her home? That man who'd been bothering Lydia? She'd called him creepy. Erik should have taken notice of the customer, but he'd been so focused on his mission to woo Lydia that he'd not paid the man much attention beyond his annoying his woman. Brad. She'd called him Brad, and he'd been in her home. Did Brad have magickal powers that somehow escaped their notice?

Panic welled inside him. Brad had been in her home. If he was magickal that meant she'd let the man in. Lydia had yet to invite him inside past the barrier spell.

Erik let the wind take him, speeding him down to her home. The subtle stench of dark power curled his nose as he rematerialized on her lawn. He ran to her open door. "Lydia!"

Reaching forward, he touched the barrier. It was weak. A steady thud sounded within the home. Erik held his breath and pushed his way inside. Passing the barrier felt a lot like being skinned alive, but he made it through. Light footsteps ran overhead, but he knew they weren't Lydia's. A door vibrated, the source of the noise. When he opened it, he frowned in irritation. A translucent figure in a green ballroom gown sat on basement steps. Her grayed complexion and vacant eyes didn't see him as it swayed back and forth. Her head had been bumping the old door, making it thud. The woman was dead so there was nothing he could do for her at the moment.

The running feet came down the steps. A girl's soft voice began to sing a light, eerie tune. "You can't hide. You can't seek. You can't find the will to speak."

Erik frowned in irritation. Ghosts were notoriously pesky creatures. He strode to the door. The dark shadow didn't fully reveal herself, but she continued to sing as another shadow danced in the living room.

"Where is she?" Erik demanded.

"We're not bound anymore. We're not leaving like before," the child song answered. Then the shadows charged him, pushing violently forward to yell in unison, their voices demonic, "And you can't make us!"

For the briefest second they consumed him, but his age-old magick was too much and they couldn't hold on to him for long. He expelled their attempt at possession and ran from the home. When he glanced back at the Victorian, he saw the window glow and the curtain shift. He would deal with that poltergeist infestation later, but right now he needed to find Lydia.

He turned on the lawn, reaching out with his feelings. He looked for her, trying to connect his emotions with hers, but felt nothing. She was gone. He was too late.

"NOT YOU, too, Lydia. They got you, too. Omigod, look at your dress," Charlotte whispered, trying to free Lydia's arms from her sides. Her hands shook and it took her much longer than it would have under normal circumstances to untie the ropes. "What did they dress you in?"

Lydia coughed, trying to expel the dust from her lungs. The sack from her head lay discarded to the side.

"They're a cult," Charlotte insisted, yanking the rope hard.

It slid from Lydia's hands, scratching her skin. At the moment she didn't care. When she could finally move, she pushed up and looked around the tiny cell. Someone had secured bars to a basement's stone foundation. The bars looked new, the foundation old. Owning an old home, Lydia had dealt with old rock foundation. It might look like it was crumbling, but it'd be sturdy. Darkening light shone through a small window near the ceiling. There was nothing special about the place. It was an old, dirty basement with an air handler, furnace, and water heater—a leaky water heater if the puddle around the base was any indication. They could be anywhere. She leaned over, trying to see up the wooden stairs.

"They're going to sacrifice us," Charlotte whispered. "We have to get out of here."

"We don't know that," Lydia answered, her throat dry.

"I heard them. When they brought me here they told me my sacrifice would be appreciated. They're sick." Charlotte stood and began shaking the bars. Yelling, she said, "Let us out!"

"Char, who? Who said that?" Lydia pulled her friend back. Her friend's face was dirty and pale. The denim jeans were stained at the knees and her T-shirt was ripped along the seam. "How long have you been down here?"

"I don't know. Hours? A day? I can't remember. I was on my way back to watch the kilt show at your place when Joe stopped me."

"Joe?" Lydia shivered. "That…" She shook her head. "No, that can't be. He's so…"

"Nice?" Charlotte gave a small laugh that held no humor. "I thought so too. Try psychotic."

"I thought I recognized a voice. He tried to disguise it, but Brad was there when they jumped me at my house." She recalled the cold chills whenever the man was near and warning flashes of Brad's memories she'd been forced to endure. When the men carried her someone had taken liberties and held her by her breast. She rubbed her wrist over her chest, trying to erase the feeling. In hindsight, it was easy to put the pieces together. At the time, a chill was a chill, and she thought she'd imagined the disgusting images because Brad repulsed her so much. "I never understood that friendship."

Charlotte gave a meaningful look around. "Oh, I'm beginning to suspect they both belong to the psycho of the month club."

"This doesn't make sense." Lydia closed her eyes and tried to concentrate. Why would Joe and Brad want to kidnap them? Ok, so Brad's motivations could be guessed at. He was a pervert. She'd gotten enough flashes into his brain to know he was a little obsessed with fucking her. But Joe? She'd never gotten a sense of evil from Joe. She'd known him for years. He went to fundraisers, tutored children, invited people to church functions and brought food around to the sick and elderly. They said sociopaths were adept at blending in, but even so she couldn't see it.

"Lydia, snap out of it," Charlotte demanded. "I know you're scared, but we have to focus. It doesn't have to make sense. We're in this situation and we need to get out of it."

Lydia realized she wasn't as scared as she should have been. She thought of Erik. He'd come to the house looking for her. He would know she was gone. He'd come looking.

Unless he thought she stood him up.

Ok, she was starting to worry.

"I'm sorry I didn't come looking for you." Lydia began systematically pushing at the bars, testing them. "I thought maybe you took a nap or had things to deal with at your apartment. I should have known something was up when you didn't answer your phone."

"They have to come for us sometime," Charlotte said, as if her plan had been formed long before Lydia arrived. "When they open the door, we fight. It doesn't matter what they say or what weapon they have. We fight."

Lydia nodded. After everything magickal that had been going on in their lives, she wondered if she should say something to Charlotte. Seeing the woman's scared face, she wasn't sure that would help. Not for the first time she regretted letting the MacGregors wipe her friend's memories of magickal events. It was quite possible their abduction had nothing to do with magick and everything to do with common sickos. Perhaps the brief visions she'd had were warnings that she'd been too stupid to pay attention to.

Lydia thought of Erik, willing him to magickally know where they were. However, simply waiting and hoping for a man to save her, even if he was a warlock, wasn't in Lydia's nature.

"Help," Lydia yelled when the bars wouldn't budge. "We're in here. Help!"

Charlotte's yell joined hers as they screamed in hopes that someone would hear and rescue them.

BRAD HUMMED SOFTLY TO HIMSELF, not hearing his wife sniveling behind him, not hearing his sons fight over the video game two rooms away. There was too much work to do. He slowly cut the image of Lydia's head from her body and carefully glued it to the perfect figure—an image torn from the pages of a sleazy magazine. That is how he wanted her, all sprawled out and ready and exposed, tied up and gagged.

Satisfied that he'd gotten the image right, he turned to his wife tied up on the bed. She'd been pretty when he married her, but age and pregnancy had taken that from her. Still, she played his games and for that he kept her around. Brad crossed naked to the bed and tacked the image to the headboard and grabbed the lotion he'd bought from Lydia's store.

LYDIA GASPED, nearly choking as she forced the image out of her mind. The visions had never been so vivid. She felt Charlotte's hand resting on hers.

Yelling had done them no good. If anyone could hear them, they weren't coming to help. The basement prison had become dark as the sun set outside. She could make out the lines of the bars, but night hid the dark corners of the room.

"Someone's coming," Charlotte whispered, gripping her arm. Soft light appeared as the door opened. The sound of creaking footsteps led their eyes to the wood stairs. Familiar uniform pants appeared in a stream of dim light.

"Sheriff?" Lydia asked.

Charlotte gasped. "Thank God it's you!"

The women rushed forward to the front of the prison.

"Sheriff, be careful," Lydia whispered. The man's gun was holstered. "I don't know where they went."

"Try to stay quiet." Hurrying down the rest of the way, Sheriff Johnson clanged a large ring of keys in search of the right one before he pushed a key into the lock. "Let's get you out of here, ladies."

Relief filled her. The man unlocked the door and gestured them to follow. He crept his way up the stairs, placing his hand on his gun. They came to the top of the stairs and he moved aside to let them up. She didn't recognize the house, but the decor looked deceptively normal.

"How did you find us?" Charlotte asked. She pulled at Lydia's arm. "How did you know which key would work in the lock? You only tried one."

Good questions. Lydia turned to study the Sheriff. The man frowned.

"Well, I almost got you all the way outside without a fight." Sheriff Johnson dropped his hand from his gun and stepped back. "Go ahead. Do it your way."

Joe, Brad, and Brad's two sons appeared holding guns. They pointed the pistols at the women.

"If you would be so kind as to join us," Joe said.

"Move," Brad ordered with a lecherous lick of his lips. He clearly got off on the power trip.

"Why would you…?" Lydia asked the sheriff. "None of this makes sense. I mean Brad I get, he's a creep, but you, Sheriff?" She turned to Joe. "Why, Joe?"

Brad tried to leap forward at the insult, but Joe calmly grabbed his arm and held him back.

"I'm sorry, Lydia. I do like you, but we have our orders," Joe answered. He smiled, as if the gesture would put her at ease. "There's no need for this to be unpleasant."

Charlotte gasped and Lydia turned to see a revolver to her friend's head. The Sheriff nodded to the front door, not lowering his arm. "Enough chatter. This one can be replaced."

Lydia got his meaning and instantly began walking. She tried to keep an eye on her friend, but Brad pushed the small of her back to make her hurry. She stumbled into the front door.

"Go," Brad ordered. "Tim, get the door." Brad's oldest son opened the door. "Tom get that gun barrel aimed nice and even at the center of the chest. That's a boy."

The women went onto a large porch. They were in the country outside of town. She recognized the Sheriff's home now that she saw it from the outside. The metal tin star hanging in front of the driveway was a dead giveaway.

Fire burned on the lawn, casting orange shadows. Charlotte stumbled into her back and grabbed hold of her. Lydia automatically turned to take Charlotte by the arm. She wasn't sure if it was her trembling or Charlotte's but they shook violently. Everyone she'd had some kind of interaction with in the last several weeks stared back at them. Flaxen ringlet girl and her mother held hands. Mrs. Callister tilted her head to the side before taking the pencil from behind her ear to write on an imaginary notepad. Chef Alana wore an apron and looked like she'd just stepped out of a kitchen. The only people missing were Jane from the nursery and the MacGregor family.

A gun barrel pushed into her back, forcing them to walk toward the light.

"Mr. Baker from the post office?" Charlotte whispered, not understanding. "Mrs. Callister? Is that our third grade teacher, Mr. Wirth? He jogs near your house every day. Lydia, what's going on? Has our entire town gone insane?"

Flaxen ringlet girl reached to the ground and grabbed an ornate goblet. The second her fingers touched it the gathering began to chant in unison like a crowd possessed. A dark shadow whipped past Charlotte causing her to scream in fright. It circled the fire and came back for them, passing over Lydia and leaving her skin cold and numb where it touched along her arm and neck. It ruffled her hair before moving once more around the flames. Another shadow joined it, fluttering like two dark moths to the bonfire's light.

The girl smiled at her as she stopped before them with the cup. Excited, she said, "Hi, lotion lady!"

Lydia didn't move.

"Hi, lotion lady," she repeated, a little darker and meaner. Her smile faltered.

"Hi," Lydia whispered. The girl's smile returned.

The girl held the cup up to Charlotte. Joe jolted Charlotte in the back and ordered, "Drink it."

"No." Charlotte refused.

Joe lifted his gun and held it to Lydia's head. Tears escaped her, but Lydia managed, "No, don't, Cha—"

Charlotte lifted the cup and drank. She coughed, spewing the thick red liquid over the little girl. It looked like blood. The girl screamed and ran to her mother.

Joe lifted his pistol and fired into the air. Charlotte cried out weakly. She nodded at him, crying as she took a drink and forced herself to swallow. Joe motioned for her to do it again. She did, gagging. Her body convulsed, and she dropped the goblet. Charlotte fell to the ground, shaking violently as a seizure erupted over her body. Lydia tried to go to her, but Brad and Tim grabbed her arms. She struggled as they tried to pull her around the fire. Joe appeared in front of her and punched her in the stomach to get her to settle down. Lydia doubled over in pain, and they tossed her face first toward the earth. She saw Charlotte through the edge of the flames still flailing on the ground. Tom leaned over the woman, watching.

Feet pinned her arms down and she couldn't crawl away. Closing her eyes, she thought, *Ok, it would be really great if you could fly in on a broomstick and save us now, Erik. Omigod, please, just save us.*

Chapter Fourteen

"Wow, great dress," Iain said to Erik, eyeing Lydia from their place in the ditch alongside the gravel road. They were across from a home isolated from town by about ten miles and surrounded trees. "Your girlfriend is really hot."

Erik smacked him across the back of his head. "Focus!"

"Sorry," Iain mumbled, "but she is."

Normally, Erik would be making jokes and laughing with his brother in the face of danger. Immortality had a way of lessening one's sense of mortal fear—even if technically there were ways to kill a warlock. Like what the *lidérc* now attempted in using Erik's *inthrall* against him. Even so, he wasn't scared for himself. He worried about Lydia. Seeing the woman he loved being hefted upright on a pole by a bunch of psychically compromised townsfolk had a way of making Mr. Grim Reaper look all too real.

The sound of chanting filled the air, the words from some ancient Magyar dialect he couldn't translate. Lydia kicked her feet, hanging by her arms. A thick log stuck in the ground with a metal ring along the top. Townsfolk pulled a rope through the ring, sliding Lydia up the pole. When they finally had her several feet off the ground, they stopped and tied off the rope on the metal star lawn decoration near the side of the road. Her feet must have found hold on something because she stopped kicking and stood straighter. Erik stared at her back, willing her to feel him, trying to give her comfort any way he could. Everything inside of him told him to save her, to rush in, forgetting what centuries of magick had taught him. She had to be terrified, how could she not be?

"Stop," Iain said. "I know ya want to comfort her, but if you're not careful with your feelings they'll detect us."

Erik withdrew his attempt to connect, hating that Iain was right.

"I love her?" Iain sounded surprised.

Erik blinked. Hissing, he demanded, "What?"

Lydia was his. Erik wasn't sharing her with Iain.

"*Ya* said, 'I love her'," Iain corrected. "Put your magick down and try to concentrate. No need to zap me. I think your lady friend is hot. I'm not going to ask her to have my babies."

Erik pointed a finger of warning at the man, but let the matter drop. "There, around the top of the fire. Do ya see it? A shadow."

"The *lidérc*." Iain nodded. "It's here."

Logs were carried from a stack on the side of the house to be thrown into the blazing fire, the possessed marching like ants in a circular pattern to do the task. Myth mistook the *lidérc* for humans or animals, but they were much harder to capture than that. They were incubi who possessed living things as they fed on them, making them do things like have promiscuous sex and race cars— anything that got the blood pumping with excitement and fear. When they were done, a person would be left comatose or crazy, or if they were lucky, dead. The *lidérc* were drawn to life just like they were drawn to the heat of the flames.

"We can't wait any longer," Erik insisted.

"Ya heard Da. We wait for them. We cannot fight the *lidérc* without the right magick. Lydia is alive. Take comfort in that."

"What are those people looking at on the far

side of the fire?" Erik didn't like waiting. He wanted to charge in, foolish as it would be, and take Lydia off the pole.

"Ya rush in and they'll simply start the process early," Iain insisted. "Ya shouldn't even be here. Your connection to Lydia is the whole reason this is happening. You're too involved."

Erik gave a low growl and ignored his brother's warning. It was his life and his magick they tried to steal through Lydia and that made this his decision. Already he could feel the tickling pull of the chanting as they called him to her. Lucky for him, they didn't seem to realize the brothers were already there. Insistent, he again asked, "What are they looking at?"

"Someone's on the ground." Iain narrowed his eyes and focused his vision. His pupils morphed, becoming large enough to take over his entire eye until there was no iris left. With the ability to metamorphosis into various birds of prey, his vision was superb. "Charlotte. She's not moving."

"Dead?" Erik stared at Lydia. She screamed as one of the shadows came near her body. Her legs kicked out as she lost her footing and she swung around by her arms. He desperately wanted to go to her, to save her and Charlotte. But his power would do him no good and that left him as helpless as a mortal man against very magickal beings.

"I can't tell." Iain focused harder. "I'm trying to find a pulse."

Suddenly, Iain exhaled, holding his chest. His eyes widened and his pupils shone with an inner light as they locked into their distorted shape. The chanting became louder. The possessed stopped what they were doing and turned to where the brothers hid. Slowly they came to form a line along the far side of the road.

Iain made a weak noise, gasping for breath. Gentle streams of light began to pull from his eyes and mouth toward the fire. Erik slashed his hand through the light to break the connection but it did little good. He felt Iain's magick move against his fingers. Erik hefted his brother up and over his shoulder only to crumble to his knees the moment he stood.

Erik's eyes turned to Lydia. Iain's light passed by her and moved to Charlotte on the ground. Erik coughed. His chest tightened. He felt Lydia inside him seconds before she ripped his magick from him. Automatically, he clutched his throat, trying to stop the life from draining out. Iain slumped onto the ground. The townsfolk crossed the road now that the warlocks were immobilized. Erik felt their hands but was petrified, unable to fight.

"TAKE HIS POWER," flaxen ringlet girl encouraged.

"Yes, take him." Tom came to stand beside the younger child.

Lydia tried to resist as Erik's power entered her. She saw his magick in the light that surrounded her. She smelled him, felt him, tasted him. Never had they been so close, or so far apart. In that moment, she understood him on a deep instinctual level. He had so much power, bound himself so tight to keep it at bay. She felt the sting of years, centuries of living, the heartache of losing mortal friends until he and his family buried themselves in their clan.

Yet there was more. As one of the shadows flew next to her head in excitement, she knew what they wanted as well. They used her to take Erik's power so that they may again take human form. They were not content to merely control humans, in fact they seemed to hate playing the puppeteers. They wanted life and had been hiding in the forest essentially sulking as they waited for it to come to them. Their eagerness shone in ringlet girl's eyes, radiated in Tom's heavy breathing, resonated in the chanting of the possessed townsfolk.

Lydia's skin itched as if it might explode. She was not built to contain so much energy. Her blood became hot. Sweat dripped into her eyes.

Charlotte's screams erupted over the distance. They didn't bind Charlotte, not like they did Lydia, because the drink they gave her would keep her immobilized on the ground. Charlotte would take whoever's power came near her first—a forced *inthrall*. But Lydia was different. Her connection to Erik made her special. The shadow could barely contain its impatience.

The tight ropes around her wrists kept her hands over her head as she was suspended on the thick wood pole like a beacon to lure Erik in. A peg at her feet helped to brace her weight but she had to stay balanced or risk dangling freely.

Joe and Sheriff Johnson dumped Erik at her feet. His eyes looked up at her but he didn't move. The shadow became more frantic, trying to syphon the magick from her before the process was finished. Lydia looked from Erik to where she could just see Charlotte's head. They'd placed Iain on the ground next to her friend. The other black shadow hovered close to them to take Iain's power.

Lydia didn't have living family or a lot of close friends. She had Charlotte and Erik, and these shadows were trying to kill them both. The shadow pulled from her as it forced her to take from Erik. His powers passed through her, and she cried out at the pain. Every inch of her body burned, inside and out, her nerves raw, her bones aching, her skin itching, her eyes watering. She was dying, a slow and painful end.

Eyes formed in the shadow before her, and she swore she saw the ghost of a smile. The dark mass took human shape. The impression of arms lifted toward her. The shadow's frozen touch contrasted the heat of her skin. Lydia gasped and jerked. The shock of cold brought her back to her senses. If the thing was going to kill her, she would take it with her. Not knowing what she was doing, she willed Erik's magick back into her body, trying to reverse the process. The shadow thrashed. It placed its hands on her shoulders and brought the single mass of what would have been feet to her stomach and pushed as if Lydia's actions trapped it to her. Beneath her ringlet girl and Tom began screeching, an unearthly sound.

The second shadow shot up to help its friend, abandoning Charlotte. The townsfolk closest to it growled in anger and rushed the pole she was on. Hands gripped her legs, rocking the post. She felt herself taking life from the surrounding trees and plants. The more magick she took inside her the harder it became to contain until finally it burst out over the yard.

The shadow convulsed violently, the darkness lightening from within until it burst into ashes. Half of those gathered fell to the ground. The second shadow's minions rocked her harder. She felt fingers digging into her skin as if to rip her apart. They loosened the pole knocking her head against the wood several times. She tried to pull at the last shadow creature as she had the first, but she was too weak. The shadow carried Iain's powers, not Erik's, and she couldn't connect with it. Warmth trickled out of her nose and she tasted blood on her lips.

"Try not to kill the humans," Angus ordered, his voice sounding far away. She blinked heavily trying to find him. "There! Niall, Euann, immobilize it."

Lydia detected a tartan rushing past her before a bright strobe light flashed. She closed her eyes against the painful pulse of light. Screaming sounded from the conscious townsfolk. Lydia's body swayed as they stopped rocking her. She fell off the peg and hung limp against the wobbling post.

Chaos erupted. She heard the slaps of flesh, the call of commands, the screeching of the shadow through his minions. When she again opened her eyes she found Niall lifted off the ground surrounded by light. Euann stood beneath him holding a small strobe pointed at the shadow. The box looked like something from a hippy's drug den—hardly an impressive magickal tool. Yet, it seemed to be working.

Rory was on the ground next to Iain and Charlotte, shielding them with his body as the battle raged above him. Tom hit at his back. The boy was one of the last people standing. Mrs. Callister stumbled around the yard in a haphazard circle as if confused.

Unlike when Lydia killed the first shadow, the second one did not turn to ash. Instead, it began pulsing with the light. Niall remained before it in the air. His stiff body acted like some kind of blockade to keep the shadow from escaping. With a tiny burst it was over. The shadow succumbed to the light, disappearing as if it had never been. Niall dropped to his knees and didn't move from the ground.

Suddenly, Mrs. Callister and Tom both dropped like dead weight. Tom slumped over Rory's back. The warlock pushed him off.

"Cut her down," Angus said. Seconds later she was falling forward, unable to catch herself. She dropped into a pair of arms. "That's it, lass, easy now." Angus laid her next to his son. "You're safe. I'll be back for ya once we clean up this mess."

Erik didn't move. His eyes were fixed open, staring at the pole where she'd been. She tried to speak, but nothing came out. Taking the last bit of her strength, she flopped her hand onto Erik's chest over his heart. It beat beneath her fingers.

"We can't do anything about the dead grass and trees so killing a few more to get the job done won't matter. It'll just have to be a mystery." Angus's voice was far away. "Boys, set up the picnic tables and put the casserole out."

Lydia heard the rush of feet and saw flashes of light behind her closed lids. Casserole? Her throat gurgled and she passed out.

Chapter Fifteen

Lydia felt a tickle along the nape of her neck. Her limbs were numb with the residual effects of deep sleep, but she was warm and safe…and really hungry. Her muscles stiffened and trembled as she gave a small stretch. The tickling traveled down to where her neck met her shoulder.

A low moan sounded, and she realized Erik lay beside her on the bed lightly kissing her. "*A stóirín*, ya are a handful of trouble, but I kind of like it."

Her eyes opened, but she had no desire to run away from him. She felt safe—safer than she had in days. It was clear the instant she saw the room that she was in the MacGregor mansion. The style of the dark wood and a portrait of Erik in full MacGregor plaid surrounded by the Scottish countryside was a dead giveaway. Feeling the wandering hands moving along her waist under the covers, she could well guess this was Erik's bedroom.

She smiled at the portrait. He did look pretty sexy with long hair, like some sort of romance novel hero. "I'm the handful? My life was tame before you MacGregors moved in next door."

"We do what we can, lass." He kissed her shoulder, the lips pressing harder this time. Erik's body shifted, and she felt the full press of his arousal against her hip. "Had I known all I had to do was save ya from mortal danger to get ya into bed I would have found trouble sooner."

His hand found the flesh of her waist and slipped around to her stomach. When she reached her arm out from beneath the covers she noticed she wore black silk pajamas. They weren't hers. "Am I still hallucinating?"

"Hallucinating?" Erik's kisses stopped. "What do ya mean, love?"

"I could have sworn I heard your dad planning a picnic before I passed out." She gave a small laugh. "Something about setting up tables and putting out casseroles."

His hips rocked against her gently. "That he would have. The townsfolk would need a reasonable explanation for a bunch of strange memories and the Sheriff's ruined lawn. They'll think someone used bad mushrooms in a potluck casserole, and they all were drugged out of their minds. The doctor will explain the rest of it away as temporary amnesia due to hallucinogens."

"I don't even want to know why you had illegal 'shrooms around." Lydia gave a small yawn. The feel of his hands made her forget all about being hungry. "Or an old strobe light."

"Niall had them. Hallucinogenic drugs leave people open to influence. The hippies had it right —black lights and strobes keep the *lidérc* away and out of their compromised brains."

Her smile fell and she turned in his arms to study his face. "What about Charlotte?"

"Safe," he assured her. Erik propped up on his elbow. The covers fell along his waist and his chest was bare. "Everyone is safe."

"What were those things? Are they coming back? Are there more of them? Why did they want to kill...?" She paused. "No, I know the answer to that last one. They needed me to take your powers from you so they could become human form again to wreak more havoc. There was so much hatred and anger in them. Right now they're confined to the shadows, but if they became full bodied monsters I can't imagine what they'd do."

"The Hungarians call them *lidérc*. Others know them as a kind of incubi or succubi. Ya killed one, and Niall banished the other for the next hundred years or so. It will not be coming back for a very long time."

"Succubus?" Lydia frowned. "Like vampires?"

"Not the blood suckers. More like psychic vampires and possessor demons. They find weaknesses in people's psyche and crawl inside the shadows of the mind to control them. We warlock have a natural immunity to them. The only way they can get our magick is through an *inthrall*. You're my natural *inthrall* so ya were used to try and take my powers." He touched the tip of her nose. His eyes flashed and instantly her skin began to tingle where he touched her, more so than normal. "I can see some of my energy is still inside you."

Her breathing deepened. Lydia's hand strayed to his waist. "And Charlotte is Iain's *inthrall?*"

"Not naturally, no. She had been exposed to Iain's magick when they petrified her, and then she was given something to make her a portal in which to take a warlock's powers. Iain was trying to see if she was harmed when her spell and his magick connected." Erik's expression fell a little. "It was a very rare collection of events. The *lidérc* must have been watching us very closely. Setting up magickal security takes time, which is why we always send a group in advance to a location before the clan moves to the area. Apparently, our normal protocols weren't enough to keep the evil out."

"Oh, no, Iain?"

"He's in a coma. My mother worked an enchantment spell to preserve him. Ya were able to reverse the process between us a little and give my strength back. Charlotte and Iain do not have our connection. It's not her fault. She didn't know what to do. The process nearly killed them both. Charlotte rests, which is the best thing for her. We're trying to pull some of the magick out of her. We need to decide what to do with her before she wakes up." Erik's hands resumed their exploration. His finger slid down her nose to her lips. Everywhere he touched erupted with tiny explosions of pleasure. "But nothing needs to be decided at this moment, except for one thing."

"Which is?" she whispered. The heat of his body drew her closer to him. The magick in his fingers worked their spell over her. She felt his powers lingering inside her. She knew if she wanted she could drain him of his magick, his life. One touch is all it would take, the simple will of her to do so. The fact made her much more powerful than the warlock next to her on the bed.

"Are ya going to stop playing hard to get and let me catch ya already, Lydia? Because ya have more than captured me, my love."

Her heart quickened. "Please tell me your sister didn't cast another misguided spell."

"No, love, those words are all mine."

"You may be a powerful warlock, but you're a silly man." Lydia pressed her lips up to meet his. She kissed him softly. "You caught me that first day we met."

Erik moaned cupping her cheek to hold her face to his. He instantly deepened the kiss, letting her feel by the subtle movements of his body just how much he wanted her. "Ya might have let a man know it, lass." A deep laugh rumbled in his chest.

"I sent you erotic dreams. I saved your life. I tamed you when you shifted into a beast." She touched his cheek, pulling at his magick only to release it back into him. The feelings it awoke were very seductive. "I'm allowing you to live at this very moment. So, what were you waiting for, a gilded invitation to spell it all out for you?"

"I'm told we men can be rather dense. It could help."

"Fine," Lydia gave a pretend sigh of exasperation. "Erik, hon, enough with all the talk. Can you shut up and kiss me already?"

He growled and buried his face in her neck. Nipping at her, he said, "Not exactly the 'I love ya' I was looking for."

"Are you kidding?" Lydia pulled him by the hair to make him look at her. "Like I'm going to commit fully before I find out if you're all talk. I mean, you did lead me to believe you were something of a god in bed."

"Oh, now ya challenge my manhood?" He flipped her over on her back and pinned her down with a heavy thigh. "I'm trying to be a gentleman and let ya recover from your ordeal, but—"

"Stop talking." Lydia leaned up and pressed her mouth to his. She let her hand glide lower to his hip. To her surprise, she discovered he didn't wear any clothes. Unable to help herself, she let her hand glide over a firm ass cheek, her fingers cupping the bottom edge.

"Aye, love, whatever ya want." His words were light and playful, but she had a feeling he meant them completely. He would give her whatever she wanted. When she'd pulled at his magick he hadn't tried to stop her. The residual effects of what happened to them lingered inside her. She felt so much of him, a connection she'd never had with another person before. It was an invisible thread reaching out of him and coming into her. She knew him intimately, not by memories but by instinct and emotions. Lydia understood him, and when she kissed him there were no doubts in her mind that this is who she was meant to be with.

His fingers skimmed over the silk of the pajamas. The material seemed to melt against her flesh from his warmth. With very little effort he undressed her. A brush of his finger against a button caused it to unfasten. A whisk of his hand drew her pants down her legs without his even needing to physically pull on them. Silk tickled her flesh, but the sensation was instantly replaced by the hard muscles of his naked thigh.

Without pulling the sleeve from her arms, he tugged the shirt out from under her body. Apparently, it had melted through her. She gave a small laugh. "Interesting magic trick. For your next act, please don't pull any rabbits out of my...well, hat."

"There's no trick to my magick," he assured her. He took her hand from his ass and glided it around to the front. Erik pushed her fingers against his arousal. "It's all very real." Then chuckling, he licked playfully at her mouth. "And ya can't call my manhood 'rabbit'. At least give it a manly name I can brag about."

She began to form a smartass answer, but instead gasped loudly as his hand moved over her flesh to leave tingling trails of magick in its wake.

She saw the blue marks of it over her breasts and arms before it dissipated. Erik cupped her sex. The tingling intensified. She gasped, arching off the bed when a finger entered her. His grin widened. Pulses of energy vibrated from his hand along her body. She jerked violently, trembling as a climax was ripped out of her with his power.

Lydia gasped for breath, completely shocked by what had just happened. Her bones felt as if they melted inside her legs. She couldn't move. Her heart hammered, pounding in her chest and ears and throat. It was all she could do to draw breath.

Erik looked very proud of himself. He kissed the corner of her lips before whispering by her ear, "And that was just my hand, love."

"Ah," was all she could manage to answer. Yes, physically he was a great lover, but there was more between them, so much more. The real pleasure came from their emotional connection. It was strong and more real than anything else she'd ever experienced with a man. The very idea of Erik left her breathless.

"I'll take that to mean ya think I'm more than proving my worth as a lover," he said playfully. Something in his happy gaze said he felt their connection too.

Taking advantage of her weakened state, he

began kissing the length of her body. Lips grazed her stomach and thighs before his tongue licked the center heat of her sex. Every thought left her as her brain focused on the moment.

Erik took his time, not rushing even as the hard length of his arousal attested to his need. He appeared to enjoy torturing himself—and Lydia while he was at it—drawing out the perfection of the moment. He kept his kisses light and constantly moving. He licked the folds of her sex, nipped at her inner thigh, sucked on the sensitive flesh of her hip. Only when her legs stirred, trying to force him up her body to finish her did he draw his cock to her pussy.

He entered her deep and sure, thrusting hard. Erik filled her and one word whispered through her mind as he did, "Finally." The restraint inside him broke. His skin glimmered with magick, coating their naked flesh with its light. She felt the power inside him building and renewing, feeding off their sexual energy, luring her to take some for herself. There was more, just behind the sexual need. After this moment, nothing would tear them apart. She belonged to him, and he to her. They were bonded.

A breeze swept over the room, but there was no natural cause for it, no open windows or doors. It blew his hair around his handsome face and cooled her heated flesh. With each thrust of his body in hers the magick around them became more fervent. He pulled out. Covers flung from the bed across the room. He pushed in. The portrait on the wall rattled. Out. The bed shook and lifted off the ground. In. The bed rocked, rotating them in a slow circle over the floor. Out. A dresser slid sideways and hit a wall. In. She couldn't take the pleasure building inside her body, couldn't think to fight the feelings growing inside her heart.

Lydia cried out, climaxing as she'd never climaxed before. Pleasure rippled over her in a wave, pulsing with a visible yellow glow over Erik and the magickally possessed room. Erik had ahold of her hips, gripping tight as if he'd fly away if he let go. His knees were braced and he managed to thrust a few more times before he too met release.

As her tremors subsided everything stopped moving and the bed dropped hard on the floor. She breathed hard, unable to get enough oxygen into her sated body. Gasping, she said, "You weren't kidding. You are like a god in bed. That was some show you put on."

Erik collapsed next to her and chuckled even as he too panted for air. "That wasn't my show, love."

Lydia stiffened. Was he saying *she* did that?

"Luckily for me, sex replenishes my magick or ya would have sucked me dry of more than my seed." He touched her thigh. "I've never had my magick pulled out of me by the tip of my cock before, well except when ya had your mouth on me in the car."

Lydia glanced around the room, mortified that someone might have heard. She wasn't ashamed of her relationship with Erik, but this was a family home.

"Don't ya worry about the mess, love," Erik said, following her gaze to his room. "As soon as I can muster the energy I'll clean it up. Though, ya keep fucking a man like that and I'll gladly let ya rearrange the whole mansion."

She wanted to answer, but she was too weak. Lydia stared up at the crooked portrait of Erik in the Highlands of Scotland, presumably done very long ago before the ancestors of her ancestors had even met and had children. She wasn't even a possibility in that world. In that moment, she felt very mortal. She had what? Another fifty years? Sixty? He would live forever.

"Ah, don't worry love," he whispered, misreading her expression. "That feeling is normal after ya expend so much magick. Just close your eyes and rest. Ya will feel great when ya wake up."

ERIK GRINNED as Lydia's eyes closed and she almost instantly fell asleep. He could tell she was exhausted. Next time he might have to temper her absorption of him, but just a little bit. There was no way he was going to stop her completely, not if she made love to him like that. Magick wasn't the only thing she'd pulled out of his cock. She'd drained him completely of his seed. Never in his life had he been so sated. In fact, he didn't think he could manage another erection at the moment if he wanted to. *That* had never happened before.

Erik couldn't have been happier. He'd waited so long to claim her like this, and it was so much more than he'd hoped.

Chapter Sixteen

"Congratulations!" Margareta announced.

Lydia froze in shock in the dining room doorway. Margareta and Angus were both staring at her with smiles on their faces. She held her breath, and thought, *Please don't let them be talking about what I did with their son.*

Yeah, the orgasm had been, well, room altering, but it wasn't something she cared to discuss with parental figures. When she awoke Erik was gone and the room had been returned to normal. She had no idea how long she slept, only that she was starving for something to eat.

"Daughter!" Angus beamed at her. "Welcome to the clan."

Now she was even more confused. They made absolutely no sense. Seeing their coffee cups she thought maybe they were both drinking a little Irish whiskey in their coffee. "I, um, huh?" She pointed behind her. "Are you aware that Malina is petrified on the staircase? She looks like she was trying to run out the front door." Lydia gestured to her shoulder. "She has a messenger bag stuck mid-motion behind her."

"Pay no mind to Malina. She tried to disobey me and follow the men out to battle. Clearly, she is not ready if that little unpleasantness with the love potion is any indication." Margareta waved her hand in dismissal. "She'll thaw out in a few more hours."

"Ya have to let the girl grow up sometime," Angus muttered.

"Erik just told us the happy news." Margareta ignored her husband's comment. "Don't ya worry none about not having a mother. I'll help ya see to all the plans. Ya will have the finest wedding a girl could hope for. I am here to help ya decide every detail."

"She should have a grand event," Angus mumbled more to himself than to his wife, "ya have been planning on throwing a wedding for one of our kids for the last three hundred years." Then to Lydia, he winked, "I'd run if I were ya, lass, and elope. This one will have your wedding looking like a fairy tale ball complete with singing horses and dancing flowers."

Good idea, Lydia thought. *Run away from this conversation.*

Lydia slowly backed out of the dining room. She might starve, but her stomach would have to wait. Clearly the MacGregor elders were suffering from some kind of delusion.

"Ya scared her," Margareta scolded her husband. The words were followed by a loud smack and Angus's unconcerned laughter. "If ya lose me my grandchildren I'll do more than brain ya!"

"There ya are." Erik grinned at her as he came bounding down the steps two at a time. He stepped around his statue of a sister as if such a thing were normal. Perhaps here it was. He paused, nodding at Malina. "Morning, banshee." He gave a small brotherly laugh and poked his thumb toward her face. "She does kind of look like a banshee with her hair flying around like that and her mouth all open. Yeah, ma froze her good. See how her eyes don't move?" Erik leaned closer to her and grinned as he looked into her mouth. "Ha, Euann put a mint in there." He patted Malina's arm.

"I'm beginning to see why Malina used me to whammy you," Lydia said.

"Hey, a mint is better than a beetle." Erik continued down the stairs until he was within kissing distance of Lydia.

"I think you need to check on your parents." Lydia pointed toward the dining room. "I don't think all of your brothers 'shrooms made it into the casserole."

"What do ya mean?" Erik frowned and made a move to go to his parents' aid.

"They think we're getting married."

Erik stopped and then gave a sheepish look to the floor. "Don't be mad I told them without ya. I was excited."

"Erik…" Lydia made a weak noise. Marriage? The idea didn't necessarily repulse her, but it all seemed a little sudden. She did love him, yet… "Isn't there something you're forgetting to do?"

"No." He shook his head in thought. Damn but he was sexy. Even now she wanted to kiss him and forget everything else. "Iain's condition is unchanged. Euann and Rory are taking turns sitting with Charlotte. Niall is out making sure the cover up worked."

"I meant a proposal."

The man actually looked confused. "Proposal for what? As far as I know I wasn't supposed to be working on a business plan for anything. Are my parents trying to expand your business? If ya don't want to, just tell them no. They'll fuss but not every family business needs to be a multi-million dollar corporation. Though, I suppose we could generate a lot of local goodwill by expanding and employing the locals. I can have that realtor man, Frank, look into properties—"

"Traditionally the man gets down on one knee and asks the woman if she'll marry him instead of just assuming she will." Lydia nodded her head slowly to prompt his agreement and then shook it in denial when the words didn't seem to fully register.

"You're my *fíorghrá*," Erik said, as if that explained it all. "Of course we'll get married. I was serious when I said you've captured me. Ya love me. I'm utterly and completely taken with—"

"We need to get this lassie to the hospital." Euann carried Charlotte in his arms. "She started to wake up. I used a little potion on her to force her asleep, but it won't keep her under for too long." Charlotte's foot bumped Malina as he carried her past his sister. Euann grimaced. "Dammit, banshee, aren't ya thawed yet?" Then to Erik, he gestured his head toward their sister and said, "She does kind of look like a banshee like that, doesn't she? If I had time, I'd dye her hair white and take pictures."

"Why a hospital?" Lydia looked at Erik. This

family really had no concept of the word emergency. "I thought you said she was safe here, that the magick just needed to wear off."

"Erik ordered us not to wipe her memory again under any circumstances, and considering the potion she drank and what she did to Iain, I don't want to be the next warlock she sucks power…well, anyway. So, I figured that leaves one option. We leached enough magick out of her that she won't accidentally throw nurses all around the room with it. If we can't erase what happened then we should get her to the hospital with the others. Niall said the townsfolk woke up and the emergency room looks like an epidemic hit. If we slip Charlotte in now they'll think she tripped balls with the others."

"Tripped balls?" Erik repeated.

"It means hallucinate, old man," Euann explained.

"That would be like lying to her again," Lydia interrupted before the brothers could start bickering. "She'll think she's crazy. You don't know what it was like in that basement, not knowing who had you or what was going to happen. I can't let her deal with that on her own. It was real. It happened."

"It's up to ya, Lyd. She's your friend. We can try to erase what happened and hope that the potion wore off, or we can get her to the hospital with the others." Erik touched her arm. "Once everything calms down we can tell her whatever truth ya think is right."

"Fine," Lydia motioned to the door. "Let's take her to the hospital with the others. It would probably be good if they did some blood tests on her anyway." Maybe it would be for the best if Charlotte thought the basement nightmare was just a bad drug trip. Perhaps then the woman could forget the fear like a bad dream. After Charlotte drank the potion she'd fallen unconscious so it was possible she knew nothing about sucking Iain's magick from him or the attempted sacrifice.

"Hey, Erik, she's getting a little heavy. Do ya think—?" Euann adjusted Charlotte in his arms.

"It looks like ya have her. I'll get the car," Erik answered.

Lydia gave him a stern look.

"My darling intended will get the car." Erik went to the table at the bottom of the stairs and produced a set of keys from a small drawer. "It's around back, love."

"Engaged?" Euann grinned. "Congratulations. That's wonderful news. It's been some time since we had a clan wedding. Ma will be thrilled. She's been filling up that wedding planning book of hers for centuries."

Lydia snatched the keys from Erik. "You have really got to quit telling people that."

ERIK GRINNED as his bride walked away from him. He couldn't help himself. Never in his life had he been this happy.

"I don't understand. Why can't I know? I'm family." Euann carried Charlotte toward Erik and thrust her at him so he was forced to catch her and help carry her weight to the car.

"Och, she's just upset because I forgot to propose to her first," Erik answered.

"Ya forgot to ask your future wife to marry ya?" Euann laughed. "Smooth, brother, very smooth."

"I forgot about that part of the custom. She would have said yes, right? We're clearly destined to be together. It's not like I've really thought about the whole marriage process over the last... ever. So I forgot a couple details." He managed a small shrug. "What do ya mean heavy? This lass barely weighs a thing."

"I know," Euann thrust Charlotte's weight completely over onto Erik and let go of her. "I just wanted to make ya carry her."

Erik adjusted Charlotte in his arms as he

watched Euann run for the stairs. "Where are ya going? We need to get up to the hospital."

"Go ahead. I'll be right behind ya." Euann stopped by Malina. "But ya really don't think I can pass up a picture of this, do ya?"

Erik gave a small laugh. He heard his car coming from around the back of the house. Lydia's driving grinded a little hard on his gears and he flinched. As he backed toward the front door, he yelled, "I want a copy!" Malina blinked. "And ya better hurry, the banshee is waking up."

"HERE." Erik dumped an armful of vending machine junk food on Lydia's lap. "I wasn't sure what ya wanted so I got one of everything."

Lydia glanced up at him from her place in the hospital lobby and smiled gratefully. She was just happy to get a chance to eat something—finally. Taking a chocolate bar off the top of the pile, she tore it open and bit into it. She barely tasted it before starting on a second bar.

Erik chuckled. "Magick can be rather draining." By the sparkle in his eye she could well imagine which magickal draining he was thinking of. "Any word on Charlotte?"

Lydia shook her head in denial. "Not really.

They wanted to do blood tests before they let us see her. I know one of the nurses from high school. She said she'd come and get me if Charlotte woke up."

"Niall," Erik called, standing.

Lydia shoved the rest of the second chocolate bar into her mouth and looked up at Erik's brother. With her mouth embarrassingly full, she couldn't speak. Niall glanced at her but didn't acknowledge her otherwise.

"It's contained," Niall said. "Since some prominent members of town were involved it was pretty easy to convince the doctors to report this as a case of accidental food poisoning versus mass hysteria caused by hallucinogenic mushrooms. I don't know that they'll even bother to test the casserole."

"What about Charlotte?" Lydia pushed the pile of vending machine treasure off her lap and stood, forcing Niall to acknowledge her as part of the conversation.

"I put a veil over myself and slipped into her room. She's alive. The doctors think she had an adverse reaction and slipped into a mini coma. Once the sleeping aid Euann gave her wears off, she'll wake up fully." He glanced at Erik.

"I know she's alive," Lydia said, slightly irritated with Niall's dismissive manners. "And I know everything that happened so you can speak freely in front of me about it."

Erik nodded that Niall should do so.

"There is something off about the woman. I can't put my finger on it, but I think it has something to do with the potion she drank. It is my recommendation that we box her up and ship her to," he studied Lydia, "the farm to be monitored."

"What's the farm?" she asked.

"A prison for clan trouble," Erik answered.

Niall frowned at his brother and then gestured to Lydia. "Do ya want me to take her out back and erase her?"

Lydia reached for Erik's arm, ready to use his magick to fight Niall off if he tried. "Don't you dare touch me."

"We're getting married," Erik inserted calmly.

"Omigod, you have to quit saying that to people!" Lydia exclaimed.

"But we are," he answered assuredly.

"Oh, then welcome to the clan," Niall answered, though his congratulations lacked the enthusiasm the others had shown. "Ma will be happy."

Erik grinned. Lydia shook her head, not sure how to argue the point or if she even wanted to. Instead, she focused on her friend. "We're not imprisoning Charlotte. We're not erasing her.

We're not doing anything to her. If there are consequences to be dealt with then so be it. We deal."

Niall hardly looked impressed by her decree. She had a feeling to him she would always be an outsider, a non-warlock.

"Find another way," Lydia told Erik.

"We can watch her." Erik patted the hand on his arm. She felt his magick warming her fingers and drawing up her arm to calm her. "We'll move her into Lydia's house. She'll be safe there."

"Charlotte loves her apartment. She calls it her sanctuary," Lydia denied. She snatched her fingers away from Erik, not wanting him to magickally alter her feelings. "I have no problem letting Charlotte live with me, but—"

"We'll move to the mansion," Erik said. He paused as two nurses walked past. When they were out of hearing range, he continued, "Charlotte can take the house."

"I'll buy her apartment building and evict her. It'll be easy enough to buy her out of her remaining lease, and we need living space for the clan anyway." Niall reached for his phone and pressed a few buttons as he walked away. "Da, give me that realtor's number. I need to buy a building today."

Lydia felt a slow rage building inside her. Yes,

she loved Erik. Yes, if he bothered to ask her properly she might do something crazy like jump into a marriage with a warlock who never aged. Yes, Charlotte would always be welcome in her home. No, she did not want to live in a house—no matter that it was the mansion she used to daydream about as a child—with a bunch of magick wielding warlocks pranking each other all the time. No, she didn't want to open a factory tomorrow to expand her business. She wanted to expand Love Potions on her own. The house and the business were her legacy from her grandmother. She wanted time to think. And she definitely wanted to make her own decisions when it came to her future.

"There love, all settled." Erik made a move to hold her.

Lydia pulled away. "No, love, not all settled."

"What did we forget?"

"Since there is clearly no stopping your family from throwing your magick and your money around, I'm going to go tell Charlotte the doctors think she should live with me for the time being to make sure there are no residual effects. Then, when she is ready I'm telling her the truth."

"Truth?" Erik sounded slightly worried.

"All of it." Lydia scowled. She reached to the pile of junk food and began gathering the majority of it into her arms. "Now you go do whatever it is you do, and I'm going to eat and stare at Charlotte until she wakes up."

"I can come with—"

"Alone." Lydia strode away from him.

"SWEET! FREE CHIPS." Euann reached down to a bag of potato chips Lydia had left behind and opened it. Grinning as he popped one into his mouth, he asked, "Where's my new sister off to?"

Erik glanced at his brother, noting his bruised eye. "Banshee woke up, didn't she?"

"Not to worry. Mission was accomplished." Euann laughed. "And already messaged to every clan phone."

"Malina's going to kill ya for that," Erik warned.

"She'll try, but first she has to wash the color out of her hair. I enchanted it, so she'll think it's clean and then it will slowly start turning gray again until she washes it, rinse and repeat for about a month." Euann ate another chip. "So, all settled here?"

"Aye." Erik nodded. "But I think Lydia's upset with me."

"Ah, she's a girl. Probably having her girlie

time or something. It did look like she raided the vending machine for junk food. Just get her some chocolate and wait it out." Euann motioned that Erik should come with him. "Da just called. He wants us to go look at some property downtown with Niall. Ya know our baby brother has no patience for business. He'll offer a million dollars for it just to be done with negotiations. I'm on security and you're on realtor duty. The elders' orders."

By elders Euann most likely meant Erik's parents, as the uncles and aunts had yet to arrive in town.

"Aye, nothing more to do here." Erik pulled his car keys out of his pocket. "Text me the address. I'll meet ya there."

"LYDIA."

Lydia stiffened at the Sheriff's voice. She slowly turned, trying to calm the sudden thundering of her heart. Joe stood next to him. They wore street clothes and hospital bracelets. She automatically looked for Brad but didn't see him.

"Hello," she answered carefully, watching their faces to see what they might remember. Even knowing what she did, she couldn't help the tremor of apprehension that wormed its way up her spine. They'd held her at gunpoint and kept her locked in a cell.

"Were you discharged as well?" Joe asked, eyeing her armful of candy. "Weird epidemic. I don't even remember organizing a church potluck at the sheriff's, but we've concluded that's what must have happened."

"No, I'm not sick. I was lucky," Lydia said. "I'm here with Charlotte and to visit the rest of you, of course. Is everyone all right? No one was seriously hurt?"

"Few bumps and bruises, nothing too serious so far," the sheriff answered. "I'm thankful my wife was out of town visiting her sister in Texas. She's not going to be happy when she sees our yard."

"I heard it was a contaminated batch of mushrooms and that some altered memories or memory loss was a side effect," Lydia lied. "I even heard a doctor say retrograde amnesia."

"We're not sure what it was," Sheriff Johnson said. "I'm trying to keep panic down. It's possible everyone caught a bad flu virus that caused dehydration. You should have the doctor check you out, just in case."

"I'll do that." Lydia nodded. She walked away

slowly, pretending to look at room numbers as she listened to the men.

"If it is hallucinogenic mushrooms," Joe said, "I'll bet it was those vandals, Brad Williams's boys. That family has been trouble since they moved in. I tried to do the Christian thing and invite him to church when he first moved here. He actually spit on me. I haven't talked to him since, but the whole town knows his sons are responsible for the spray paint. I wouldn't put it past them to drop a few drugs in the town supermarket as a prank."

Lydia stiffened, recalling one of the *lidérc's* memories. It watched Joe and Brad interact outside a gas station and entered both of their minds at the moment of heightened irritation. That single display of negative emotions let the creature slip inside and make himself at home within the men. It was the same way the two creatures had taken over the rest of the town, slipping in while their human hosts were emotionally vulnerable.

She shivered, not liking the sensation of being inside the creature's thoughts. Hopefully, the after-effects of her pulling Erik's magick away from the shadow would wear off in time. It would appear she'd taken in some of the creature when she did so.

"No one is happy about this. I'm already

looking into the vandalism," Sheriff Johnson assured him. "We can't go accusing people without proof. The school is already aware the boys have behavioral issues, and they're keeping an eye on them. Legally, I can't arrest them for being misfits."

The men walked down the hall, their words no longer detectable. Whatever the *lidérc* had done, it seemed its influences over Joe had worn off. That was a good sign. Maybe Erik was right that things in town were becoming normal again.

"Normal?" Lydia gave a dismissive laugh as she walked into Charlotte's hospital room. "I'm in love with a hardheaded warlock. Nothing will ever be normal again."

Chapter Seventeen

Lydia hated the blank look on Charlotte's face as she drove her friend home from the hospital. The doctors had finally released her that morning into Lydia's care. Their insistences that Charlotte not live alone for the foreseeable future felt an awful lot like a MacGregor spell and not real doctorly advice. They refused to let Charlotte leave until she agreed. Charlotte only agreed because she'd received a special delivery letter about her immediate eviction.

Erik pulled his car to a stop outside the old Victorian. Lydia had been trying her best to ignore him out of principle. He'd have to learn that she wasn't going to submit to his will whenever he wanted. Ok, so she apparently would because they'd made love in his car outside the hospital. Lucky for them no one saw. A few charming words, that damned MacGregor accent, that handsome devilish smile, and she'd been drawn to him like Gramma Annabelle to moonshine.

"Wow. You really got the storm damage fixed fast," Charlotte said, looking up at the house. Then, frowning, she said, "There was a storm right? I didn't imagine that too?"

"There was a storm," Lydia said, trying to hide the guilt she felt at not telling the whole truth. She wasn't sure Charlotte could handle it. Her friend looked fragile, as if a stiff breeze might knock her over. "Erik and his brothers came and helped me. Malina helped me inside the house. Gramma's old room is ready for you. I hope you don't mind staying in there."

Charlotte nodded and continued to look around the yard as if she was trying to recall something and couldn't.

Lydia looked helplessly at Erik. He stepped around the car to take Charlotte's elbow. "Iain and Rory will bring the rest of your things from your apartment later today."

"I don't want them in my house." Charlotte pulled away from him.

"I went through and got anything that might be private," Lydia said. "I promise I didn't look, just put it all in boxes for you to go through when you're up to it. They're just bringing over the heavy stuff."

Charlotte relaxed some and nodded. "I'm going to go rest." She walked into the house.

When they were alone, Lydia said, "You should go. Charlotte needs me."

"I don't want to leave ya," Erik said. "Ya have been at the hospital since we admitted her. Now that you're home I want ya close. I need to know you're safe."

"I'm safe. You said it yourself, the threat is gone," Lydia reasoned. "Charlotte needs me and your being here won't help her relax. I have your number. I'll call if I need you."

Glancing over the Victorian, he said, "Yes, go and help her get settled. If ya get an idea of what you'd like to take up to the mansion I can have Rory and Iain help me grab the heavy stuff tonight and start moving ya in."

Lydia could have argued, but she wasn't sure it would do any good. Sighing, she said, "You really don't hear me when I talk to you, do you?"

"What do ya mean, love?"

"Never mind. Just see if Malina will meet the guys here when they're ready to drop off Charlotte's stuff? I could use her help with a few things."

Erik smiled. "It will be done." He kissed her, and she felt his love and happiness pouring into her. It was hard to be mad at him when he was so free with his emotions toward her.

She waited on the drive as she watched him drive away. Then, going inside, she said, "Gramma, where's the grimmie? We have protection spells to cast."

"This house needs a good smudging." Gramma Annabelle appeared. She looked around. "I don't know who let all those little monsters in, but I think I've chased most of them away. Those field ghosts should just stay outside where they belong."

"Field ghosts?" Lydia arched a brow.

"Don't worry about them, dear. They died back in the Old West. You know in the 1800s they were always massacring each other or dying from pandemics." Annabelle fluttered around the kitchen. "Violent deaths tend to keep the spirits around."

"That's comforting," Lydia mumbled sarcastically.

"So who's the handsome devil of a man who dropped you off?" Annabelle disappeared and reappeared beside the door.

"Erik MacGregor."

"And why were you kissing Erik MacGregor?"

Her grandmother shimmered, leaving the door to reappear in front of Lydia.

Gasping, Lydia stepped back as her grand-mother surprised her. She covered her heart to still its rapid beating. "Apparently we're engaged."

"Really?" Gramma Annabelle clapped her hands. "Tell me everything. And don't leave out a single detail."

"Only if you help me re-cast all of your old protection spells while I talk," Lydia said.

"Done," Annabelle agreed. "So, who are we trying to keep out?"

"Erik MacGregor," Lydia answered.

"Oh, intrigue! I can see I'm going to like this man of yours." Her grandmother swept her way to the basement door. "Well, come on, let's go get the book. You might want to grab your gardening gloves."

"YOU WANT me to magickally help you carry Charlotte's furniture upstairs so that my brothers don't have to be invited into the house?" Malina looked from Lydia to Annabelle's spirit. "Then you want me to help make sure your barrier spell is strong again because you plan on torturing Erik by keeping him out?"

"Well, not torture really, just give him a reality check until—" Lydia began.

"I'm in," Malina interrupted.

"But I'm not going to hurt him," Lydia insisted. "This is just to make him realize he can't dictate the terms of our life together."

"Yeah, torture him a bit, I'm in." Malina nodded, rubbing her hands.

"Ah, dear," Annabelle said, floating sideways over Malina's head. "You know you look much too young to let your hair go gray. Hair color will take care of that. If you need help, Lydia will show you where you can buy box color. It's not like your day. We have modern advances."

"Gramma, this is her day," Lydia said. "She was just born several hundred years ago."

Malina frowned and marched into the living room to a small antique mirror they'd managed to magickally mend the day before. As she watched the color drain out of her hair to be replaced by banshee white, Malina growled. "Euann."

"Gramma, go keep an eye on Charlotte. She should be sleeping," Lydia said. "But don't show yourself. She's been through enough."

"Malina, are you going to help me test the barrier? I did everything Gramma said, but I want to be sure the house is safe. Not just for me, but for Charlotte."

"Yeah, coming," Malina mumbled, glaring at her reflection.

IAIN AND RORY were not happy about being banned from the house. Erik and Niall had come down to join them. The men kept trying to find a way inside, as if it was a personal challenge between Malina and her male relatives. It didn't help that Malina taunted them from the kitchen doorway.

Hearing the shuffle of footsteps, Lydia hissed, "Malina, stop. Charlotte's up."

"Charlotte," Malina repeated. Rory lowered a glowing ball of light and Iain's taunt died on his lips. As the magick settled, the lawn became darker in the evening light. Malina had assured her that Euann's security kept people from the town from seeing the magickal glow. When Lydia gave Malina an insistent look, she said, "What? You wanted the barrier tested. It's tested. They can't get in."

"I thought you'd do some kind of mumbo-jumbo spell sensing thing," Lydia answered quietly, mindful of where Charlotte's steps sounded on the top of the stairs.

Malina shrugged. "This way is more fun."

"Charlotte," Lydia called, instantly softening her voice and making it light and non-threatening. The lights were off so it was hard to see Charlotte's face. "How did you sleep?"

Charlotte walked down the stairs like a zombie —stepping and pausing, stepping and pausing. Her hands hung at her sides, and she gave a little moan.

"That good, huh?" Lydia said. "What would you like? Tea or coffee?"

Charlotte moaned again.

"Charlotte?" Lydia frowned as her friend came closer. Her eyes were glazed and she carried a small blue bag clutched in her dusty hand. "Uh, Malina, help, please."

"What is it?" Malina joined them. "Oh, I see!" Matter-of-factly, she said, "Your friend has a hitchhiker."

"A what? The *lidérc*?" Lydia panicked.

"No." Malina smirked. "I'd say the grandma."

Lydia let loose her captured breath. "Gramma, put Charlotte back!"

Charlotte's mouth opened, and she drooled.

"Gramma, now!" Lydia ordered. "Put Charlotte back and get out of my friend."

Charlotte slowly turned to make her slow way back upstairs. She dropped the bag on the floor. Lydia picked it up and peeked inside. A small cloth with blood and strands of her grandmother's hair were inside. She tossed it on the table. "Ew."

"Malina, enough play, go get Lydia." Erik's voice actually made her smile. Lydia stepped where he could see her.

"*Fíorghrá,* let me in," Erik said, giving her a handsomely charming look.

Lydia grinned. "No."

"But," he glanced around the part of the kitchen he could see without getting too close. "Why'd ya reinforce the barrier spells? It had come down. I was in your house looking for ya the night ya disappeared, and I noticed ya had an infestation. I want to make sure those spirits are gone."

"Ah…" Lydia pretended to think. "No."

"They're gone. We took care of it." Malina offered, smirking at her brother as she leaned against the countertop. "Well, almost all of it. There's a dead grandma in here wearing Charlotte, but we made her put the woman back to bed so it's fine."

"*Cum do theanga ablaich gun fheum,* banshee." Erik growled.

"*Thalla gu Taigh na Galla,*" Malina retorted.

"English," Lydia demanded.

"He told me to shut up. I told him to go to hell," Malina translated.

"What is this about, love?" Erik asked Lydia.

"It's the only way I can think of to make you stop and listen to me." Lydia stood on her side of the barrier. Even though he was near the bottom of the outside steps, with his height she didn't have to look down far to see him.

"I'm listening," he said.

"We are not engaged," Lydia stated.

"But you're my *fiorghrá*," Erik protested. "Of course we'll get married. I want to be with ya, forever."

"*Fiorghrá* means true love," Malina piped in.

"And I am not living in your mansion. This is my home. I'm staying right here and my business, for now, is staying right here." Lydia crossed her arms over her chest.

"But, the mansion is safer," Erik said.

"And full of crazy warlocks throwing magickal pranks on each other," Lydia insisted.

"She has a point," Malina put forth.

Erik glared as his sister.

"If you want to be with me, Mr. MacGregor, then you need to understand I won't be dictated to, no matter how cute you are naked." Lydia pictured him naked and was instantly sorry for it.

"Yeah, I'm not touching that one," Malina mumbled.

"Enough with the peanut gallery comments,"

Lydia said, glancing over her shoulder to get the woman to shut up.

Malina grinned, completely unconcerned.

"Is this because I didn't ask ya?" he inquired.

"The MacGregor men are a bit dense, Lyd," Malina said. "You'll have to spell it out for him."

"Yes. You just assumed I'd say yes to everything you wanted to do. You didn't respect me by asking me what I wanted. That's not how this works." She smiled at him, thinking of how his chest moved when they made love. Crap. Now her focus would go completely off course and she'd soon start coming on to him.

"And ya couldn't just say that? Ya had to block me from the house?" He again looked around, as trying to find a way in.

Lydia leaned closer and lowered her tone. "That's to keep me from falling for your charms and your magickal touch so I don't lose myself again."

He grinned. Now that detail he seemed to fully understand. "I don't care if we live here, but you'll have to let me in." His eyes shimmered with meaning and she felt him trying to seduce her.

"I do plan on living here. I'm not sure where you'll live." She arched a challenging brow.

"Well, then," he lifted his hands to the side in

a small gesture, "will ya marry me, Lydia Barratt?"

"No." She smiled victoriously.

Erik frowned. "But…"

Malina's hard laughter cut him off. Even his brothers and cousins chuckled at her answer. Iain said, "Ma is going to be so mad ya messed this up, Erik."

"That's not a proposal," Lydia said. "That's a question in the middle of a forced conversation. I want a proposal. I want a story I can tell my friends. I want a ring and I want to feel special and I want to announce it together. I want to feel all giddy inside not irritated that my man is so dense I have to spell out the obvious to him."

"But…?" Erik tried to speak.

"Oh, you heard her," Malina said, whipping her hand forward to slam the kitchen door in Erik's face. The blue barrier lit up a few times as Erik knocked on it. Malina touched her shoulder. Her tone uncharacteristically serious, she said, "Good for you, sis. It takes a stubborn woman to put a MacGregor warlock in his place. You truly are his *fíorghrá* because you know just how to handle him. Make him sweat it a bit. I can guarantee he'll never take your opinion for granted again."

LYDIA WAITED UP FOR HOURS, expecting Erik to show up with flowers and candles to recite bad poetry on her lawn, or even—heaven forbid—sing her one of his horrible ballads. The proposal never came. Malina went home to the mansion. Charlotte slept in her new room. Gramma Annabelle pouted at the kitchen table staring at the spell bag she couldn't move for about an hour before disappearing.

"What? There was an empty place in Charlotte where they took her memories. I just slipped in." Annabelle had defended her actions. "Charlotte will never know the difference, and I needed a body." Apparently, the ghost had been attempting to walk the spell bag outside to expand her haunting territory. Lydia wasn't sure letting her grandmother loose on the town was a good idea.

Now, as she lay in bed alone, Lydia missed Erik. She knew she had to make a point, but it was hard. After all she'd been through, she just wanted to snuggle into his arms and never leave them. She was still awake as the clock flicked over to 3 a.m.. The window was open so she could better hear outside and the curtains rustled in the breeze. She turned on her side to stare at the night when she detected a small sound from downstairs. Frowning, she sat up and tilted her head to better listen.

Something was off. She could feel it.

"Char?" she called softly. Lydia crept into the hall and went to open Charlotte's door. The woman still slept. "Gramma?" She tiptoed to the stairs and made her way slowly down.

Her nerves prickled with awareness, but not the kind of tingling Erik caused. This was a warning. A cold chill swept over her, filling her with fear. She couldn't run, couldn't leave Charlotte alone in the house. Her eyes were used to the dark, but it was still hard to make out details in the shadows. She remembered the spine-chilling spirits. Had they found their way back in?

"Get out of my house," she stated loudly. "I command you to leave. This is my house. You don't belong here."

She heard a shuffle near her front door and quickly ran to the kitchen. Foolish though it was, she flung open a low cupboard and grabbed a cast iron skillet. Supernatural things hated iron, right? She wasn't sure but it sounded like something she might have heard once...on television.

Footsteps came toward her. She held the handle tight. Brad appeared in the doorway. He looked at her with possessive eyes. She let go of her captured breath, relieved for a brief moment that he was human and not demonic. Then she realized he'd broken into her home in the middle of the night.

"Hi Lydia," he said. The smarmy tone of his words made her skin crawl. She never did like this guy. His friendship with Joe had been his only redeeming factor and she'd discovered that had been forced.

"What are you doing in my house?" She thought of the barrier spell, but knew Brad must not have been magickal if he made it inside. No, he was all human scumbag.

As if to answer her own question she got a flash of him standing outside her window where the rose bushes used to be, masturbating. He was the one who'd ordered the flowers replaced and he wasn't pleased when the storm blew them away. Brad had been watching her since he'd first seen her. She thought of him pinning her picture over his wife's head before he fucked the woman.

Brad used her moment of distraction to step closer. "I think you know what I'm doing here. We've been dancing around this moment for a long time."

This man was evil. She felt it in him, so much more sharply now that part of Erik's magick resided inside her. Erik's powers gave her the ability to see him for who he was. A rush of images flooded her, every gesture she'd given him blown out of proportion, every word, every look. He'd been stalking her, creating a relationship where there wasn't one. Oddly, the *lidérc's* agenda had kept the man's natural tendencies at bay, but with the creature gone, Brad was free to be Brad. And she wasn't his first victim. He'd done this to another woman in the town he'd lived in before Green Vallis, and another in the town before that.

Brad's hand strayed to his pants and she saw him rub at his erection through his jeans.

Lydia dropped her arm and smiled, not letting go of the pan. "You're right. We have."

She'd shocked him. His hand stopped stroking. He tilted his head to the side as if accessing his options.

Lydia stepped closer, lowering her chin to give him the most seductive look she could muster. "I have wanted to get you alone for a very, very," she paused, coming to stand before him, "very long time…"

He opened his mouth to speak and Lydia took her chance. She gripped the handle and swung the cast iron skillet at his head. The pan made contact with his skull with an awful crack.

"…to tell you to shut the hell up and stop looking at me, you creepy asshole."

Brad didn't have time to react. He slammed into the doorway and dropped to the floor. A knife fell near his hand. Lydia had no doubt he'd planned on killing her and doing unspeakable things to her dead body as he had his other victims.

Keeping an eye on him, she set the pan on the table and went to the phone to call the police. Her hands shook as she dialed. Now that the danger had passed, she felt tears sliding down her cheeks. Lydia stretched the cord as she went to a drawer to pull out a butcher knife. She inched toward his fallen body and stretched out with her toes to drag his knife out of his reach.

ERIK RAN DOWN THE HILL. He'd been trying and failing to sleep as he attempted to work out just how he'd get Lydia to say yes to him. He hoped he was up to the challenge and every detail of his proposal had to be perfect. With the barrier spell so newly in place, he was finding it hard to detect Lydia inside the Victorian. And then he'd felt her, as if she called to him. At first he'd smiled, thinking she was having one of her erotic dreams. Then he heard the police sirens in the distance.

His heart nearly stopped as Lydia's home

came into view. Sheriff Johnson already stood on her lawn, out of uniform, and deputies were walking around the perimeter of her house. Two paramedics pushed a gurney toward their ambulance.

"Lydia?" He ran onto the lawn in worry only to have guns drawn on him. His eyes followed the gurney. He lifted his hands.

"It's all right," Lydia said.

The words filled him with relief as he found her unharmed next to the sheriff. He didn't move as he kept his hands up. The bullets didn't worry him, but concealing his identity did. "What happened? Are ya injured?"

"Erik," she said, his name coming out on a sob.

"Let him through," the sheriff ordered. "That's the fiancé."

Erik went to pull Lydia into his arms. She trembled and buried her face in his chest. "What happened?"

"That's one brave lady you have there," Sheriff Johnson said. "She fought off an attacker. Brad Williams broke into her home tonight and had her at knifepoint."

Lydia lifted her head. Tears flowed down her cheeks. "Stalker."

The sheriff nodded. "It would appear that way."

"Sheriff," one of the deputy's called. Both men turned to look. He carried over a bag and held it open. Erik saw rope, knives and a gun inside. Hugging Lydia tighter, he kept her from looking as he stroked her hair. "I found this close to the front door."

"Get it into evidence," Johnson said.

"No," Lydia managed, still gripping Erik's arms. "He is a stalker. He, ah, he told me. I'm not the first. There were others. He killed them. You have to look in the woods near water. He likes to wash up after. One in each town he's lived in. Ask his wife, she'll know where they've lived." Lydia took a deep breath, trying to calm herself. "They'll look like me."

Sheriff Johnson nodded grimly. "All right, Lydia, I promise I'll look into it."

"And he did the mushrooms," she added weakly. "I don't know why."

"Charlotte's in the living room with one of my men," the sheriff said. "Is there some place you ladies can go for the night?"

"They'll come home with me," Erik said.

"I'll get the crime scene clean up guys out first thing in the morning. They're from out of town so it takes them a few hours to get here. They'll make it look good as new." The sheriff went to some of his men.

"Crime scene? Were ya injured?" Erik asked.

"I hit him on the head with a skillet. He bled." She trembled. "I didn't know what else to do. I just kept seeing all his victims through his eyes, and I knew what he was going to do to me. I had to tell the sheriff something so I lied and said he bragged about it."

"And the mushrooms?"

"Those two Williams boys have had it hard enough with a father like that. They don't need to be blamed for the mushrooms too," she whispered. "Omigod, and Charlotte. These things can't keep happening to Charlotte. She's already so confused."

"Come on, let's get ya ladies to the mansion," Erik said. Even with everything going on she was thinking of others. There was no way he'd ever let his woman go. If he spent an eternity begging, he'd get her to marry him. But for now, all that matter is that she was safe. "I promise, Charlotte is going to be safe. Ya need to worry about yourself, love."

***

"Ya poor things," Margareta declared as Erik

brought the women inside. Lydia didn't even bother asking how the woman knew what had happened. Niall and Rory came from the dining room. Rory carried a glass of whiskey. Niall held the bottle.

Charlotte stood close to Lydia. "So tonight is real? Brad is a stalker and you killed him."

"He's alive," Lydia answered. Though, the paramedics didn't seem to think he'd live through the night. She'd whapped him pretty hard. She tried not to think about it, not when everyone was looking at her for a reaction.

"Anything to handle?" Niall asked gruffly.

Erik shook his head. "No."

Niall nodded and swung back the bottle to drink.

"Niall, show Charlotte to a guest room," Margareta ordered her son. She snatched the bottle from him. "And use a glass. You're not a Neanderthal."

"Come on then," Niall said to Charlotte.

Lydia nodded to her friend that she should go. Charlotte didn't protest. After her friend disappeared upstairs, she said, "I don't like this. She's not herself. She doubts everything."

Margareta came forward and placed her hand on Lydia's cheek. "Time is sometimes the best magick of all. Give her that." Then to Erik, she said, "And there is also great magick in rest. Niall will make sure Charlotte is safe. He won't be great company, but then I imagine she'll just want to rest. Ya two go to bed." When Margareta removed her hand she took a few strands of Lydia's hair with her. Lydia flinched in surprise but it didn't hurt. The woman continued, "Rory will find Euann, and they'll do a sweep of the property just to be sure. I'm going to my lair."

Erik nodded in understanding.

"I could really use a shower," Lydia said as they walked up the stairs. She moved slowly and he paused long enough to sweep her up into his arms to carry her. She leaned her head against his shoulder. "I really miss normal."

"My mother is going to make sure the danger has passed for ya once and for all. We won't see much of her for several days. Such future telling magick takes a lot out of her and is rarely performed, but as perfect as Green Vallis seems to be, we've already encountered many threats. Such is the way with places of great power—all sorts of people, both good and bad, will be drawn to it."

"Perhaps they just follow you," she said.

"Brad was here before we were," Erik countered.

"You're right." Lydia sighed and closed her eyes. "If you hadn't of come, I wouldn't have had the ability to detect what he truly was until it was too late. Your magick saved my life."

"Lydia, ya are my life," he whispered, kissing the top of her head. "All I want is to protect ya, forever."

Lydia felt his love for her and held him close. Who cared if he was a little domineering? She loved him and wanted to be with him. Everything else would work itself out.

"Ok," she whispered. "I'll marry you."

"Sorry, love, but I didn't propose to ya." Erik chuckled as she lightly smacked him on the chest. "But I will gladly help ya take a shower."

Chapter Eighteen

"I can't believe your fiancé's brother evicted me," Charlotte said, staring at the fresh paint on the door frame. Lydia had found the color in the basement and painted over the area where Brad's blood had splattered. The cleanup crew did a good job, but it just made her feel better to erase him from her house completely.

"He probably didn't know you were the tenant." Lydia hated the lie. She stood to wash out the paintbrush in the sink. "And I for one am very happy to have you here. I don't want to be alone right now, so really you're doing me a favor."

A car sounded outside, and she hurried to the window to look for Erik. She knew a proposal was coming, she just didn't know when or how. At least, she hoped a proposal was coming. It was only a truck passing and she sighed, going back to the sink.

"It's the principle of the thing," Charlotte said. She stuck a label on a bottle and moved it over to the side.

With everything that had happened they were backlogged on orders. The smell of lavender came from the stove. They'd been making batches of lotion since they arrived back at the house early that morning. The place reeked like a perfumery.

"Niall evicted me while I was sick in the hospital, poisoned by your stalker," Charlotte continued. "What kind of asshat does that? And then he mutters a half-ass, drunken apology to me right after the stalker tried to kill you. I didn't see Niall yesterday. I hope that means he's gone for good."

"I'm glad to see some of your fighting spirit is coming back," Lydia said, smiling. This sounded more like the old Charlotte. Margareta had been right. Time had done wonders. Ok, so it had only been a little over a day since Brad's attack, but still, wonders.

"Like a bad mushroom trip is going to slow me down for long," she said. "It's still messing with me. I thought I saw a ghost last night, but I was half-asleep so it was no big deal."

Lydia stopped washing and set the brush on an old towel she'd laid out on the counter. This might be the perfect time to ease Charlotte into some of the truth. "Well…"

"Well?"

"You remember the Gramma Annabelle thing, right? We didn't really get a chance to talk about it." Lydia glanced around the room. She saw the ghost appear in the living room out of Charlotte's eye line. Annabelle nodded eagerly. "When you left my house, you were going to get a spirit board."

"No way! I thought I hallucinated that part. Have you seen her? Did she try to communicate?"

Lydia nodded. "Yeah, she's appeared a few times."

"Gramma Annabelle, if you're here, make this bottle move," Charlotte placed one of the labeled bottles away from the others and stared at it.

Annabelle floated into the kitchen and placed her hand over the bottle, letting the solid object sink through her transparent fingers as she held her hand flat over the table. Charlotte gave a little scream and shot out of her chair.

"Not as easy as it looks, dear," Annabelle stated. She pushed her hand through the table and then stood. "It's all I can do to not sink through the floorboards."

From her place against the wall, Charlotte

stared at the ghost. "It's talking. Please tell me you hear it talking, Lydia."

"You're not crazy. Gramma is here." Lydia frowned at her grandmother. "You could have been a little more subtle."

"*It* can hear you," Annabelle said. "You want to touch me?"

Charlotte nodded and stepped hesitantly closer to the ghost. She reached her hand out to poke Annabelle's arm. "You're freezing."

"You look like hell," Annabelle answered.

"I was dosed with magic mushrooms and the doctors think I may be crazy now." Charlotte stepped a little closer to better swipe her fingers through the spirit. "It's possible I'm hallucinating you."

Lydia watched Charlotte's face only relaxing when her friend didn't panic or pass out. A distant sound caught her attention and she tilted her head. "Shh, do you hear that?"

The ghost turned to look at her.

"Bagpipes?" Charlotte guessed, not taking her eyes off Annabelle. She poked her finger at her again.

Lydia gave a little jump of excitement and smoothed down her hair. "How do I look?"

"Good," Charlotte and Annabelle said in unison.

"What's with her?" Annabelle asked.

"Proposal time," Charlotte answered.

"Stop staring at me. It's a little creepy." Annabelle mimicked Charlotte and poked at the woman a few times.

"I can't," Charlotte said, poking the ghost again.

Lydia hurried to the kitchen door and out onto her lawn, unable to contain her excitement. She looked down the hill to where the sound came from. A group of men in kilts turned the corner followed soon after by a crowd of townsfolk. The musicians stepped in time to the music, as they played their bagpipes. Two horses flanked each side of them carrying flags with the MacGregor family crest on them. In the front was Erik, leading the way. With him were his brothers, father, and Rory. There were also a few men she didn't know but who had the MacGregor look about them. Malina followed in her tartan gown pushing a wheelchair. The old lady in the chair looked like an older, withered version of Margareta. Wrinkled skin clung to her bony frame. An out of breath English bulldog dressed in tartan plaids followed Malina on a leash. Behind her a group of women in various forms of tartan gowns followed.

Mrs. Callister scribbled notes furiously on her

notepad as she half-ran, half-walked to stay in front of the others. Chef Alana walked with Jane Turner. She gave a small wave when she saw Lydia. Joe and Mr. Baker from the post office stood next to a group of men from the Eternal Order of the Elk men's club. They were a harmless group that sat around smoking and playing cards all night away from their wives. Several people had their cell phones out recording the Scotsmen. Others flashed pictures.

Lydia smiled at Erik as he stopped the procession in front of her. He dropped the blowpipe from his mouth and placed the instrument on the old lady's lap. "Thanks, Ma."

"Margareta?" Lydia whispered when Erik neared her.

"The spell took a lot out of her. She'll be fine, and more importantly, you'll be fine," he whispered back. The bagpipe music stopped. Then louder, as he took her hands in his, he said, "Lydia Barratt, *táim i ngrá leat.*"

He paused and a few of the MacGregor women vocalized, "*Ahh.*"

Erik kneeled on one knee. He lifted two fingers in front of his heart where the crowd couldn't see them. A thin smoke formed before materializing a diamond ring with a heart-shaped stone. "Say ya will marry me, lass."

Lydia was aware of the eyes on her, but she didn't care. She only saw Erik. A tear slipped over her cheek, and she felt the nervous excitement welling inside her chest. She nodded. "Yes."

He surged to his feet and pulled her into his arms. Kissing her soundly, he turned her to the side so she lost balance and fell into his arms. Her foot kicked up to the side to help counterweight her upper body. The crowd cheered. Erik righted her.

"Are ya feeling giddy now, love?" he asked, stroking his thumb along her temple and cheek.

"A bouquet of flowers would have done nicely," she said. "You didn't have to pied piper the whole town."

"Och, no, lass, only a grand gesture will do for my heart." He slid the ring onto her finger. "I want everyone to know you're Erik MacGregor's woman. Besides, it was only a little harmless spell to get them to follow. The other option was for me to sing." He glanced behind him. "I still can if ya wish." He opened his mouth wide.

"No, don't." She laughed, grabbing his face and kissing him. "There's no need for threats. I already said yes."

The light sound of music caught her attention, and she looked at Margareta in the wheelchair.

Next to her a horse stood. Lydia leaned in to Erik. "Is that horse humming?"

Erik looked at his mother and then the humming animal. "Ma."

Margareta shrugged and stroked the animal's side with a shaking hand. It stopped.

"Come on, lads, drinks on me!" Angus shouted. Cheers answered his cry. The Eternal Order of the Elk seemed particularly excited by this turn of events. Suddenly, the bagpipes started up again as Angus led the people back down the hill.

"Come on then, Traitor!" A Scottish accent yelled from within the group of musicians. The bulldog pulled at his leash and hurried after his master. Malina handed her mother's chair off to a tartan covered woman and jogged after the men.

"You, Mr. MacGregor, are going to be a handful," Lydia said. Then, sighing as she watched the departing crowd, she added, "And so is your family."

"I think ya can handle us, lass." He lifted her into his arms. "Now, how about ya finally invite me into our home? If I'm going to live here, ya might as well let me inside."

"I don't know. You're pretty entertaining when I don't let you in." Lydia laughed. Happiness bubbled over inside her.

"Are they gone?" the woman holding the wheelchair asked.

"Aye, Aunt Cait, it's safe," Erik said. "This house is protected. The townsfolk won't see anything magickal."

Cait pulled a square mirror out of the back of the wheelchair and lifted it toward one of the other women to take. "Hold the end, lad. We need to get your ma home to rest."

Erik obeyed, pulling at the mirror. It stretched wider and taller. Then when it was full length, Cait pushed the wheelchair toward it.

"Nice to meet ya, lass, welcome to the family," Cait said before wheeling Margareta into the mirror. She disappeared into the waving reflective surface.

Lydia gasped and looked around. Charlotte peeked out of the doorway. She pointed weakly behind her. "Um, Lyd, I'm going to lay down. I think the mushrooms are acting up again." She disappeared into the house.

When the other women went through leaving Erik holding the mirror on her lawn, Lydia reached to touch the surface. Her fingers slipped into the mirror, and she jerked them back.

"Peek inside," Erik said. "No one is watching."

Lydia glanced to make sure Charlotte had left and then leaned her head toward the mirror and closed her eyes. She felt warmth as she passed through the glass and then opened her eyes to look. Her head was in Erik's bedroom at the mansion. She saw Cait's back as she pushed Margareta out of Erik's room. Lydia pulled out of the mirror.

"It's a compromise," Erik said. "Now we live in both places. If anything happens, we can be in the mansion in two steps." He pushed the mirror so that it became smaller and easier to carry. "Is that all right, love? The portal will make my family happy, and this way we have their protection at all times. Don't worry, we'll leave our room locked on the other side. No one will be coming over uninvited."

"It's actually kind of perfect," Lydia said, chuckling. "With us, Charlotte and my grandmother's ghost flitting around, the Victorian might feel a little crowded. This will give us some privacy. Though, maybe not so much magick around Charlotte right now. She's been through enough and I just reintroduced her to my grandmother's ghost."

"Aye, sorry about that," he murmured. He held the mirror with one hand and pulled her close with the other. "She looks better though. Euann wants me to put in a good word for him with Charlotte."

"So naturally you'll sabotage him?" Lydia wrapped her arms around his neck and held him close.

"Oh, aye, definitely. I still owe him for a few things he did to me back in the seventeen-hundreds." He took her offered lips and kissed her. "See, lass, ya understand us MacGregors perfectly."

"Seventeen-hundreds," she whispered. No matter how she tried to ignore that little fact, it kept coming back to trouble her.

"Aye, he got me drunk and I ended up conscripted into the navy," Erik chuckled. Then, seeing her expression, he said, "Ah, love, don't worry. It's just pranks between brothers. I'm unharmed, and Euann didn't mean for it to happen."

"Have you been married before?" Lydia pushed a strand of his hair out of his face to study his eyes.

"No, lass, ya will be my first and only." He returned the gesture, brushing the hair out of her face.

"Only? But I'm not a warlock. I'm human. I'm not like you, Erik. I'll grow old and die. I'm not magickal." Inside she shook with emotions. Trying to lighten what she was saying with a joke, she said, "You know, unless I come back to haunt you. I'm sure Gramma Annabelle can tell me how it's done."

"All I have is yours, Lydia." Erik let the mirror drop on the ground and slipped his arm around her waist. A light breeze swept around them. She shivered, feeling him in the wind. "That includes my immortality and my magick. Aye, death can find us all, but ya will live as I live. My magick will infuse ya and, after time, ya will grow your own power and become immortal as well. Of course, until that time you'll have to stay close to me." A seductively playful smile curled his lips. "I'll need to feed ya my power." He wagged his brows and pulled her hips flush to his to feel his desire for her. "It's a way to make sure we're the real thing. If we part, the process will stop. This is how the non-magick become magick."

Lydia felt his magick slipping into her fingers, tingling down her arms. "Are you sure that last part isn't a line? If we part, the process will stop?"

"We best not risk it." He rocked into her. "Though, might I suggest we take the rest of this conversation up to our room, and through the mirror? Ya can rearrange anything ya like, love, but maybe it's best not to scare Charlotte."

"I suppose it's time you came inside, Mr. MacGregor," Lydia whispered, leaning her mouth close to his ear, "to give me my magickal feeding."

"Aye, *fíorghrá,* whatever ya wish." He grabbed the mirror and whisked into the home.

"I love you, too, Erik." Lydia laughed when he didn't bother to look around the house he'd been trying so hard to get into but instead hurried her upstairs toward her room. "You crazy warlock, I love you too."

The End

The Series Continues...

WARLOCKS MACGREGOR® 2: SPELLBOUND

Let Sleeping Warlocks Lie…

Iain MacGregor knows how his warlock family feels about outsiders discovering the truth of their powers, its forbidden. That doesn't seem to stop him from having accidental magickal discharges whenever he's around the woman who has captured his attention. Apparently his magick and other "parts" don't seem to care what the rules are, or that the object of his affection just might be his undoing.

Warning: Contains yummy, hot, mischievous MacGregor boys who may or may not be wearing clothing and who are almost certainly up to no good on their quest to find true love.

For more information, visit www.
MichellePillow.com

Warlocks MacGregor® 2: Spellbound: Extended Excerpt

"*Dè tha thu ag iarraidh?*"

"What do I want?" Jane whispered, looking around in confusion for the speaker. She was unsure as to how she'd come to be outside. One moment she'd been in bed, the next in a garden. "I'm losing my mind."

She knew this garden. She'd itched to get her hands on it ever since she'd moved to Green Vallis, Wisconsin. The plants were choking from neglect, but beneath their twisted wildness was rich soil. Most of the trees and shrubs would be salvageable—if not at their current location, then transplanted elsewhere. The grounds were expansive and had so much potential. Being located on a hill above the small town, it had ample sunlight and natural drainage when it rained. It belonged to an old mansion that had just recently been purchased after decades of sitting empty. Everyone in town knew the story of its builder— the displaced English lord. He'd been a rake or a rogue or whatever they called the rambunctiously decadent men of the time.

Despite whatever the nobleman had lacked in his personal life, he'd had a great eye for creating picturesque beauty. The property came with eighty acres of land, including part of the surrounding forest with a stream running through it and the old English landscape garden. Yes, the giant house was nice, but Jane saw it more as a backdrop to the nature surrounding it. She couldn't imagine owning eighty acres of land. The mere idea of it was a kind of what-would-you-do-if-you-won-a-million-dollars pipe dream.

"*Dè tha thu ag iarraidh!*"

Jane flinched as she found the bearer of the mysterious voice. Why was a Scottish woman screaming at her? And why was the woman's tiny frame aging so rapidly Jane could see the wrinkles forming on the pretty face as if the woman was living an entire lifetime in a single afternoon?

Jane knew she was hallucinating. What else could this be? The doctors had warned her that her mind would eventually deteriorate. Even so, this hallucination felt very familiar as if she'd lived this moment but couldn't remember it.

"*Thalla's cagainn bruis!*"

"Chew a brush?" Jane tried to translate the woman's words. It made no logical sense that she understood any of it, as she didn't speak Gaelic. She frowned, looking at an overgrown gooseberry bush a few feet from where she stood on the cobblestone path. Not knowing why she tried to obey, she lifted her arm in its direction but couldn't reach. Why couldn't she reach it?

She looked down. A light fog surrounded her legs. It held her immobile like metal shackles. Fog like shackles? She should be able to run through the fog.

"*Dè tha thu ag iarraidh?*"

"I don't know what I want," Jane answered, blinking rapidly as a wrinkled finger pointed a little too close to her nose. How could the finger be so close? The woman was nearly twelve feet away down the path near the mansion's exterior wall. Fear filled her, nearly choking the breath from her lungs. "Why can I understand what you're saying? Who are you? How did I get here? What do you want?" She remained rooted in place, like the wild overgrowth around her yearning to be saved. "I don't understand why you're yelling at me."

The aging woman's finger dissipated into mist but did not disappear. Instead, the mist surrounded Jane's head. She swatted it away, but the action only caused the mist to swirl up her nose. Around her, the plants moved, coming to animated life. They stretched and grew, aging like the now-old woman before her, then transforming into a beautiful combination of lilac and purple Scottish heather. The heady scent of flowers and honey was so strong it burned her nostrils and caused her eyes to water. Bagpipes sounded in the distance, impossibly carried on a wind that did not stir.

And then…nothingness.

Warlocks MacGregor® Series

Love Potions
Spellbound
Stirring Up Trouble
Cauldrons and Confessions
Spirits and Spells
Kisses and Curses
Magick and Mischief
A Dash of Destiny

More Coming Soon

Visit www.MichellePillow.com for details.

Newsletter

To stay informed about when a new book in the series installments is released, sign up for updates:

Sign up for Michelle's Newsletter
michellepillow.com/author-updates

About Michelle M. Pillow

New York Times & *USA TODAY* Bestselling Author

Michelle loves to travel and try new things, whether it's a paranormal investigation of an old Vaudeville Theatre or climbing Mayan temples in Belize. She believes life is an adventure fueled by copious amounts of coffee.

Newly relocated to the American South, Michelle is involved in various film and documentary projects with her talented director husband. She is mom to a fantastic artist. And she's managed by a dog and cat who make sure she's meeting her deadlines.

For the most part she can be found wearing pajama pants and working in her office. There may or may not be dancing. It's all part of the creative process.

**Come say hello! Michelle loves talking
with readers on social media!**

www.MichellePillow.com

facebook.com/AuthorMichellePillow

twitter.com/michellepillow

instagram.com/michellempillow

bookbub.com/authors/michelle-m-pillow

goodreads.com/Michelle_Pillow

amazon.com/author/michellepillow

youtube.com/michellepillow

pinterest.com/michellepillow

Complimentary Material

The Savage King

BY MICHELLE M. PILLOW

Lords of the Var® Book One
by Michelle M. Pillow

Bestselling Catshifter Romance Series

Cat-shifting King Kirill knows he must do his duty by his people. When his father unexpectedly dies, it's his destiny to take the throne and all of the responsibility that entails. What he hadn't prepared for is the troublesome prisoner that's now his to deal with.

Undercover Agent Ulyssa is no man's captive. Trapped in a primitive forest awaiting pickup, she's going to make the best out of a bad situation…which doesn't include falling for the seductions of a king.

~

About *Lords of the Var*® (Books 1-5)

You met their father, King Attor, in Dragon Lords Books 1-4, now meet the Var Princes!

The cat-shifter princes were raised to not believe in love, especially love for one woman, and they will do everything in their power to live up to their father's expectations. Oh, how the mighty will fall.

~

The Savage King Excerpt

Kirill watched the door to his bedroom open. He'd been sitting in the dark, trying to relieve the stress headache that had built behind his eyes for the last week. The pain started at the base of his skull and radiated up to his temples until he could hardly see straight.

A heavy responsibility had been thrust on his shoulders, a responsibility he really hadn't prepared himself for, the welfare of the Var people. King Attor had not left him in a good position. He'd rallied the people to the brink of war, convinced them that the Draig were their enemy, and even went so far as to attack the Draig royal family.

Kirill wanted to see peace in the land. However, he knew the facts didn't bode well for it. The Draig had a long list of grievances against King Attor and the Var kingdom.

Before his death, the king had ordered an attack on the four Draig princes, all of which ended horribly for the Var. The worst was when Prince Yusef was stabbed in the back, a most cowardly embarrassment for the Var guard who did it. If he hadn't been executed in the Draig prisons, he would've been ostracized from the Var community. Luckily, Prince Yusef survived or they'd already be at battle.

Attor had also arranged for the kidnapping of Yusef's new bride. The Draig Princess Olena had been rescued, or that too would've led to war. The old king had even tried to poison Princess Morrigan, the future Draig queen, on two separate occasions. She too lived. And those were only a few of the offenses Kirill knew about in the few weeks before King Attor's death. He could just imagine what he didn't know.

Kirill sighed, feeling very tired. He'd known since birth that the day would come when he'd be expected to step up and lead the Var as their new king. He just hadn't expected it to be for another hundred or so years. His father had been a hard man, whom he'd foolishly believed was invincible.

"Here kitty, kitty, kitty." His lovely houseguest's whisper drew his complete attention from his heavy thoughts.

Ulyssa bent over like she expected him to answer to the insulting call. He dropped his fingers from his temple into his lap, and a quizzical smile came to his lips. As he watched her, he wasn't sure if he was angered or amused by her words.

"Are you in here, you little furball?" she said, a little louder.

She wore his clothes. Never had the outfit looked sexier. His jaw tightened in masculine interest, as he unabashedly looked her over. All too well did he remember the softness of her body against his and the gentle, offering pleasure of her sweet lips. She'd made soft whimpering noises when he'd touched her, yielding, purring sounds in the back of her throat. Even with the aid of nef, he was surprised by how easily and confidently she melted into him. The Var were wild, passionate people and were drawn to the same qualities in others. He suspected she'd be an untamed lover.

Too bad she'd belonged to his father first. In his mind, that made her completely untouchable though none would dare question his claim if he were to take her to his bed. Technically, by Var law, she belonged to him until he chose to release her. For an insane moment, he thought about keeping her as a lover. He knew he wouldn't, but the thought was entertaining.

Kirill's grin deepened. Ulyssa strode across his home to the bathroom door with an irritated scowl. It was obvious she didn't see him in the darkened corner, watching her. He detected her engaging smell from across the room, the smell of a woman's desire. It stirred his blood, making his limbs heavy with arousal. And, for the first time since his father's death, his headache relieved itself.

"Hum, maybe I'm looking too high. I'm sure there has to be a little cat door here somewhere. Come here, little kitty. Where are you hiding?"

His slight smile fell at her words. It was easy to detect her mocking tone.

"Where's your little kitty door, huh?" Ulyssa whispered to herself, her blue gaze searching around in the dark.

Kirill grimaced in further displeasure. He watched her open the door to his weapons cabinet. Her eyes rounded, and he thought she might take one. She didn't. Instead, she nodded in appreciation before closing the door and continuing her search for an exit.

She stopped at a narrow window by his kitchen doorway. Her neck craned to the side, as she tried to see out over the distance. Kirill knew she looked at the forest. From under her breath, he heard her vehement whisper, "Where exactly did you little fur balls bring me? Ugh, I need to get out of this flea trap, even if I have to fight every one of you cowardly felines to do it. I've fought species twice as big and three times as frightening. A couple of little kitty cats don't scare me."

If this insolent woman wanted to play tough, oh, he'd play. Curling gracefully forward, Kirill shifted before his hands even touched the ground. He let one thick paw land silently on the floor, followed by a second. Short black fur rippled over his tanned flesh, blending him into the shadows. His clothes fell from his body, and he lowered his head as he crept forward. A low sound of warning started in the back of his throat. He was livid.

To find out more about Michelle's books visit www.MichellePillow.com

Please Leave a Review

Please take a moment to share your thoughts by reviewing this book.

Be sure to check out Michelle's other titles at www.MichellePillow.com